Alice-Miranda
Holds the Key

Books by Jacqueline Harvey

Alice-Miranda at School
Alice-Miranda on Holiday
Alice-Miranda Takes the Lead
Alice-Miranda at Sea
Alice-Miranda in New York
Alice-Miranda Shows the Way
Alice-Miranda in Paris
Alice-Miranda Shines Bright
Alice-Miranda in Japan
Alice-Miranda at Camp
Alice-Miranda at the Palace
Alice-Miranda in the Alps
Alice-Miranda to the Rescue
Alice-Miranda in China
Alice-Miranda Holds the Key

Clementine Rose and the Surprise Visitor
Clementine Rose and the Pet Day Disaster
Clementine Rose and the Perfect Present
Clementine Rose and the Farm Fiasco
Clementine Rose and the Seaside Escape
Clementine Rose and the Treasure Box
Clementine Rose and the Famous Friend
Clementine Rose and the Ballet Break-In
Clementine Rose and the Movie Magic
Clementine Rose and the Birthday Emergency
Clementine Rose and the Special Promise
Clementine Rose and the Paris Puzzle

Alice-Miranda
Holds the Key

Jacqueline Harvey

RANDOM HOUSE AUSTRALIA

A Random House book
Published by Penguin Random House Australia Pty Ltd
Level 3, 100 Pacific Highway, North Sydney NSW 2060
www.penguin.com.au

 Penguin
Random House
Australia

First published by Random House Australia in 2017

Addresses for the Penguin Random House group of companies can be found at
global.penguinrandomhouse.com/offices.

National Library of Australia
Cataloguing-in-Publication entry

Creator: Harvey, Jacqueline, author
Title: Alice-Miranda holds the key/Jacqueline Harvey
ISBN: 978 0 14378 070 0 (paperback)
Series: Harvey, Jacqueline. Alice-Miranda; 15
Target audience: For primary school age
Subjects: Friendship – Juvenile fiction
          Holidays – Juvenile fiction
          Children's stories

Cover and internal illustrations by J.Yi
Cover design by Mathematics www.xy-1.com
Internal design by Midland Typesetters, Australia
Typeset in 13/18 pt Adobe Garamond by Midland Typesetters, Australia
Printed in Australia by Griffin Press, an accredited ISO AS/NZS 14001:2004
Environmental Management System printer

Penguin Random House Australia uses papers that are natural, renewable
and recyclable products and made from wood grown in sustainable forests.
The logging and manufacturing processes are expected to conform to the
environmental regulations of the country of origin.

For Ian and Sandy — who would have thought we'd get to fifteen!

Prologue

Down below, the factory whirred and thumped as the machines jolted back and forth, spitting their contents onto the conveyors. From the control room, the plant supervisor looked out over the vast floor and marvelled at how far things had come in the past few years. Not so long ago there would have been a hundred workers attending the stations, but these days human intervention just wasn't necessary – most of the time. He was fortunate they still employed someone like him. No doubt in the future there would be a machine to do his job too.

The man's stomach grumbled. Tonight already felt like one of those shifts that would never end. He stood up and walked to the small refrigerator, where he pulled out the ham-and-pickle sandwich he'd packed for his dinner. He carried it back to his work station and sat down, then picked at the edge of the cling film when an alarm began to bleat.

'Not now,' he sighed, hoping that one of the workers would sort it out. He could feel the beeping sound working its way inside his head, a dull ache rising. As the alarm continued, he huffed and stood up. He left his sandwich on the bench and hurried downstairs towards the offending machine, which of course was at the furthest corner of the building. He didn't notice the shadowy figure dart into the control room, closing the door softly behind them.

It didn't take long for the supervisor to recalibrate the injector. It was the second time it had happened this week, which was somewhat disconcerting, given the machines had recently been serviced and usually ran like clockwork. He glanced back towards the control room, which was suspended like an eagle's nest at the end of the factory. It was strange – he didn't remember closing the blinds. Or had he? Working the night shift on too little sleep wasn't exactly ideal and he did seem to be more forgetful these days.

Once more, the shadowy figure went unnoticed as they slipped back out through the control-room door, shoving a piece of paper into their pocket. The deed was done. You couldn't change the past, but the future? Well, that was something else altogether.

Chapter 1

Millie studied her cards again, willing the one at the top of the deck to be either a black seven or a red three. She looked across the table at her friend, wondering how it was that Alice-Miranda always managed to keep such a straight face.

'It's your turn,' Millie reminded her.

The tiny brunette child hummed, then reached out and placed her hand on top of the deck before retracting it quickly and fanning her cards onto the table. 'Full house,' she declared with a cheeky grin.

Millie threw hers away in disgust. 'Seriously! I thought this game was mine. What's that? Six in a row?'

Alice-Miranda shrugged and wrinkled her nose. 'Seven, I think. But who's counting? Sorry, Millie. Some days you win, and some days . . . you know how it goes.'

Millie sighed and swept the cards towards her. 'I'm not giving up yet. Your winning streak has to come to an end sooner or later, although I'm glad your luck held out for the engineering competition. I still can't believe our tower managed to withstand Plumpy's wind-machine test.'

Alice-Miranda looked at her friend. 'I think that was definitely more luck than skill, especially when he upped the fan level to typhoon strength.'

'No, it wasn't,' Caprice piped up from the centre of the sitting room. The girl was cocooned within a beanbag and snuggled up to Fudge, their resident cavoodle.

As it was Saturday night, the students of Grimthorpe House had gathered in front of the television to watch a movie. There was barely an inch of room, with girls lounging all over the place in chairs, on beanbags and duvets and pillows raided from their bedrooms.

'We were amazing. Well, at least, *I* was,' Caprice conceded. 'And the rest of you weren't such a bad support crew, I suppose.'

Winchesterfield-Downsfordvale Academy for Proper Young Ladies had recently held its very first Science, Technology and Engineering Fair, where the girls had spent a whole week engaged in a series of challenges ranging from chemistry and physics, to robotics and construction. Millie had almost choked when she'd been placed in the same group as Caprice. Luckily, so had Sloane and Alice-Miranda, and in the end their group was named the overall champion, receiving a giant silver cup engraved with their names. Caprice had argued that she and Sloane should be able to keep it in their room until next year's competition – the girl was quite convinced they'd only won because of her – but Miss Grimm had other ideas, promptly placing it under lock and key in the school trophy cabinet.

'You know, your modesty is always so refreshing, Caprice,' Millie replied with a roll of her eyes. She shuffled the cards and somehow managed to spray them up into the air.

Caprice snorted and waved her hand dismissively. 'What's the point of winning if you can't rub everyone's noses in it? Not that *you* would have much experience with that.'

Sloane wriggled out of the beanbag she was lying on and picked her way across the sitting-room floor. 'Can I play? she asked, joining Alice-Miranda and Millie at the table. 'I think I'd rather watch Miss Wall's instructional video on javelin throwing techniques than this boring movie. At least there's that funny part when Mr Plumpton wanders onto the field and doesn't realise he's in the line of fire. I don't think I've ever seen him move so fast.'

Alice-Miranda grinned. 'He was lucky Miss Wall was off her game that day.'

'Well, I think it's a lovely film,' Mrs Howard said. The housemistress was wedged into her favourite armchair, her knitting needles clacking away as the body of the jumper she was making for her grand-daughter grew longer.

'Me too,' Sofia said. 'That dog is adorable.'

'Not as cute as Fudge,' Caprice said, stroking the pup's curly caramel fur.

'Mrs Howard, could I make some hot choco-late?' Sofia asked.

There was a chorus of agreement from the rest of the girls as the movie was interrupted by the catchy new jingle for the Kennington's grocery chain.

'I'll give you a hand, dear,' the woman said, setting her knitting aside. 'I think we'd best make a large pot.' She muted the sound and left the television remote on the seat cushion as she stood up and navigated her way to the door.

'Change the channel, someone,' Caprice ordered.

'Don't you even think about it,' Mrs Howard called from the kitchenette. 'Who knows what rubbish is on the other stations.'

'Whatever,' Caprice griped. 'Hey, isn't that your father, Alice-Miranda?' The girl pointed at the television, which had just cut to a news bulletin. Emblazoned across the bottom of the screen were the words: *Kennington's food-poisoning outbreak.*

Alice-Miranda put down her cards and stood up to get a better view. 'What are they saying?' she asked as she watched a clip of her father walking from his car to the front doors of the Kennington's offices.

'Turn it up, someone,' Caprice demanded, before stretching back to Mrs Howard's chair and unmuting the television herself.

'The Kennington's grocery empire is tonight under threat as police investigate the cause of a food-poisoning

outbreak that has left scores in hospital with a range of symptoms including nausea, headaches and general confusion. The national food authority is working with Kennington's to isolate possible contaminants. However, at this stage the source remains a mystery. Owner Hugh Kennington-Jones has said that all avenues are being thoroughly investigated, and he and his wife are keeping those affected in their thoughts.'

The story ended with Alice-Miranda's father facing the cameras, a look of grave concern etched into his features.

Alice-Miranda shivered as if her blood had just run cold. What a terrible thing to happen. This morning she'd been prattling on about typhoon-resistant towers while her parents were dealing with a crisis. Now she felt positively foolish.

A quiet murmur rippled around the room.

'Wow, that sounds pretty bad,' Caprice said.

Alice-Miranda's brow puckered as all eyes fell on her. 'I'm sure Daddy will get to the bottom of it. I only hope all the people affected get better very quickly.'

'Yeah, because if anyone dies, your dad will probably go to jail,' Caprice said matter-of-factly.

Millie glared at the girl. 'Did you really have to say that?'

'Well, it's true,' Caprice retorted.

But Alice-Miranda hadn't even heard her. She was lost in her own thoughts.

Millie slipped off her chair and walked over to her friend. 'Are you okay?' she asked.

Alice-Miranda nodded. 'I might sit out this round and give Mummy a call.'

Mrs Howard walked back into the room, carrying a tray laden with mugs of steaming hot chocolate. She set it down at the end of the table as Sofia walked in behind her with a second lot. The sweet aroma filled the air, and the girls descended upon them like seagulls.

'Would you mind if I used the telephone?' Alice-Miranda asked the woman once the melee had died down.

'Go ahead, dear,' Mrs Howard said. She paused, taking note of the uncharacteristically sombre tone of Alice-Miranda's voice. 'Is everything all right?'

'Her father's in *big* trouble. People might die because of stuff they've sold in their shops,' Caprice jumped in, relishing the opportunity to deliver the bad news. She took a sip of her milk, which she immediately spat back into the mug. 'Ow! That's scalding hot.'

'Good, maybe it will shut you up for a while,' Millie grumbled.

'I heard that,' Caprice sniped, and poked out her burning tongue.

Mrs Howard turned to Alice-Miranda. 'Off you go, dear. Make that call,' she said. 'And you can take the telephone to your room if you'd prefer.'

'Thank you,' the child said, and scampered away down the hall.

'That's so unfair,' Caprice whined. '*We* never get to make calls in *our* rooms.'

'Did I just hear you volunteer to clear out the attic all day tomorrow?' Mrs Howard said, arching an eyebrow.

'No,' the girl sulked, hunkering back down beside Fudge.

'Then I'd do as Millie suggested and keep a still tongue for the rest of the evening,' the woman harrumphed.

Millie's eyes were rooted to the doorway as she fidgeted, unsure of what to do. Her instinct was to go after Alice-Miranda, but she didn't want to pry either.

'Why don't you play another round of cards?' Mrs Howard said, gently placing her hand on the girl's shoulder and giving it a reassuring squeeze. 'Give her a few minutes, Millie – you can check on Alice-Miranda in a little while.'

Chapter 2

Sleep had not come easily to Alice-Miranda that night. She'd been reading since just after four o'clock, hoping the book would finally send her off, but each time the sandman beckoned, her brain would click back into gear. Despite her mother's assurances that everything was under control, there had been a waver in the woman's voice that hadn't filled her with confidence. Though, the knowledge that Mrs Oliver was undertaking a barrage of testing in her laboratory that was housed in the ancient cellars of Highton Hall did somewhat quell her unease. If anyone could get to the bottom of the problem, Alice-Miranda felt sure that Dolly Oliver could. Not only was she the family's spectacular cook, Dolly's work in food science had earned her accolades around the world – particularly for her Just Add Water creation of freeze-dried foods, which had made inroads into feeding many of the world's impoverished nations.

Now, as the first rays of morning sun streamed through the gap in the curtains, Millie rolled over and yawned loudly.

Alice-Miranda smiled across at her friend. 'Good morning,' she said softly. She slipped her bookmark, with its picture of a pony that bore a striking resemblance to Bonaparte, between the pages and placed her book on her bedside table.

Millie stretched her arms above her head and sat up. 'Have you been awake long?'

'A while,' Alice-Miranda said, not wanting to cause concern.

Millie peeled back the covers and bounced across to Alice-Miranda's bed, snuggling in beside her. 'Okay, out with it,' she demanded. 'What else did your mother say last night?'

'Nothing,' Alice-Miranda said, tying her wild curls back into a ponytail. 'I told you everything I know.'

'Then what are those suitcases doing there?' Millie pointed at the puffy crescent-shaped bags under Alice-Miranda's big brown eyes.

Alice-Miranda giggled. 'Not just bags but suitcases? How impressive.'

'Have you slept at all?' Millie asked.

'Not really. I couldn't stop thinking about all the people who have fallen ill and how upset their families must be, which made me think about my own family. I suppose I've never seen Daddy look so very tired and stressed – it was quite a shock. I even tried counting sheep but, believe me, it doesn't work. Perhaps I should have a word with Shilly and Mrs Oliver. I have a feeling Mummy was putting on a brave face, but she did say that Mrs Oliver is on the case.' Alice-Miranda stopped and looked over at her friend. 'Do you think there's anything we could do to help?'

Millie rolled onto her back and examined the ceiling for a full minute. 'I don't really see what we could do from here. Between the doctors and scientists and Mrs Oliver, they'll surely find the cause soon.'

Alice-Miranda nodded. 'I just feel so helpless. What if more people get sick in the meantime? Maybe Daddy should close all the stores until they know exactly what's going on.'

Millie jumped down onto the floor and put on her glasses. 'It's not the first time your parents have had trouble with their companies and they've always managed to pull through,' the girl said, gathering up her bathroom bag and towel.

'That's true. I'd almost forgotten about the awful business with Mr Finkelstein and the reopening of Highton's on Fifth Avenue. Now I think of it, Daddy also had quite a drama at Pelham Park when we were on camp,' Alice-Miranda said. She yawned widely, a wave of exhaustion rolling over her.

'And who knows how many other things have happened that your parents haven't told you. You can't fix everything,' Millie said sternly.

Alice-Miranda grinned at her flame-haired friend. 'How come you're always the voice of reason these days, Millie?'

'I have to be good at something, seeing as though I'm abysmal at cards,' Millie said, grinning back. 'Do you want to go for a ride this morning? It might take your mind off things.'

'That's a great idea,' Alice-Miranda said, perking up. 'Mummy always says that a dose of fresh air does wonders, and Bony definitely needs the exercise. I had to let his girth strap out another notch last week.'

'We'd better get a move on, then. I can see a Chops and Bonaparte derby coming up and this time I've got a winning feeling in my bones,' Millie said. She donned her floral shower cap and charged out the door.

Chapter 3

Francesca Compton-Halls hid in the cupboard under the stairs and brushed away the tears that simply refused to stop falling. In the weeks since her arrival at Bodlington School for Girls, someone had very kindly rearranged the linen and towels so that there was a spare shelf just big enough for her to neatly fit into. Sadly, that shelf had soon become her favourite place in the whole school.

There was a light tap on the door followed by the familiar voice of Mrs Fairbanks. 'Chessie, dear, are you in there? Why don't you come out and help me make some pikelets?'

The girl pulled a tissue from the bundle in her pocket and blew her nose as quietly as she could. She took a deep breath, then opened the door and tumbled into the housemistress's outstretched arms. The scene had been played out numerous times since Chessie had discovered the cupboard.

'There, there,' the woman soothed, looking at the girl's red-rimmed eyes.

'I don't know what's wrong with me,' Chessie blubbered, clutching the ratty toy dog that was her constant companion. 'Everyone's been so kind. It's just me.'

Ettie Fairbanks rubbed the girl's back and gave her an extra squeeze. Francesca Compton-Halls had one of the worst cases of homesickness the woman had ever encountered and she'd dealt with more than a few in her almost thirty-five years of service. The poor poppet had cried enough tears to fill a dozen buckets and it made not an ounce of difference that they were nearing the end of term. The woman was also in two minds about what effect the holidays would have on the child. Although Chessie would have some time with her mother, Ettie feared it would make her return to Bodlington all that much harder to bear.

Just this afternoon Ettie had telephoned her dear friend Peggy Howard, who was the housemistress at Winchesterfield-Downsfordvale Academy for Proper Young Ladies, for some much-needed advice. The two ladies met eons ago at a conference called *Tales, Tantrums and Turmoil: How cheese toast and hot chocolate can beat the boarding-school blues* and had struck up a wonderful friendship. Over the years they'd often consulted one another regarding particularly tricky students or parents. Unfortunately, the distance between Bodlington and Winchesterfield-Downsfordvale rarely allowed for them to meet in person, but they didn't let that deter them from keeping in touch. Ettie always felt better after she'd talked with Mrs Howard. Having a friend who knew exactly what she was going through was a godsend.

To be fair, the other girls had been incredibly patient with Chessie. Except, of course, Madagascar Slewt, who delighted in making the child's life even more difficult. Then again, that girl delighted in making just about everyone's life a nightmare, including Ettie's. Apparently, Mrs Howard was dealing with a similar creature. There was always one.

'Why don't we make those pikelets and some milkshakes too?' Ettie suggested. She glanced at her watch and decided she'd best make a smaller batch than usual or risk the wrath of Mrs Pinkerton, the school cook. She'd been in trouble with the woman a few times lately, when that blabbermouth Madagascar had relayed their penchant for late afternoon teas.

Chessie nodded and wiped away her tears, trying to muster a smile. 'I'll go and wash my face,' she whispered, and headed off down the dark panelled hallway.

She opened the door to the bedroom she shared with three other girls and breathed a sigh of relief to find it empty. Chessie's mother had been terribly impressed that the dormitories at Bodlington were made up of compact little units for four or six students, each with their own ensuite. Chessie's room mates were a lovely bunch, but she hadn't really got to know any of them in the past eight weeks. Her sadness had been much too paralysing, which was odd given that, until recently, she'd never been a shy or difficult child.

Chessie was cross with herself for being so pitiful yet she had no idea what to do to pull herself out of this horrible fug. Maybe if she had boarded at a school closer to home, and her mother visited during the term, things might have turned out differently. A six-hour train journey wasn't exactly easy to fit into an afternoon, so she hadn't seen her mother once since her arrival at Bodlington.

Perhaps it was the circumstances of her departure that had caused her misery. Her mother's marriage had come as a huge surprise to Chessie and then she'd been bundled off to boarding school without any discussion whatsoever. She had to wonder if her stepfather wasn't especially keen on children. Chessie loved her mother dearly and had always felt loved in return, but the two-minute telephone calls had made her second-guess everything.

Chessie washed her face and quickly brushed her long, curly brown hair. She pulled it back into a taut ponytail, but couldn't quite catch all the rogue ringlets. She wandered down to the kitchenette, where Mrs Fairbanks was busy stirring a large bowl of batter. Unfortunately, Madagascar was there too.

All term Chessie had pondered what it was that made the girl so powerful. She wasn't remarkably funny or clever, and she seemed to spend most of her time being rude to the teachers and students yet no one ever stood up to her. Worst of all, Chessie had a feeling it was Madagascar who had stolen Rodney, her toy dog, at the very beginning of term. Chessie had been inconsolable until he was found stuffed into one of Mrs Fairbanks's wellington boots. It was fortunate the woman had cause to wear them that day, or who knows how long he would have been missing.

'How's our resident misery guts this afternoon?' the girl sneered from under her mouse-brown fringe.

'Maddie,' Ettie chided.

'Mrs Fairbanks, my name is Madagascar and only *I* get to decide who calls me Maddie,' the child replied snootily.

The housemistress almost imperceptibly shook her head at the girl but didn't bite back. Madagascar was one of those children who loved to spar and Ettie was not in the mood.

'Maybe I'll just call *you* whatever I like and see if you enjoy it,' the girl challenged. '*Fairy.*'

Chessie gulped. Madagascar was tricky at the best of times, but she seemed particularly nasty this afternoon. Chessie didn't understand at all why

Madagascar thought it was acceptable to speak to anyone in such a dreadful way. To her horror, words to that effect slipped out of her mouth before she had time to stop them.

Madagascar's eyes narrowed and an evil grin spread across her face. 'What did you say, crybaby?'

'Nothing,' Chessie whispered, and shrank back behind Mrs Fairbanks. She could feel her bottom lip begin to tremble and willed it to behave.

'Ha! Are you going to blubber again?' Madagascar rolled her eyes. 'We've had some babies here before but, honestly, you take the biscuit.'

'Right, that's it! Madagascar, go and do your homework before you say something we will all regret,' Mrs Fairbanks ordered. She glared at the girl, then felt a small stab of remorse herself. She wouldn't put it past the little snipe to complain that she'd been sent to her room.

Regrettably, the fact remained that Madagascar's father was the chairman of the school council and Ettie had had several run-ins with him previously about his daughter's appalling behaviour. To make matters worse, he was one of those parents who wore blinkers when it came to his own child. The last time she'd worked up the nerve to report

Madagascar's misdeeds, the man had delivered a not-so-veiled threat about Ettie perhaps needing to look for employment elsewhere.

'Fine! I'm leaving because I have better things to do with my time. Call me when the pikelets are ready.' Madagascar ran her forefinger through the batter and promptly stuck it in her mouth, then swanned out the door.

Chapter 4

Alice-Miranda stood up in her stirrups to stretch her legs, then sat back down and shivered. The blue morning sky had given way to gathering grey clouds as she and Millie set off, loaded up with a small picnic consisting of four slices of devil's food cake, two ham-and-cheese baguettes and two bottles of Mrs Smith's home-made lemonade. When Millie had told the cook they were planning a long ride at lunchtime, the woman had gone into overdrive. Mrs Smith had caught wind of the Kennington's news and hoped that Alice-Miranda wasn't too upset by what was going on. In any case, she reasoned that some special treats could help to take the child's mind off recent events.

'So where exactly do you want to go?' Alice-Miranda asked, giving Bonaparte a rub on the neck.

They'd seen Charlie Weatherly at the stables and mentioned a few different routes they might take, including popping over to Wood End to visit Mr Frost. Alice-Miranda had bumped into the man in the village the weekend before and he was keen to hear all about their trip to China. Although, as she pointed out, it seemed a rather long time ago now, given there was only a week of term left. He mentioned that his daughter, Ursula, was planning to spend Sunday with him too and Alice-Miranda was interested to see how she was getting on with her teaching studies. Alice-Miranda hoped Ursula might even be able to work at Winchesterfield-Downsfordvale once she was qualified.

'What about Wood End?' Millie suggested, apparently reading the girl's mind.

'I was just about to say the same thing,' Alice-Miranda said. 'We can share our picnic with Mr Frost and Ursula.'

'Only if Cherry and Pickles don't sniff it out first,' Millie quipped.

It was common knowledge that Mr Frost's goats had a predilection for eating everything in sight, including car windscreen wipers and hub caps.

'Cynthia will be glad to have some company for a little while. I think those two creatures terrorise that poor old donkey,' Alice-Miranda said.

Millie clicked her tongue and Chops began to trot. Bony followed suit to keep up beside him.

'Do you feel like a race?' Millie asked.

Alice-Miranda yawned and shook her head. 'Maybe later.'

Millie looked across at her. 'I'm beginning to wonder if the real Alice-Miranda was abducted by aliens last night and replaced with this girl that looks like, but certainly doesn't sound like, my friend. I'm not sure who this worry wart is beside me.'

'I'm sorry,' Alice-Miranda sighed. 'You're right – about the worrying, not the part about me being an alien impostor. I promise I'll do my best to stop fretting, but you know I have to try to help wherever I can.'

'Now, that's more like the girl I know and love,' Millie said. 'And you'd better have cheered up by the time we head home, because I've got to be able to beat you at something this weekend.'

She reached out and punched Alice-Miranda gently on the arm. Bonaparte swiftly turned his head and nipped at Millie's hand.

'Oi, you monster,' she barked, glaring at the black beast. 'Behave yourself.'

Chops turned and threw the bit up and down in his teeth as if to agree.

'Bony!' Alice-Miranda chided. She reached forward and scratched the naughty pony between his ears, which twitched back and forth as he picked up the pace. Without missing a beat, Millie and Chops trotted after them through the woods and down across the bubbling creek that led to Mr Frost's farm.

✴

The girls were greeted by the squeaky heehaws of Cynthia, who was stationed by the gate and doing her best to let everyone know that visitors had arrived.

'She sounds like one of those plastic toys that you squeeze the air in and out of,' Millie observed as Chops slowed to a walk.

As if to prove a point, Cynthia bellowed another round of breathy hacks.

Alice-Miranda grimaced. 'She reminds me of the rubber ducks I used to fill the bath with when I was little. I was convinced I could make music with them, but if they sounded anything like Cynthia, it's no wonder Mummy used to pull such terrible faces.'

The girls wheeled their ponies into the yard at the rear of Mr Frost's immaculate cottage. The back door opened and a flurry of fur raced out to greet the girls, followed by their master.

'Hello Maudie, hello Itch,' Alice-Miranda called to the two cocker spaniels that were excitedly dashing in and out of Bony's and Chops's legs. She looked down at their owner and beamed. 'Hello Mr Frost. Don't you look dapper today.'

And indeed he did. It seemed the fellow had swapped his usual khaki overalls for more elegant attire. He was dressed in a crisp white shirt and a new pair of jeans, with his brown boots so highly polished you could almost see your reflection in them.

'I was hoping you'd come,' Stan said with a broad grin. 'Ursula is due any minute now. She'll be very pleased to see you both. She's bringing Myrtle and Reg with her too, so I thought I'd better make an effort.' He tugged at the shoulder of his shirt. 'That sister-in-law of mine has high standards.'

Alice-Miranda glanced at the satchel containing their lunch. 'Oh dear, we brought a picnic to share, but I don't know if there'll be enough for six of us.'

'Not to worry,' Stan replied cheerfully. 'I've been busy cooking this morning myself. I'm sure we can just add it all together.'

'That's a good idea.' Alice-Miranda slipped down from the saddle and pulled the reins over Bony's head, hitching them out of the way so he wouldn't trip over them. She and Millie led the ponies around to the field before turning them out with Cynthia, who looked for all the world as if she were smiling. She was nodding her head and making quite the commotion.

Millie scanned the field. 'Where are Cherry and Pickles?'

Stan Frost squinted into the middle distance. 'I hope they haven't escaped again. Little blighters got into the front garden last week and made a right old mess of my petunias.'

'There they are!' Alice-Miranda exclaimed, pointing at the oak tree in the far corner. The two goats were perched high up on a branch.

Stan shook his head. 'Don't ask me how they get themselves into any of the predicaments they do. I've decided that they're not goats but magicians.'

Millie and Alice-Miranda giggled. It was a truly ridiculous scene.

The girls followed Stan inside the house and Alice-Miranda unpacked her satchel, depositing their offerings on the table alongside the feast Mr Frost had prepared. There was an orange cake and a platter of sandwiches, some freshly baked scones and a pot of whipped cream.

Millie surveyed the generous spread. 'Wow! You *have* been busy.'

'My baking has definitely improved,' he said, patting his tummy to prove it. 'I don't know why I've started to enjoy it at my age, but it might have something to do with that lovely Venetia Baldini and her television show.'

'Everyone adores *Sweet Things*,' Alice-Miranda said. 'And Ms Baldini *is* the loveliest lady. You should have seen the treats she created for Aunty Gee's silver jubilee. They were scrumptious! Her daughter, Caprice, goes to our school.'

'But there's nothing sweet about *her*, believe me,' Millie added with a cheeky grin.

Car tyres crunched on the gravel outside. Alice-Miranda skipped to the back door and pulled it open just as Myrtle Parker had been about to knock. The woman stumbled forward as the door gave way ahead of her.

'Good heavens,' Myrtle squawked as she righted herself and her pillbox hat, which had slipped over her eyes. 'What are *you* doing here?'

Alice-Miranda smiled. 'Hello Mrs Parker. Millie and I thought we'd pop by to visit Mr Frost and Ursula and now you and Mr Parker are here too. What a wonderful surprise. Mummy says that times like these are pure serendipity.'

'Hello Mrs Parker,' Millie called from a safe distance. She was on the other side of the cottage kitchen, helping Mr Frost pull teacups and saucers out of the cupboard. 'It's lovely to see you too,' she mumbled.

Stan stuffed his fist into his mouth to stop himself from laughing.

Myrtle looked across at her brother-in-law and Millie, wondering what they were carrying on about.

As Reginald Parker followed his wife inside, Alice-Miranda launched herself around the man's middle before hugging Ursula too.

Mrs Parker bustled over to the kitchen table and sat down, placing her beige handbag on the seat beside her. 'That's a terrible business with your father,' the woman said with a cluck of her tongue.

'Myrtle,' Reg warned, shooting her a fierce stare.

'Well, it is,' the woman insisted. 'By the sounds of the television reports, people are *very* sick and may even –' her voice petered to a whisper – 'die.'

Millie cast a reproachful glare in the old woman's direction.

Stan Frost looked up from where he was making the tea. 'What's all this about, then?'

Alice-Miranda sighed and sat down beside Reg. With a deep breath, she explained as much as she knew.

When the girl had finished, Ursula patted her hand. 'You mustn't worry yourself, sweetheart.'

'Yes, I'm sure your parents will get to the bottom of it very soon,' Stan said, smiling sympathetically from the other side of the room. He brought over the teapot and began to fill their cups, then fetched a jar of strawberry jam from the pantry and set it down on the table. 'We'll be needing this for the scones.'

Myrtle Parker's lip curled at the label on the jar. 'We most certainly will not. It's Kennington's own brand.'

'It's not even opened yet,' Stan objected.

Myrtle's nostrils quivered like jelly in a stiff breeze. '*Precisely*. You know none of us can be too careful.'

Alice-Miranda bit her lip and glanced at Millie. The woman had a point.

Reg Parker stirred his tea and reached over to take a scone. 'These look absolutely delicious, but you couldn't possibly have them *without* the jam and cream.' He picked up the jar and scooped a teaspoon of the crimson condiment onto the side of his plate.

Alice-Miranda leaned across and touched the old man's arm. 'That is an awfully kind gesture but you really don't have to,' she said. 'I completely understand if you'd rather not.'

'My dear girl, I am less likely to get sick from eating this than the leftovers in the refrigerator at home,' Reg said firmly.

Myrtle Parker glared at her husband. 'Well, don't come crying to me when you're back in the hospital.'

'You mean from Thursday night's meatloaf?' he teased.

Myrtle huffed and jabbed her slice of orange cake with her fork. Stan thought it best not to mention that all of the ingredients in that had come from Kennington's too.

Millie racked her brain for something to say, eager to change the mood. Her eyes twinkled as she happened upon just the thing. 'Do you want to hear about our trip to China? I ate a scorpion on a stick in the night market.'

Myrtle blanched and choked on her cake. 'Good heavens! How ghastly.'

'Oh, that's fantastic!' Ursula gasped. 'I did that too, years ago.'

For twenty years Ursula had travelled the globe, amassing a wealth of experiences before only quite recently being reunited with her father.

Alice-Miranda grinned. 'And we helped to solve a case involving a huge robbery.'

'Of priceless Ming Dynasty chicken cups,' Millie added. 'I know that doesn't sound like much, but Alice-Miranda brought down some really big crooks – whales, actually.'

Alice-Miranda blushed. 'I didn't do it on my own, Millie.'

'What on earth are you talking about now?' Myrtle tutted before sipping her tea. The old woman was also keeping one eye on the jam jar, as though the spoon might suddenly levitate and drop its red peril onto her plate if she dared turn her cheek.

'Whales, high rollers, super-big gamblers,' Millie replied. 'The Chinese government gave Alice-Miranda a hefty reward too, which she donated to the Wongs' new acrobatic school.'

Silence fell over the table and all three adults leaned in, their curiosity piqued.

Reg winked at Alice-Miranda. 'Well, come on then, sweetheart. You'd better start from the beginning.'

Chapter 5

Adrienne Treloar folded the shirt and placed it on top of the clothes that were already packed neatly into her suitcase. She could hear the thumping of tiny feet in the hallway before the bedroom door burst open and a small boy with a mop of orange locks, and an even smaller girl with two feathery pigtails, flew into the room squealing. The boy leapt onto the middle of the bed, where his sister couldn't climb.

'Martha can't get me! Martha can't get me!' he teased.

The little girl's face crumpled and she began to cry. 'Mama!' she yelled. 'Leo's a poo.'

The boy giggled. 'Martha said poo-oo! Martha said poo-oo!' he chanted.

'Leo, please stop tormenting your sister.' Adrienne reached down and picked up the baby, who clawed at her neck. 'It's all right, blossom,' she cooed, but it was too late. Martha was wound up like a top and no amount of cuddles and kisses were going to curb the impending wobbly.

Adrienne looked at the clock on the bedside table.

'Bentley!' she shouted over the ruckus. 'I need you to take Martha so I can finish packing.'

Leo stopped his teasing. 'Daddy's in the shed,' he said.

'Of course he is,' Adrienne muttered. She often wondered what her husband did all the time he spent out there. He claimed to be thinking. Well, that was a load of piffle if ever she'd heard it. He couldn't even remember to take his swipe card to work. Adrienne had had to make a trip to the factory on a rare night off the other evening to deliver it. She really wished he'd do less thinking and more doing. If Bentley better acquainted himself with the housework and cooking and all the other things that needed to be done around the place, she wouldn't have to rely so much on their nanny, Penny. Heaven knows his work was hardly what she'd have called stressful. It annoyed her no end that he'd settled for something so far beneath him. 'Come on, then. We'd better go and find him.'

Adrienne reached for Leo with her free hand, but the boy ignored her and jumped off the bed, racing ahead.

'Be careful on the stairs,' she called after him, her words falling on deaf ears.

There was a huge crash as the lad missed the last step and hit the timber floor at the bottom with a thud. For a second Martha stopped screaming and a long, lung-sucking silence filled the house.

'Leo!' the woman cried out and scurried downstairs.

She picked the boy up in her other arm and he clung to her, sobbing his almost-five-year-old heart out. She wished Dottie was home. Her older daughter was marvellous with the little ones and seemed to be able to calm them down better than anyone. It was hard to imagine she was only in the third grade.

Adrienne walked through the house to the back door. She adjusted Leo's dead weight on her hip. 'Do you want to go and find Daddy for me?'

Leo blinked his long wet lashes and nodded, then slipped from her grasp and ran into the garden, shouting out to his father.

Adrienne watched after him, thinking how he had the most beautiful green eyes, just like her husband, until the kitchen clock refocused her attention. She cuddled Martha, whose bellowing had softened to a whimper, and headed back upstairs. If she didn't leave in twenty minutes, she'd be late and that wasn't part of her plan. She needed to be firing on all cylinders. This time she wasn't going to be overlooked. She deserved this promotion more than anyone else and nothing and no one was going to stand in her way.

Chapter 6

After three attempts to entice Bonaparte to the gate with a variety of treats, Alice-Miranda finally succeeded with a handful of juicy carrots Mr Frost had pulled from his garden. Millie had only to whistle and Chops galloped over, but Bony was having far too much fun playing chasings with Cynthia and the goats.

Alice-Miranda's first try saw Cherry sprint from the other side of the field and snatch the apple from her outstretched hand, while her second go involved

Pickles leaping more like a gazelle than skittering like the goat she was, to hoover up some lettuce leaves.

'Poor Cynthia. There's never anything left for you with those two bandits about,' Mr Frost said. He pulled another carrot from his back pocket and made sure that the donkey had it all to herself.

Alice-Miranda hugged the man. 'Thank you for a lovely lunch. It's just what I needed.'

'Thank you for taking the time to drop by and for that delicious chocolate cake,' Stan replied. 'Mrs Smith has truly outdone herself this time.'

'We'll be sure to pass on the compliment,' Alice-Miranda said as she placed her left foot into the stirrup and swung up into the saddle.

'And I'm sorry about Myrtle's nonsense earlier on in there.' Stan looked pink around the ears. 'She's always been one for saying the first thing that pops into her head.'

Millie rolled her eyes. 'If it only came into her head it wouldn't be a problem – it's the flying out of her mouth that's the issue.'

Stan grinned. 'I'm pretty sure she has a broken filter, Millie. I've never known her to be any different.'

'Mrs Parker didn't mean any harm and I rather like the fact that you always know where you stand with her,' Alice-Miranda reasoned. 'Besides, she is right. We can't be too careful. We wouldn't want anyone else to fall ill.'

Millie quickly mounted Chops as Stan opened the gate.

'It was lovely hearing your stories of China,' he said. 'I might even consider a little trip of my own one of these days.'

'Good for you, Mr Frost,' Alice-Miranda said. 'My granny says that you're never too old for an adventure. Apparently, she and Aunty Gee are planning a trekking holiday in Patagonia next spring. Granny says they've been on quite a few explorations incognito over the years.'

'Aunty Gee's the best,' Millie said fondly. 'I can just see her and your granny with their backpacks, dressed in their safari suits, cutting a swathe through the jungle.'

Alice-Miranda smiled. 'Aunty Gee, yes – she's up for anything – but it's harder to imagine Granny Valentina out there. I guess it must be true, though, and Granny has been known to surprise us.'

'Take care, girls,' the man said, waving them farewell. 'I'd better make sure Maudie and Itch haven't demolished the kitchen. It probably wasn't a good idea to leave those two inside with food on the table.'

'Goodbye, Mr Frost,' Alice-Miranda said, waving back. 'Thank you for having us.'

Cynthia heehawed, and Cherry and Pickles bleated loudly.

'Bye!' Millie called as the ponies began to trot.

Bony and Chops quickened their pace and in no time the girls had crossed the creek and were bounding up the other side of the bank, heading for home.

'I love Wood End,' Millie sighed wistfully. 'We should visit more often. I could sit and watch those silly goats forever.'

'They're comedians, all right,' Alice-Miranda agreed. 'As well as magicians.'

'Wouldn't you like to know how they get themselves on the roof of the shed and in that tree?' Millie thought for a moment. 'Maybe they have a ladder.'

Alice-Miranda giggled, picturing the two creatures whipping out a ladder and scurrying up the rungs.

As the two girls wove their way through the woods to the meadow known as Gertrude's Grove, Millie turned to her friend. 'How are you feeling?' she asked.

Alice-Miranda smiled. 'Much better. It was good to get out and think about other things.'

'Even if Mrs Parker does have the tact of a pig in a pie shop,' Millie grumbled.

Alice-Miranda chuckled. 'I seem to remember I promised you a race, so we'd better give you one.'

Millie looked at her sideways. 'You're on, but just don't cry about coming second. Countdown from three, two, one!' she shouted.

Both girls dug their heels into their ponies' flanks and the little beasts took off. It was neck and neck as they traversed the field and galloped over the hill into the dale below. They slowed down to splash across the stream, then charged up the bank. Bony was doing well to keep up alongside Chops, who was renowned for his speed. Both ponies thundered on as they headed for the woods that separated the grove from the school.

'Come on, Chops!' Millie urged.

'Go, Bony!' Alice-Miranda called. She leaned forward in the saddle, ducking under a low-slung branch, which narrowly missed the top of her head.

Chops surged ahead. Millie stole a glance, hoping they'd put some distance between their rivals. 'Come on, boy, they're gaining!' she cried out.

As Millie turned back to the track ahead there was an almighty shriek. She tugged hard on Chops's reins and managed to bring him to a halt. As she wheeled around, her freckles disappeared under a complexion the colour of milk.

Millie leapt from the saddle and ran to her friend. 'Oh no, no, no, no!'

Alice-Miranda was lying on her back, a trickle of red oozing from her lip. The silence was sickening. Millie crumpled beside her friend. Bonaparte stood over them, as if keeping guard. Millie realised there was blood coming from somewhere on the back of Alice-Miranda's head. She gently removed the girl's helmet, then tore off her jersey and wedged the garment between Alice-Miranda's head and the ground to keep an even pressure and stop the flow. Tears began to cloud Millie's eyes.

'Wake up, wake up, please wake up,' she whimpered. She tried desperately to remember what she should do first. What was that acronym? Doctor something. Dr ABC.

'Danger,' she said out loud.

Millie cast around for any signs of danger, but there was none as far as she could see.

'Response.'

She lightly tapped Alice-Miranda's cheek and called her name, but the girl was out cold.

'Airway.'

Millie leaned in close. She could feel Alice-Miranda's breath on her cheek and see her chest rising and falling.

'Good, that all looks good,' the girl rambled to herself. 'She's breathing.'

Millie noticed that her jersey was now soaked through. She needed something else to wrap around Alice-Miranda's head. She stood up and ran to Chops, grabbing the tea towel Mrs Smith had used to package their picnic from her saddlebag. She bit the fabric, creating a tiny tear, then ripped it into two long strips to use as bandages. She tied them as tightly as she dared.

'Be strong. Be brave. Be bold,' she chanted under her breath. 'It's just a cut. Head wounds always bleed a lot. Remember when you had that tiny cut on your forehead? There was loads of blood, but you weren't even really hurt. It doesn't mean anything.'

In the distance Millie heard a tractor engine start up. She jumped to her feet, trying to see where it was, and spotted a puff of dark smoke against the light grey sky.

Chops was standing near the fence, his head in a thick clump of grass, tearing at the long tufts. She whistled and called him over to her. The pony looked up and did exactly as she'd asked. Millie hauled herself into the saddle.

'Bonaparte – don't move,' she ordered.

The little black pony whinnied loudly, and it sounded almost as if he were saying sorry.

'And you,' she said to her friend, 'don't you dare go anywhere either. I'll be back in just a minute.' Without another moment to spare, Millie dug in her heels, and she and Chops shot off in search of help.

Chapter 7

Millie picked at the skin around her thumbnail, replaying the events of the past several hours on a loop inside her mind. Her stomach twisted, perhaps from hunger, but she couldn't contemplate eating a thing. Fortunately, she'd found Charlie Weatherly on the tractor quite close to the scene of the accident. He'd called for an ambulance, then raced off to open the gates while Millie had hurried back to Alice-Miranda and held her hand until help arrived. There had been no change, but at least the bleeding had

almost stopped and the paramedics had congratu-
lated Millie on her quick thinking with the make-
shift bandages. Now, sitting in the hospital room
with Alice-Miranda's parents, there was nothing
anyone could do but wait. She glanced over at the
bed just as Alice-Miranda's eyelids fluttered open.

'She's waking up!' Millie exclaimed, rousing
Cecelia and Hugh from their dozy states.

'I'll get the doctor,' Hugh said groggily, and
pushed himself out of the armchair in the corner.

Cecelia rushed to her feet and stood beside
Millie, watching her daughter. 'Darling, we're all
here,' she said softly.

And she wasn't understating the fact. Down
the hallway, Miss Grimm, Miss Reedy, Mr Charles,
Mrs Smith, Dolly Oliver, Mrs Shillingsworth,
Mrs Greening, Jacinta and Sloane were all eagerly
awaiting any news. Myrtle and Reg Parker were
there too, along with Stan Frost. Even Evelyn
Pepper had joined the group a couple of hours ago
to see if there was anything she could do.

Alice-Miranda ran her tongue around the
inside of her mouth. 'Water, please,' she whispered
hoarsely. She wrinkled her nose at the strong smell
of antiseptic in the air.

Cecelia quickly poured a glass from the jug on the side table and popped in a straw. 'Take it slowly, darling,' the woman said. 'You've got some stitches inside your lip.'

Alice-Miranda reached up and felt the back of her head. There was a tender bump and her hair was matted and crusty.

'How are you feeling?' Millie asked, a warm rush of relief spreading through her veins.

'Strange,' Alice-Miranda replied, her brows furrowing. 'And really tired.'

Her father reappeared with the doctor in tow. The woman wore a white coat and had a stethoscope slung around her neck.

'Hello there, Alice-Miranda,' she said. 'I'm Dr Miller and you're in the children's hospital in Chattering. You have a nasty bump on your forehead and there's a cut inside your mouth, which we've had to stitch up, along with a gash at the base of your skull.'

Alice-Miranda began to nod, then grimaced.

'I'm afraid you've also got a badly sprained ankle. It's bandaged now and we've done some X-rays. There's nothing broken, so I'm sure you'll be up and about in no time,' the woman said as she checked the child's pulse and blood pressure and shone a small torchlight into her eyes. 'There are a lot of people who are going to be very happy to hear that you've woken up.'

'How long have I been asleep?' Alice-Miranda asked.

Millie checked her watch. 'About six hours.'

'Goodness, I must have given you all a terrible fright,' the girl said apologetically. 'Is Bony all right?'

Millie smiled. 'He's fine.'

'And he's in our bad books,' Cecelia said, her mouth set into a grim line.

Alice-Miranda frowned as a memory scratched at the back of her mind. 'But it wasn't Bony's fault, Mummy,' she said quietly. 'We were having a race and of course Millie and Chops were in the lead when suddenly there was a hare. It jumped out of the grass in front of us and Bony tried to avoid it. I remember now. He went one way and I went the other and that's why I fell off.'

'Well, we can work out what to do with Bony later.' Hugh kissed the child's forehead, then hastily brushed at the side of his face.

Alice-Miranda smiled at him. 'There's no need to be upset, Daddy. I'm already much better than I was an hour ago.'

'Thank heavens for that,' the man said, not attempting to stem the tide of tears this time.

Cecelia sniffled into a bundle of tissues.

'Shall I tell everyone she's awake?' Millie asked. She thought it best to give Cecelia and Hugh some time alone with Alice-Miranda.

'Why don't you and I both go?' Dr Miller suggested. 'But Alice-Miranda won't be able to have any more visitors until tomorrow at the earliest. She needs to rest.'

Millie nodded, and the pair walked outside into the hallway.

'You're a lovely friend, Millie,' the woman said. 'Alice-Miranda's very lucky you were there when the accident happened. All that blood must have given you quite a scare.'

'My mother's a vet, so I've actually seen plenty of blood before, but I guess it's different when it's your best friend. It was a bit frightening,' Millie admitted, chewing her thumbnail. 'I can still remember the thud when she fell – it was so loud. I have to say, I'm amazed I managed to do anything useful. My brain felt like a lump of dough. It must have been the adrenaline.'

Sloane spotted the pair and nudged Jacinta, who had fallen asleep on her shoulder. Some of the adults were sipping coffee and thumbing through magazines, but sat to attention as soon as they caught sight of Millie and the doctor.

Ophelia Grimm hurried over to them. 'How is she?'

Millie looked at the headmistress and promptly burst into tears.

'Good heavens,' the woman gasped, fearing the worst. 'Has something happened?'

'Alice-Miranda's awake and she's going to be fine,' Millie sobbed, unable to stop the flood.

'Yes!' Sloane exclaimed, grabbing hold of Jacinta.

Dolly embraced Shilly and then Miss Reedy. Charlie clenched his fists together and dropped his head as if he were praying. There was a cheer from Mr Parker and Stan Frost, while Myrtle Parker sobbed and Evelyn Pepper sighed with relief.

'Oh, Millie, dear girl.' Miss Grimm hugged the child tightly. 'You've had an awful shock and been so brave.'

'What that child needs is a honey sandwich and a cup of tea,' Dolly said. Glad to be of some use, she stood up and bustled out of the room in search of a kitchenette.

Millie quickly pulled herself together. Having a good cry for the first time since the accident had made her feel almost instantly better.

'Will Alice-Miranda really be okay?' Charlie asked. He was still in his work clothes, having accompanied Millie and Alice-Miranda in the ambulance to the hospital.

Dr Miller put her hands into her white coat pockets. 'All signs are pointing to a full recovery, but Alice-Miranda needs to sleep. She's had a nasty bump on the head and a concussion as well as the sprained ankle. We'll keep her under observation for the next few days and then she'll need to go home and take it easy for a while before she's completely mobile again. I'm afraid she won't be going back to school until next term.'

Millie's heart sank. She hated the thought of being at Winchesterfield-Downsfordvale without her best friend, but at least Alice-Miranda was going be fine. It was only a week, really. Maybe she could stay with her grandpa for a few days in the holidays so she could visit Alice-Miranda at Highton Hall.

'When can we see her?' Jacinta asked.

'I think it would be best if you all went home and got some rest yourselves,' the doctor instructed.

'You can come back tomorrow afternoon – but, please, one or two at a time. We don't want to wear the girl out.'

'Thank you, Dr Miller,' Ophelia Grimm said. 'I'm glad to be returning to school with some happy news. I know everyone has been worried sick.'

The doctor excused herself and the group stood up. There were lots of hugs and relieved smiles and even a few more tears. Mrs Oliver reappeared with Millie's sandwich and tea, and the girl took just a few minutes to wolf it down. She hadn't realised how ravenous she was until the food was directly in front of her.

'Now, I think it's time we make a move or none of us will be able to wake up for school tomorrow,' the headmistress said to the girls.

Millie excused herself to say goodbye to Alice-Miranda. She poked her head inside the door and saw that her friend had already fallen back to sleep. 'We're heading off,' she whispered, tiptoeing into the room.

'Darling girl, thank you so much for looking after her,' Cecelia said, sweeping Millie into her arms.

Hugh hugged Millie too. 'Thank you – we're both very proud of what you did.'

'She's my best friend,' Millie said, a deep crimson blush darkening her cheeks. 'I wouldn't know what to do without her.'

Hugh Kennington-Jones's phone rang in his pocket. He pulled it out and stared at the screen. 'Sorry, I have to take this,' he said, and stepped into the corridor.

With everything that had happened that day, Millie had almost forgotten about the Kennington's crisis. 'Have you had any breakthroughs?' she asked tentatively, wondering if she should even bring it up.

Cecelia shook her head. 'No, but perhaps this will be good news,' she said with a tight smile on her lips. 'Although I'm not sure who could be calling at this hour.' It was approaching ten o'clock in the evening.

From the colour of Hugh's face when he returned, it didn't look like the call had been positive.

'What is it?' Cecelia asked.

'Another forty-six people have fallen ill,' Hugh said, running a hand through his hair.

Cecelia's hand flew to her mouth. 'Oh, how awful. Have they at least discovered the cause of all this?'

He shook his head. 'The only thing the victims have in common is that they've bought and consumed goods from Kennington's in the past week. There are certain products that many more customers have purchased, such as milk and bread, but so far nothing has shown up in the tests.'

Millie noticed Miss Grimm hovering by the open door. She hated having to leave Hugh and Cecelia right at this moment. 'I have to go,' she whispered, and leaned in to give Alice-Miranda a kiss on the cheek before hugging Cecelia and Hugh again. 'You know everything will work out,' she said, trying to sound more confident than she felt.

Cecelia nodded, mustering a brave smile. 'Of course it will. We've got the best minds in the country working on it.'

Millie gave them a wave and hurried out the door.

Cecelia turned to her husband and hugged him fiercely. 'Hugh, what are we going to do?'

'I'll make some calls,' he said with a nod. He gazed at Alice-Miranda lying asleep on the bed. 'This can't go on a minute longer.'

★

The glow of a lamp illuminated the desk at the nurse's station located at the end of the eerily quiet ward.

A woman entered Alice-Miranda's room and picked up the chart hanging at the foot of the bed. She scanned the page.

'Oh.' She smirked when she caught sight of the name. 'What an unlucky week for your lot.'

The woman lingered a while, muttering to herself, when the door suddenly opened and Cecelia Highton-Smith walked through.

'Hello doctor,' Cecelia said, a look of concern creeping onto her face. 'Is everything all right?'

'Yes, fine,' the woman replied and quickly walked back out into the corridor, a bubble of anger rising in her throat. She stormed along the hallway and was almost barrelled over by a nurse pushing a trolley out of another room.

'I'm so sorry, Dr Treloar. Are you all right?' the young man asked.

'Perfect,' she replied through gritted teeth. 'Absolutely perfect.'

'Good,' the nurse said. 'Another three children have just been admitted with symptoms that suggest food poisoning. Would you be able to take a look at them?'

'Yes, of course.' Adrienne rubbed her neck. 'Show me where they are and then get me a list of everything they've eaten in the past forty-eight hours.'

'Certainly, doctor.'

Chapter 8

'We're going to miss you,' the young nurse said as she fluffed the pillows behind Alice-Miranda's head. She stepped back and surveyed the room. 'I don't ever remember a patient getting as many flowers as you. I hope your mother has a very large car.'

Word of Alice-Miranda's accident had swiftly spread to family and friends and, within hours of the girl's admittance to Room 2B of Chattering Children's Hospital, the ward had taken on the appearance of an upmarket flower shop. There were roses, peonies, daffodils, lilies and chrysanthemums, among numerous others. There was even the very exotic but extremely unpleasant *Stapelia Gigantea*, more commonly known as the African starfish. It had been a gift from Dudley Wainscott, who was one of the world's leading botanists and an old friend of Alice-Miranda's father from school. Knowing him, he would have thought Alice-Miranda would find the flower fascinating, but its putrid smell of rotting flesh saw Matron promptly relegate it to the garbage after they took a few photographs for proof of receipt.

Alice-Miranda smiled. 'I think my friends have gone slightly overboard, but it's touching to know that everyone has been thinking of me. I'm sure that's helped me make such a speedy recovery.'

The last delivery to arrive had been sent from Lucinda Finkelstein and her family in New York. It was the most spectacular spray of purple orchids accompanied by a lovely card. Alice-Miranda had made sure to take down the names of every friend who had sent her flowers so she could write person-alised thank-you letters as soon as she returned home to Highton Hall.

'I think these peonies are the most stunning I've ever seen,' the nurse said as she inhaled the scent of the pink blooms that were sitting on the bedside table.

'Please take them,' Alice-Miranda said, pushing them into her arms. 'Mummy can't possibly fit all these flowers in her car, so I'll just keep a few and everyone else can have the rest.'

The woman's face lit up. 'Are you sure?'

'Absolutely,' the child replied with a decisive nod, as her mother breezed into the room.

'Good morning darling, how are you feeling?' Cecelia asked.

'Much better, Mummy, although my bruises are getting more colourful.' The child tilted her face upwards. Her left eye and the patch around her mouth were now both murky shades of yellow and green with some purple highlights too.

'I wonder what the other fellow looks like,' Mrs Shillingsworth remarked from behind Cecelia. She walked over to give Alice-Miranda a hug.

'Oh, he's black and blue,' Alice-Miranda joked, as if she'd acquired the marks in a fist fight.

Dr Miller knocked and stepped into the room, negotiating her way through the dozens of bouquets that were covering every shelf and half the floor.

'Hello Dr Miller, please help yourself to some flowers. There's no way we can take them all with us,' the child said. She looked expectantly at the woman. 'I am going home, aren't I?'

'Let me give you one final check and we'll get the last of the paperwork sorted,' the doctor said. 'How's your headache?'

'Still there,' Alice-Miranda admitted begrudgingly, 'but it feels more like a dull ache now. It's hardly bothering me – well, not compared to the feeling that someone was practising tennis inside my skull.'

The doctor smiled. 'That's a very good description, Alice-Miranda. I'll have to remember that one in future. And what about your ankle?'

'It's a touch sore but not too bad. The stitches inside my mouth feel a bit scratchy, but won't they dissolve soon?'

Dr Miller nodded. She took Alice-Miranda's blood pressure and listened to her chest, then checked her eyes with her tiny torch before pulling the sheets back and examining her ankle. 'On behalf of all of us here at the children's hospital, I'm a little sad to say that you're right to go.'

Cecelia dabbed at the moisture gathering in the corners of her eyes.

'Now, Mummy, we've talked about this,' Alice-Miranda said sternly. 'There is absolutely no need to cry – not when it's good news. I'm coming home sooner than expected. Look at it as having me all to yourself for a couple of extra days. Although I'm afraid I'm going to be more of a bother than a help.'

'I'm sorry for being so emotional,' Cecelia said, sniffling into her tissue. 'It's just that this is the best news we've had all week.'

'We've been to collect your things from school this morning,' Shilly said. 'And Millie's very keen to chat on the phone once you're home.' She picked up Alice-Miranda's suitcase in one hand and a pot plant in the other. 'Ma'am, why don't we take some of the flowers out to the car while we wait for the paperwork?'

'Just the orchids and those beautiful violets from school and that gorgeous arrangement from Granny and the vase full of tulips from Aunty Gee,' Alice-Miranda instructed. 'I'm going to give the rest of the flowers to the staff. They've looked after me so well, they all deserve something lovely in return.'

News quickly travelled that Chattering's favourite patient was being released. Matron Evans was the first to drop by, followed by a procession of other staff members and patients. To their great delight and surprise, every single one of them left with flowers. But there was one bouquet, of the most divine irises and roses, that was reserved for a very special someone.

'Hello, hello, my dear, top of the morning to you,' Mrs Tigwell trilled, wheeling her trolley into Room 2B.

Alice-Miranda beamed at the tea lady. 'Good morning, Mrs Tigwell. You won't believe what wonderful news I have. It seems I'm going home.'

The woman's smile faltered. 'I'm glad you're on the mend, lovely one, but I'll miss seeing your sunny face each day. I don't remember having such a happy patient for a long time.'

'I've saved these for you,' Alice-Miranda said, pointing to the last stand of flowers.

Mrs Tigwell shook her head and blushed. 'I couldn't possibly take them.'

'I insist,' Alice-Miranda said. 'And Mummy can tell you that once I've made up my mind, there's not much point in trying to convince me otherwise. You've been so kind and I have more than enough.'

'Well, if you're sure, then I won't say no. They're far too beautiful to leave behind and they'd look superb in the middle of my kitchen table.' The woman smiled. 'Would you like a hot chocolate before you go?'

'Oh, Mrs Tigwell, you know I couldn't resist,' Alice-Miranda said, her eyes sparkling.

The woman swiftly produced a pot from the bottom tray of her trolley, which, unbeknown to Alice-Miranda, she'd been making every day just for her.

Chapter 9

'I don't know why *I* wasn't allowed to go to the hospital,' Caprice griped as the girls neared the assembly hall. 'I mean, she's my friend as well. It's not fair that only you two and Jacinta got to go every day, and I heard Sep and Lucas were there yesterday.'

'You could send her a card,' Sloane suggested. 'She wasn't in hospital having a picnic, you know. Alice-Miranda was quite badly injured in the fall.'

Millie hadn't said a word. She didn't feel like getting into a fight with Caprice right now.

Miss Grimm had been very particular about not overloading Alice-Miranda for a reason and, as it was, the girls were only permitted to stay a short time on each occasion.

Josiah Plumpton scurried along behind the trio, urging them to hurry up. He could hear Mr Trout playing the school song, which generally meant the headmistress was ready and waiting for the processional to start. The girls inched past the teachers, who were assembled at the door, and quickly slid into their seats as Mr Trout's chorus reached its crescendo. On stage, Miss Reedy asked the assembly to stand and Miss Grimm and the other staff members marched down the aisle, their academic gowns flowing. Mr Plumpton was the only teacher who insisted on wearing his mortar board these days, despite Miss Grimm having long ago decreed them as an optional extra as she hated the way hers messed up her hair.

'Is Miss Grimm all right?' Sloane whispered, nudging Millie.

The woman looked wobbly at best. She reached the stairs and managed to make it onto the stage, but by then her face had taken on a rather peaky shade of green.

'I think she's going to be sick,' Caprice said, a little louder than she'd intended. All eyes immediately focused on the headmistress.

Ophelia Grimm felt hot and cold and clammy at the same time. Her stomach was roiling and she soon realised that, if she didn't get out of there within seconds, this assembly could possibly turn into the worst moment of her life.

'Livinia, please take over,' she said, and desperately turned to look for something to catch what was coming. She snatched the closest thing next to her, which just so happened to be Mr Plumpton's mortar board, before fleeing as fast as she could off the side of the stage and into the wings. The assembly hall fell deathly silent until all of a sudden the sound of the headmistress losing her lunch echoed through the building.

'Gross!' Caprice groaned, scrunching up her face. 'Miss Grimm threw up.'

'In Mr Plumpton's hat, I'd say,' Sloane added.

The man's face distorted and he shuddered at the thought.

A wave of sympathetic retching filled the hall. Benitha Wall raced after the headmistress as Livinia Reedy stood speechless for a moment, before she took a deep breath and pulled herself together. 'Girls, stop that nonsense at once. You're all fine. Miss Grimm, though, is obviously unwell. We will continue with our assembly and you will not make another sound.'

'But, Miss Reedy, I don't feel so good either,' a voice squeaked from the front row. It was little Mimi Theopolis.

'Anna, take Mimi outside for some air,' the woman directed. 'And if you need to go back to the boarding house and lie down, ask Mrs Derby to phone Mrs Howard to make sure she's there.'

Livinia looked out at the girls and noticed a general malaise. Surely they weren't going to be hit with a dreadful epidemic just before the end of the term. That was the last thing they needed. Livinia read some notices and handed out the weekly awards before giving an update on Alice-Miranda's progress.

'Girls, I know that many of you have been extremely worried about Alice-Miranda. I am pleased to report that she should be leaving hospital right about now. She's going home for the remainder of the term and her mother has promised to let us know how she is. Suffice to say, she's a lucky girl as it was an especially nasty fall. Which leads me to the next announcement. Will Millie please make her way to the stage?'

Millie could feel her freckles firing up as she stood uncertainly. She walked to the stairs and took her place beside the teacher.

Livinia Reedy held a large embossed certificate in the air. 'On behalf of the headmistress and all the staff here at Winchesterfield-Downsfordvale Academy for Proper Young Ladies, I am so very proud to present Millicent Jane McLoughlin-McTavish-McNoughton-McGill with the Eleanor and Algernon Bateman Memorial Award for her calm and sensible actions in the face of great shock and calamity.'

The teacher reached out to shake the child's hand.

'Thank you, Miss Reedy,' Millie said quietly. 'You didn't have to do this. I'm just glad that Alice-Miranda is going to be okay.'

'You were terribly brave, Millie – and we're all very grateful,' the teacher whispered, then stepped back to the microphone. 'Please join me in a round of applause.'

Within seconds, the entire assembly was on their feet, stamping and clapping and cheering.

'Thank you, girls,' the woman said. 'With only two days to go, I'd like to congratulate everyone on an excellent term. We have some certificates to hand out, but I think we should wait until dinner tomorrow evening so that Miss Grimm can join us.'

There were a few groans, which Livinia managed to silence with a raised eyebrow and a glare. Noticing that Miss Wall had returned to the stage, she called the woman over to give a run-down on end-of-term activities and transport arrangements for Saturday. The PE teacher stood up and walked to the microphone, but not before whispering something in Miss Reedy's ear.

Livinia stepped back and, while Benitha talked about pack-ups and pick-ups, her thoughts drifted to the headmistress. She hoped with all her might that the woman's current state didn't have anything to do with the recent Kennington's food-poisoning outbreak.

Chapter 10

Daisy Rumble thumbed through the patient files, ensuring they were all in perfect alphabetical order. Mrs Minchin would be back from her holidays tomorrow and the woman was a stickler for detail. Daisy remembered the last time the woman had almost bitten her head off, when she'd put McDonald before MacMahon. Daisy enjoyed her work at the surgery and was quite hopeful that Mrs Minchin might retire soon. The woman's husband seemed keen to spend a lot more time on the road in their caravan, but when Daisy had mentioned something about becoming grey nomads, Mrs Minchin had suddenly grown short of breath and wild-eyed.

Dr Everingham was such a kind fellow, Daisy knew she'd enjoy a permanent position in the practice. Although, Daisy still had her work at Highton Hall and spent at least two days of the week going to visit Granny over at Pelham Park. Daisy had also picked up some part-time cleaning work there too, for Matron Bright.

The telephone rang, interrupting her thoughts.

'Good afternoon. Dr Everingham's surgery, how may I help you?' Daisy chirped into the handset.

Clearly, the man on the other end of the line hadn't realised who she was as he asked twice if she could give him Daisy Rumble's number. Finally, she managed to convince him that *she* was in fact Daisy Rumble and she'd be delighted to fill in for their nanny, who was unwell. Daisy could well attest to the girl's miseries as Penny had been in the surgery earlier with a head full of flu. She couldn't possibly have managed the children in that state. Daisy liked the Treloar youngsters, having looked after them a couple of times before when Penny had been away on holiday. Their father, Bentley, was a bit of an odd bod, and the wife seemed wound up like a clock most of the time, but it wasn't as if she was going to be looking after either of them. Their oldest, Dottie, was such a sweet little girl and Leo and the baby were adorable.

Daisy hung up the telephone and glanced at her watch. She'd have to dash home first and collect a change of clothes as she was required to stay overnight. Bentley Treloar was on the night shift and his wife worked away during the week. The man had sounded quite desperate and had even offered to pay twice her normal rate. That wasn't necessary, of course. Daisy Rumble had been brought up never to take advantage.

★

Adrienne Treloar kicked off her shoes and plonked down on the ancient armchair in the tiny flat she called home during the week. She'd just worked a double shift and was due back in six hours, but for now she had to attend to some important matters before snatching a couple of hours' sleep.

Today she'd received the call she'd been waiting for. There was a second interview, and with the work she was currently doing, there was no way she could be overlooked again. Head of Paediatrics at a major children's hospital was something Adrienne had dreamed of since she was a little girl, having been overlooked for everything else in life. But she'd show them all – especially that slimy hospital administrator, Edwin Rochester. It was his fault that her last tilt at a promotion had fallen through. Well, perhaps not entirely his fault, but he was the one who ultimately put the kybosh on things. She had been going to head up a research team with funding from the Paper Moon Foundation until it all went sour, thanks to the rotten man who made off with every last cent.

Adrienne opened her laptop and checked the news websites. The Kennington's food-poisoning scare was certainly dominating the nation's headlines. Her eyes skimmed the list of research sites she'd bookmarked for reading. It was a good thing she enjoyed work and could exist on an extremely minimal amount of sleep.

For a moment, her mind wandered to Bentley. He was the smartest person she knew yet, in the ten years since everything he'd been working towards had been ripped from his hands, he'd changed. Instead of trying to reclaim what was rightfully his, a sort of malaise had taken possession of her husband. It was almost breathtaking how one person's actions could affect the lives of so many others. Since then Adrienne had had to work twice as hard and aim twice as high to keep a roof over their heads and to pay back the loan Bentley had taken out to fund his research and development – all of which had amounted to absolutely nothing.

It was disappointing, to say the least. Bentley could have won the Nobel Prize by now if only he hadn't been such a coward. Adrienne sighed and returned to the task at hand. If she had any say in the matter, things would come right in the end and perhaps she'd be the one with the Nobel Prize instead.

Chapter 11

Cecelia Highton-Smith pulled up to the side entrance of Highton Hall and turned off the ignition. If she hadn't been so preoccupied, she might have noticed the standard roses had been trimmed into the most perfect round balls, their delectable pink blooms fragrant in the evening air. Mr Greening and Max were on hand to greet them, having received a call from Mrs Greening at the gatehouse a few minutes earlier, alerting them to Cecelia's impending arrival.

'Hello Mr Greening, hello Max,' Alice-Miranda called. She waved from the back seat, where she had been positioned with her leg elevated and a pillow tucked behind her head. Apart from a few bumps in the road and a slightly twisted seatbelt, the journey had been a relatively comfortable one.

'Hello there, poppet,' Mr Greening replied, carefully opening the door so she wouldn't tumble out. 'It's good to have you home. You gave us quite a scare, you know.' He peered into the back of the Range Rover. 'Did you happen to rob a florist on the way here?'

Alice-Miranda grinned. 'This isn't half of it, I'm afraid. There were so many stunning arrangements, but nothing compares to seeing your roses here at home,' she said, and wrapped her arms around the man's neck. She pecked his cheek as he lifted her out of the car. 'You won't have to do this for long, I promise. I've had a few days of practice on my crutches and I'm certain I'll be wheeling about the grounds in no time.'

'I think we'll get you inside and then you can show off to your heart's content. But I'm not trusting this loose gravel out here,' the man said.

'Just wait until I get my hands on Bonaparte,' Max growled. 'It's extra training for that little blighter over the next few weeks. Teach him to baulk at hares in the grass.'

'Please don't be cross with him, Max,' Alice-Miranda said. 'It wasn't entirely his fault, and the loyal beast stayed with me the whole time. When Millie came back with help, they found him nibbling at my hair and licking my face.'

'Well, perhaps I won't be too hard on him then,' the young man relented. 'I'm off to pick him up tomorrow.'

'Poor Chops will miss him,' Alice-Miranda said.

But there was no point having Bony over at school when there was no one to ride him, and at least here at home Max could keep him lunged and out of the long grass.

'Where's Daddy?' Alice-Miranda asked, realising that her father was missing.

Cecelia looked at Shilly, who frowned. 'He's had to go away for a couple of days. They're investigating one of the factories and he was anxious to be there.'

Alice-Miranda stared at her mother blankly. Then it all came rushing back to her. 'Oh, Mummy, I'd completely forgotten about Kennington's,' she gasped. 'I haven't thought of it once since I hit my head. Anyone would think I had a touch of amnesia! Here I was worrying about flowers – how thoughtless of me. Have you found the source of the contamination?'

'That's not for you to worry about,' Shilly said firmly. 'You need to devote all your energy to getting better.'

'Please tell me what's going on,' the child implored. 'I'm sure I could do something to help.'

But it was no use. It seemed the entire household had closed ranks against her. She looked to Mr Greening, who remained tight-lipped. Even Max shook his head.

'Shilly's right, darling,' her mother said softly. 'Leave it to Daddy and me to sort out the business. I'm sure we're very close to a breakthrough.'

Mr Shillingsworth glanced at Cecelia. The pair knew that was an out-and-out lie. So far there had been no progress whatsoever.

Dolly appeared at the kitchen door, wiping her hands on her apron. Her immovable brown helmet of curls sat immaculately in place, as always, and she'd even managed to put on some lipstick just as the car had pulled up. She rushed out and gave Alice-Miranda a kiss on the forehead before hugging

Cecelia tightly. Alice-Miranda didn't miss the look that passed between the two women. It felt as if everyone knew something and they weren't telling.

'Welcome home, darling girl,' Dolly trilled. 'Come on inside, then. I've got soup and bread fresh from the oven for everyone. Then, young lady, it's off to bed for you.'

'But I feel so much better than I did yesterday,' Alice-Miranda protested.

'Nevertheless, *I'll* feel better when you're tucked up in your own bed and getting the rest you need.' Dolly reached into her apron pocket for a tissue but pulled out a potato peeler instead. She wondered how long it had been there and why. With everything that was going on, she was beginning to feel a bit addled.

Mr Greening carried the child inside. Dolly had laid the scrubbed pine table in the kitchen for supper and there was a special seat with a stool for Alice-Miranda to rest her leg at the end.

The child raised her nose into the air. 'Something smells delicious,' she said, sighing happily. 'Is it pumpkin and sweet potato with just a hint of ginger?'

Dolly tapped the side of her nose. 'I see your sense of smell is as good as ever.'

'Mrs Smith insisted on bringing me meals from school because she said that the hospital offerings were atrocious, but I had a couple of snacks and they weren't too bad at all,' Alice-Miranda said. 'I didn't want to hurt the hospital cook's feelings by not eating their food, so I gave my helping to one of the orderlies. Mr Kendall always looked hungry and he was very grateful. I think he had a tear in his eye when I insisted he take that beautiful bouquet of lilies from Prince Shivaji for his wife too. He was such a kind fellow – they all were. I don't think I could have had a lovelier experience for my first time in hospital.'

'That's wonderful, dear,' Dolly said, slicing up a fresh loaf of bread. 'I just hope it will be your last time in hospital for a very long while.'

There was a knock on the door followed by the sound of Mrs Greening's cheery voice. The woman had been eager to see for herself that Alice-Miranda was doing as well as had been reported. 'Hello, everyone,' she called, then bustled over to Alice-Miranda. 'How are you, sweetheart?'

Alice-Miranda smiled up at her. 'Much better, thank you,' she said, yawning widely. 'Oh, perhaps the drive has taken more out of me than I thought.'

The family and friends took their seats around the table and in no time flat Mrs Oliver and Shilly had served steaming bowls of soup and chunks of warm bread. Alice-Miranda managed to eat half of her helping before her head began to nod and she was having trouble keeping her eyes open.

'I think that's enough for you, darling,' Cecelia said, looking at her daughter. 'Mr Greening, would you mind helping me take Alice-Miranda up to her room? It's bedtime for our lady of the hour.'

'But it's not even dark outside,' the child said, yawning again.

'Goodnight,' the group chorused.

Harold Greening scooped Alice-Miranda into his arms. She held on as he followed Cecelia up the back stairs to the second-floor landing.

'We've made some changes so you'll have everything you need up here,' her mother said.

Cecelia pushed open the door to the child's pretty bedroom, with its huge four-poster bed, pair of cedar armoires and black marble fireplace. In one corner was an enormous doll's house, which was an exact replica of Highton Hall right down to the cellars and secret passageways. The evening before their arrival, Shilly had been up dusting and polishing and arranging several bouquets of flowers that had been sent directly to the house. The most gorgeous array of blue hydrangeas sat in the middle of the mantelpiece, in one of Shilly's favourite crystal vases. She hadn't thought Cecelia would mind her using it on this occasion.

'There's a bell you can ring if you need us, and we've installed an intercom system too. Well, it's your old baby monitor, but it still works perfectly,' Cecelia prattled. She drew the curtains and turned to find Mr Greening holding a finger to his lips. It seemed Alice-Miranda hadn't heard a word, as she was already fast asleep.

Chapter 12

'The food-poisoning outbreak that has now affected more than two hundred people around the country remains a mystery as Hugh Kennington-Jones prepares to hold his first press conference since the riding accident last weekend, which landed his nine-year-old daughter in hospital for several days,' the newsreader announced. 'We're going to throw to our man on the ground, Simon Brent. Good morning, Simon,' the woman said.

'Turn it off, Shilly,' Dolly said wearily as she walked into the side sitting room. 'We know what he's going to say.' She plucked some lint from the front of her navy cardigan and yawned.

Mrs Shillingsworth picked up the remote and did as she was bid. 'It's terrible how many children are among the sick. I wonder if it's something they particularly like to eat.'

'That's a very good point, Shill. They recalled all the bread and milk, as they were the things most shoppers had purchased in common, but I've tested the samples myself and there is nothing wrong with any of those products. It just doesn't make any sense. I'll speak with Hugh and see if there's an abundance of school snacks or juice pops on the grocery receipts,' Dolly replied.

'What about the stores?' Shilly asked. 'Could it be some sort of environmental contaminant?'

Dolly Oliver placed the tea tray on the small table and proceeded to pour her and Shilly a strong brew. 'Hugh's had each one thoroughly investigated and scrubbed from top to bottom. I've never seen the man so anxious – and with Alice-Miranda's accident at the same time. I can't tell you what this whole fiasco has done to my nerves.'

The ladies sat in silence, both lost in their own thoughts about the events of the past week. It had been a challenging time, to say the least, but there was one bright spot with Alice-Miranda now home and on the mend and the house full of gorgeous flowers. Despite leaving most of them behind with the hospital staff, well-wishers had continued sending more and Highton Hall was beginning to resemble the village flower show. The last arrangement that had arrived from Baron and Baroness von Zwicky required two men to carry it into the house and it now sat pride of place in the front entrance hall.

Shilly reached for her diary, which she had tucked into the side of the armchair, and flipped it open on her lap. She looked at the page then at her friend, her mug frozen midway to her lips.

Dolly glanced up from her brew. 'What is it?'

'It seems, with everything that's been going on, I've put the garden party and open house completely out of my head. It's the weekend after next – that's not even ten days away!' Shilly gasped, feeling the full weight of the revelation. 'Good heavens, Dolly, I must have lost my mind. Perhaps I've got Alzheimer's. Can one get such a thing overnight?'

Dolly reached across and patted the woman's arm. 'There, there. I'm sure you don't have anything of the sort, my dear. We've had quite a few shocks this week. I'd completely forgotten about it myself.'

Shilly's mind was reeling. 'There's so much to be done. I've got to clean the house from top to bottom and sort the flowers and what am I going to do with all those arrangements that have been arriving? They'll be dead by then and I'll have to deal with them all over again. We need to move the furniture in the large drawing room, and there are some carpets that must be steamed. Never mind fetching the endless miles of rope barriers from the attic – I won't have any little horrors going places they shouldn't. Not to mention the gardens. Is Harold on top of that? Heavens! Her Majesty will be here to relaunch the foundation. Oh, whatever am I going to do?'

'Shilly, please calm down. The last thing we need is for you to have a heart attack on top of everything else,' Dolly urged. 'Fortunately, I've already planned the catering and ordered most of the food for the tea tent, but I have yet to organise any additional staff. Perhaps I can ask Doreen if she can come and help, given it's school holidays next week and she told me last time we spoke that she didn't have any plans.'

'Good idea. Why don't you call her now?' Shilly took a deep breath, then smacked her forehead.

'No wonder Lily rang to ask when I needed her again. She must think I've lost the plot.'

Dolly shot her a reproachful look. 'Don't be ridiculous. There's no one who runs a household like you. I'm sure you can galvanise the troops and have everything done in time. At least we never have a minute to sit still and think too much around here.'

'Right. Lists,' Shilly muttered to herself. 'I need to make some lists.'

'I'll call Doreen and then I'm going to head back downstairs for a little while,' Dolly said, pushing herself out of the armchair. 'There was a delivery this morning of some more food samples to test. I'll also ask Hugh for copies of the grocery receipts to see if there's anything youngsters particularly like to eat.'

'Children are notorious for sharing their food in the playground – perhaps there are some who are sick and their parents haven't even shopped at Kennington's recently. That might explain why a pattern hasn't yet emerged,' Shilly said.

Dolly nodded, a faraway look in her eyes. 'I wonder . . .'

'Well, I'd better pop upstairs and check on the patient before I get on with my planning. She's been very quiet this morning.' Shilly stood up and went to take the tray.

'Leave that, dear. I'll see to it,' Dolly said.

Mrs Shillingsworth headed up the back stairs to the second-floor landing. She gave the wide hallway an appraising glance, mentally calculating if there would be time to have the Chinese carpet that ran down the middle of the wide timber boards steam-cleaned before the garden party. Although, after last year's muddy debacle, perhaps she wouldn't bother. It was just that she'd spotted the smallest hint of a stain in one corner and knowing it was there would be a source of constant irritation until it was removed.

She straightened a huge portrait of Cecelia's father and whipped out a dusting cloth from her apron. Desperate times called for desperate measures – she couldn't afford to walk past a stick of furniture without giving it the once-over. Along the hallway, three matching French side tables on elegant cabriole legs stood with their bulbous inlaid bodies like overweight sentries. Their cream marble tops played host to an array of family photographs, ceramic vases and other dust-gathering antiquities collected over the decades. She gave each surface a quick spit and polish before rapping quietly on Alice-Miranda's bedroom door.

'Are you awake, dear?' she said, turning the ancient ceramic handle.

'Hello Shilly,' the child chirped from a cloud of pillows. Alice-Miranda slotted her bookmark between the pages and set *Anne of Green Gables* onto her bedside table.

'How are you feeling?' The woman ran her dusting cloth along the roof of Alice-Miranda's doll's house.

'Much better, thank you. I managed five chapters this morning and my head isn't hurting at all. I think the concussion must be better because I couldn't read so much as a label in hospital before the world began to spin before my eyes. And I've been to the toilet on my own this morning too,' Alice-Miranda said proudly.

'You were supposed to call down so I could help you,' the woman scolded. 'What if you'd slipped?'

'But I didn't, Shilly,' Alice-Miranda pointed out. 'And I'd really like to have a shower, if I may. My hair feels awful. Mummy tried to give it a sponge but it needs a proper wash. Speaking of Mummy, is she home?'

'She and your father are at Kennington's head office. She'll be back tonight,' the woman said as she dusted the windowsills and the rocking horse in the corner. 'I think your father won't be home until tomorrow evening.'

'Is there any news?' Alice-Miranda asked. 'Please don't keep me in the dark, Shilly. I know you think I can't do anything to help, but it won't hurt to know what's going on.'

The older woman looked at the child and hesitated. 'Why don't we get you into the shower and I'll fill you in then?'

The girl smiled at her. 'Thank you,' she said. 'And maybe afterwards I can come downstairs and keep you company. We could even play Old Maid. I've become quite good, you know. But first I should write my thank-you messages and then maybe I could make some get-well cards for all the people who've fallen ill from this nasty bout of food poisoning. I know the cards I got while I was in hospital made me feel so much better. It's always nice to know that people are thinking of you when you're not at your best.'

'I don't think I have time for games, my dear. I've got a lot of work to do. There's a certain garden party and open day at the end of next week,' Shilly said, paling at the thought.

Alice-Miranda's eyes widened. 'Of course! I love the garden party,' she gushed. 'It's one of my favourite days of the year.'

'I'm glad the garden party is somebody's favourite time of year. All those people traipsing through the house and me worrying myself into a stupor that things will go missing, let alone losing sleep over the weather forecast. I was still getting the mud out of the carpets months after last year's disaster,' Shilly huffed as she vigorously polished the nostrils of Alice-Miranda's rocking horse.

'Be careful, you'll make him sneeze,' Alice-Miranda laughed.

Shilly sighed. 'Well, if I could do that, I'd have some sort of magic powers and cleaning this house would be a cinch.'

'Anyway, no one knew we were going to have the worst storms in a hundred years that weekend,' Alice-Miranda said. 'I thought everyone was very well behaved, all things considered. That is, except Mummy's cousin Richard's son.'

'I warned your mother after last year's garden party that I'll lock that boy in the larder if he shows his face again,' Shilly blustered. 'By accident, of course.'

Alice-Miranda giggled at the naughty grin on Mrs Shillingsworth's face. She could only agree, seeing as though she had been the one who had caught the reprobate seven-year-old smearing Vaseline on the banister rail and pouring his lemonade into the coffee urn. He had even found time to sprinkle salt all over the cinnamon donuts Mrs Oliver had made. He was definitely tricky.

'Lucky for you, Mummy said they've gone to live in the Middle East,' Alice-Miranda reported.

Shilly scoffed. 'I wish the Arabs luck teaching that little mischief-maker some manners.'

Chapter 13

Jemima Tavistock strolled through the third-floor hallway, wondering how soon she could get the builders in. The classical decor was not to her taste and she was dying to redo the ceilings. Those hand-painted frescos were so fussy. If she had her way, she'd get rid of most of the furniture too. It was all terribly . . . brown. She was excited to finally be able to put that interiors course she'd done a few summers ago to practice.

Her husband, Anthony, had never fancied himself taking on the stately pile, but Jemima had managed to convince him that it was his duty by virtue of his lineage. Besides, it wasn't a long trip into the city. They still had the townhouse and could travel back and forth when necessary, which seemed to be every week as far as her husband was concerned. Jemima, on the other hand, had spent much of her childhood dreaming of a country estate. She was going to have dogs and horses and learn to ride. She would host the most splendid garden parties and fundraisers, and her new friends would turn green with envy. She'd get to meet all the right people and attend the most exclusive events. The opportunities would be endless. There were other things she needed to do too – things that would correct past injustices.

She was counting on the fact that their neighbours Cecelia Highton-Smith and Hugh Kennington-Jones would invite them over to dinner soon. Jemima had expected it to happen long before now and was actually feeling a bit miffed. They had sent her and Anthony a wedding present – a beautifully useless antique silver tea set, which she'd half considered selling – but there was still no word of a face-to-face meeting. Cecelia and Hugh knew *everyone* worth knowing, and Cecelia's sister was married to that dreamy actor Lawrence Ridley.

Jemima stopped to check her reflection in an enormous gilded mirror and thought about how many generations of Tavistock women must have stood in that spot doing the exact same thing. Their portraits stared down at her from the stairwell. She wanted hers up there as soon as possible but was yet to choose an artist and line up the sittings. As the most recent Lady of Bedford Manor, she needed to make her mark.

She tucked a rogue strand of blonde hair behind her ear and ran her forefinger down her brand-new nose. It had certainly made a difference – that and the iris recolouring. Who knew that, when she had copped a wayward bag of cement to the face while walking past a building site a couple of years ago, it would actually work out for the best. For a few months she'd been shocked whenever she'd seen her reflection, but overall she was pleased with her fresh look. Jemima had also gone from brunette to blonde. Though none of it was planned, the changes were probably best, given recent events.

Her husband bounded up the staircase to meet her halfway. 'I'm afraid I must be off, darling,' he said, kissing Jemima goodbye. 'I'll call you when I get to town.'

'Goodbye, my love,' Jemima sighed wistfully.

Anthony Tavistock could hardly believe his good fortune. His parents had at times despaired that their only son and heir would never marry. There had been girlfriends over the years, but it wasn't until recently that he had known what it was to fall head over heels in love. It was one gloomy day ten months ago that he'd been introduced to Jemima at a party and she had quite literally taken his breath away. The rest, as they say, was history. Jemima made him feel so worthy, when he had often struggled with the idea of his dumb luck. He was painfully aware that he'd done nothing to deserve his title, and the wealth that went with it, and lived with the nagging guilt that he could enjoy a life of relative luxury compared to most. It just didn't seem fair, really.

His father had always encouraged him to study hard and make something of himself. He said that everyone needed a career and doing nothing was not an option – for which Anthony was now very grateful. He loved working for a non-profit low-cost housing provider and, no matter what happened, he wasn't about to give it up anytime soon. He had no desire to swan about being Lord of the Manor when there were people who didn't even have a roof over their heads. In any case, Jemima was perfectly capable of running the house. She'd told him so herself. And she seemed to revel in the ways of country life.

✯

Alice-Miranda hung up the telephone. It was wonderful to hear Millie's voice and to catch up on the Winchesterfield-Downsfordvale news, but it was rather strange not being there with all her friends. She'd never been at home during the school term and found there was something especially peculiar about it. At least she had the reading list for next term, which she planned to work her way through over the break.

Alice-Miranda snuggled in under the blanket on the couch, where Shilly had set her up with her cards and pencil case and a little tray to work on. There was a glass of water and a plate of cheese and crackers on the coffee table in front of her. She picked up a black felt-tip pen and started to draw a smiling Bonaparte, having decided that he would make quite a fetching subject for a get-well card.

The sound of heels tripping on the timber floor echoed through the kitchen.

'Is that you, Mummy?' Alice-Miranda called.

'Darling, what are you doing down here?' Cecelia walked into the room and gave Alice-Miranda a big hug and kiss.

'I thought Shilly might like some company,' the child replied. 'Well, that's not entirely true. I was mind-numbingly bored upstairs. I've tried to keep myself busy and have written lots of thank-you cards and had a chat with Millie. Apparently, Miss Grimm threw up in Mr Plumpton's mortar board at assembly – can you imagine it?' Alice-Miranda giggled, then quickly sobered. 'I hope she hasn't been struck down with food poisoning. That would be too awful for words. And Millie said that Chops is coming home with Bony because Bony refused to get on the truck this afternoon without him. Apparently, the stables at Millie's place are being renovated, so that works out well for everyone. Millie might come to visit in the holidays and we can go riding,' the child said, stopping to catch her breath.

Cecelia frowned. 'Steady on, darling, we'll have to see about that.'

'I was also thinking that maybe Mrs Oliver would like some help downstairs. I could write lists and check things off for her,' Alice-Miranda said.

'I could even assist her with some of the testing. I'm quite good at Science and Mr Plumpton said that my lab work was excellent this past term.'

'Perhaps not today,' Cecelia began, then, spotting the look of disappointment on her daughter's face, added, 'but we could run the idea past her tomorrow. Now, I think I might make a cup of tea and have some of that delicious hummingbird cake I spied in the kitchen. Would you like a slice?'

Alice-Miranda grinned and nodded. 'Yes, please.'

'And why don't you set us up a game of Scrabble?' Cecelia called as she walked back out to put the kettle on. 'Work can wait a little while. It's not often I get you at home to myself.'

Alice-Miranda hastily set aside her stationery. Maybe being home from school wasn't such a bad thing after all.

Chapter 14

Queen Georgiana tossed and turned. She usually slept like a stone but, tonight, despite a mug of cocoa before bed, her mind simply refused to switch off. She had lain awake for hours, a showreel of worries playing in her head. On the one hand, she was relieved to hear that Alice-Miranda was on the mend, but there was still this nonsense with Kennington's. People were dropping like flies yet there were apparently no clues as to the source of the contamination. The whole thing beggared belief.

Poor Cecelia also had the garden party coming up too. It was a terribly important occasion, particularly with the relaunching of the Paper Moon Foundation after that dreadful swindler made off with all the money. Her Majesty sighed and reached across to snuggle the feather-down pillow beside her. She almost went through the bed canopy when the object yelped loudly.

She tore off her eye mask and came face to face with one of her beagles. The pooch resentfully wriggled from her grasp and leapt to the floor.

'Oh heavens, I am sorry, Petunia,' the Queen apologised.

She looked around for Archie and saw that he was sound asleep in his basket in front of the hearth.

'This is a nonsense,' she muttered, pushing back the covers and swivelling her feet to the ground. 'A snack is what we need. Are you two coming?' She pulled on her dressing-gown and stuffed her feet into her favourite pair of lamb's-wool slippers.

Archie raised his head and hopped out of his bed. Petunia scampered to the door. Neither creature wanted to be left behind if there was a pantry raid in the offing.

The Queen and her dogs tripped along the hallway towards the back stairs. Although it was the middle of the night, Evesbury Palace was far from silent with its abundant creaks and groans, not to mention the ticking of the thousand or so clocks which seemed to grow louder in the evenings. She reached the kitchens, comprised of a labyrinth of rooms beneath the palace, and was glad to find the place empty. She hated startling the staff and quite liked being able to make herself a cup of tea and some toast every now and again.

Archie and Petunia danced around her feet, eager for a treat.

Queen Georgiana walked into the larder and pulled the cord to switch on the lights. She squinted, then rubbed her eyes.

'Heavens, we've been robbed!' the Queen exclaimed as she surveyed the empty shelves. Her Majesty hurried to the nearest telephone and punched in three numbers. 'Mrs Marmalade, get down here immediately,' she ordered. 'I think we have had an intruder.'

Not a minute later, Marian Marmalade thudded down the stairs. She was a sight to behold in her floral robe and her hair in rollers, clutching the brass candelabra she'd thought to snatch up along the way.

'Ma'am, what is it?' The woman cast a bewildered glance around the seemingly undisturbed room, wondering why Her Majesty hadn't thought to call Dalton, her personal bodyguard, instead of her lady-in-waiting. Marian had been having the most marvellous dream and had not appreciated the call one bit.

'The larder is practically empty,' the Queen blustered.

Marian gulped and lowered her weapon. If only Her Majesty had stayed out of the servants' quarters, she'd have been none the wiser. 'Ma'am, I'm afraid the staff have removed all of the Kennington's products. On Dalton's orders.' The woman wasn't averse to that silly old trout being blamed.

The Queen's nostrils flared. 'And what about my favourite marmalade? I came down for some tea and toast and you know I cannot take my toast without Kennington's marmalade.'

'Gone,' her lady-in-waiting squeaked.

Queen Georgiana balled her fists. 'Well, this is utterly preposterous! I've been eating Kennington's marmalade my whole life and I do not intend to stop now. There's only one thing for it.' Her Majesty nodded to herself. 'Get Marjorie on the phone. This business with Kennington's cannot go on a minute longer.'

Marian Marmalade scurried away and pressed the red emergency button hidden behind a tin of shortbread. It was the direct line for Marjorie Plunkett, Head of the Secret Protection League of Defence.

Chapter 15

Alice-Miranda woke with a start. She'd had the same troubling dream ever since she'd returned from Chattering. Each time, she imagined someone standing over her bed, muttering a stream of incoherent babble. The words weren't audible or in any sensible sequence but were spouting forth like speech bubbles in a cartoon. Suddenly, the voice would stop and the person's mouth would lift into a sinister smile. No matter how hard Alice-Miranda tried, the rest of the person's face refused to come into focus.

She pushed back the covers and carefully manoeuvred her way out of bed, using her crutches to hobble to the closest of two double-hung windows in her room. She leaned them against the wall and wriggled behind the billowing cream curtains. Pink rays streamed between tufts of fluffy white clouds and onto the emerald fields below. Beyond the walled garden, Heinrich was out early on the tractor. There was a small herd of cattle milling about near the western fence and wisps of smoke unfurling from the chimney at the Bauers' farmhouse. Perhaps she should invite Jasper and Poppy to visit after school today.

She was hoping to see Daisy soon too. Granny Bert had moved into Pelham Park some time ago and was apparently wreaking havoc with Matron Bright and her nurses. It was only after the old woman had almost burned down Rose Cottage that she'd agreed it was probably time to go into care, but that didn't mean she hadn't resisted it all the way. Granny Bert sang quite a different tune once she had sampled the Pelham Park food and questioned what on earth she'd been thinking to avoid the place for so long. Alice-Miranda wondered if she and her mother could pay Granny a visit while she was home from school.

She heard the bedroom door creak open, followed by a small gasp.

'Darling, where are you?' Cecelia called, a note of panic in her voice.

'I'm here, behind the curtains, Mummy,' came Alice-Miranda's muffled reply.

Cecelia rushed over and pulled them aside, worried that her daughter had somehow got herself tangled. 'Goodness, are you all right?' she asked, tying back the voluminous fabric with the silver tassled rope.

'I was watching the sun rise,' Alice-Miranda said. 'It's going to be a lovely day and I was thinking how much I'd like to say hello to Bony and Chops.'

'Oh, I don't know about that. I'm still a bit cross with Bonaparte,' Cecelia confessed.

'Now, Mummy, we've been through this. And what have you always told me about making amends?' Alice-Miranda said, batting her eyelashes. 'Besides, we can't punish Chops just because you're upset with Bony.'

'You do raise a good point, darling.' Cecelia gave her daughter a hug. 'Come on, then. Hop back into bed and I'll get you some breakfast.'

'I'd really like to come downstairs, if I may?' the child asked. 'I feel a lot better. My head is absolutely fine and my ankle isn't even hurting much, although the colours are rather spectacular.'

Cecelia considered the proposal. She knew that once Alice-Miranda began to improve she was going to be impossible to contain. 'All right, I'll help you get dressed. And how would you feel about being my offsider for the day?'

Alice-Miranda nodded. 'Yes, please! But do you promise we can stop by the stables and say hello to Bonaparte?'

'Well, I have a list of jobs as long as my arm what with the open day and garden party coming up, but we should be able to squeeze in a very quick visit. And I might have a small surprise for you later on, if things go to plan,' Cecelia said mysteriously.

The child's eyes widened and she felt a flutter in her tummy. 'What is it?'

Cecelia grinned and tapped the tip of Alice-Miranda's button nose. 'Oh, no you don't. If I tell you, it won't be a surprise and that's no fun at all.'

★

Jemima Tavistock flicked through another of the dozen interior design magazines piled up beside her at the breakfast table.

A man in a grey suit with matching coloured hair walked into the room. 'Would you like a fresh pot, ma'am?'

'Good grief, no,' she sighed. 'If I drink any more I'll turn into a puddle of tea.'

The butler gave a slight nod and began to clear the plates.

'Oh, Prigg,' Jemima said, flipping her magazine shut, 'I've been meaning to ask you to run some errands. I need you to find me some horses.'

The man seemed almost at a loss for words. 'Horses, ma'am?' he repeated.

'It seems ridiculous to have perfectly beautiful stables standing empty,' Jemima explained. 'I'll need a riding instructor too. And a dog. Better make it two. Or perhaps four. Find out what sort of hounds people prefer around here and hunt down a reputable breeder. But I don't want anything too cutesy. I'd rather have proper country dogs with a bit of a bite to them.'

Prigg's top lip seemed to curl involuntarily as he contemplated her requests.

Jemima's thoughts wandered to Chessie and what she might be up to. Her heart ached every time she spoke to the girl, who would just cry and cry. The headmistress had told Jemima very early on that the only way the child would ever get over her homesickness would be to leave her to get on with things, so that's exactly what she'd done. But it hadn't been easy. That reminded her to call the school to inform them of the change of plan. Mrs Fairbanks would be apoplectic and Chessie would be terribly upset, but what was Jemima to do? It was just too risky to have Chessie around at the minute – at least not until things were sorted out.

Prigg cleared his throat, bringing her crashing back to the moment.

'Oh yes, there's one more thing. Please phone Ms Highton-Smith and tell her that I'll be paying her a visit this morning,' Jemima said.

Prigg recoiled at the proposition, almost dropping his tray in the process. Never in his life would he have dreamt of making such an audacious call. 'Perhaps you would like to invite Ms Highton-Smith over for tea. She hasn't been to Bedford Manor in such a long time and has always had a great affection for the house and the family,' he said, once he had regained his composure. 'I think the last time Ms Highton-Smith was here, she asked Lord Tavistock to join her and Mr Kennington-Jones on their table for a gala dinner Her Majesty was hosting. I can ask Mrs Mudge to whip up a batch of scones and I think she's already baked a lemon curd cake this morning.'

Jemima rolled her eyes. She desperately wanted to see the inside of Cecelia's house. Everyone said it had the most tasteful decor, and she could use some ideas for her own remodelling. 'But I'd prefer to go over there,' Jemima whined. Although, the thought of entrees to spectacular social events, with the Queen no less, held quite an appeal too.

'Might I suggest that an invitation to Ms Highton-Smith would no doubt be repaid in due course,' said the butler.

Jemima was about to object but thought better of it. Prigg was a prickly old pear at the best of times and she needed to have him onside rather than off. When her husband inherited Bedford Manor, she hadn't realised he would also stand to gain the staff who had served his parents for years. As well as the butler, there was Mrs Mudge the cook, Mr Wilson the gardener, and a couple of lads who helped out around the property. Considering the size of the place, though, it all seemed a bit light on. She had half a mind to employ a maid or two.

'Could you make the call then?' Jemima asked.

Prigg looked at his watch and then back at Lady Tavistock.

'All right, wait another hour in case she's a late sleeper,' Jemima relented. 'But don't forget.'

Cedric Prigg doubted that Ms Highton-Smith would be available at such short notice, but at least it would keep Lady Tavistock and her braying at bay for a little while. She'd have no doubt found some other amusement by the time he relayed the bad news.

Chapter 16

Saddled with a formidable list of errands, Cecelia and Alice-Miranda set off to the village early that morning. While the woman's mind was still awhirl with thoughts about the food-poisoning outbreak, she absolutely had to get back on top of the preparations for the garden party. She didn't want to let anyone down. Although it was held at Highton Hall, the annual event saw just about everyone in the village pitching in and either supplying goods or tending a stall. Having evolved from simply opening the house to the public for the day, it now comprised of house tours, a giant tea party on the lawn and a farmers' market with delicious local produce.

Cecelia had raised money for various charities over the years, and this year she was thrilled that the garden party would see the relaunching of an organisation close to her heart. The Paper Moon Foundation supported several of the largest children's hospitals in the country as well as smaller children's wards in rural areas. She and Hugh had both been longtime patrons of the charity until the man running it made off with the funds a couple of years ago. He'd been sent to jail, albeit with a lighter sentence, but the money had never been recovered and it had taken all this time to get things up and running again.

Cecelia had just hopped into the car, having made her last stop at the patisserie. Alice-Miranda had managed to accompany her mother on all their other errands in the village but, as Pierre's was a bit of a walk and they were taking some things back to the car, she'd elected to stay put for this last excursion.

'Well, that was odd,' Cecelia said as she turned the key in the ignition.

Alice-Miranda buckled her seatbelt. 'What was, Mummy?'

'I just spoke to Mr Prigg from Bedford Manor. He called Pierre's while I was there. Apparently, the poor man had rung around half the shops in the village trying to hunt me down,' Cecelia said, shaking her head in puzzlement.

'How peculiar. Why didn't he call your number?' Alice-Miranda asked.

'He phoned the Hall and Shilly told him we were in the village, but she was in such a fluster that she hung up before the man could ask for it,' Cecelia explained with a laugh. 'Anyway, we've been invited to morning tea with Lady Tavistock.'

Alice-Miranda clapped her hands. 'Wonderful! I've been so looking forward to meeting her. I hope she loves Bedford Manor as much as old Lord Tavistock did. You know, I've got just the perfect dress to wear. Which date does she have in mind?'

'Lady Tavistock would like us to come today. Now, actually.' Cecelia raised her eyebrows. 'But I said I'd call Mr Prigg back after I spoke to you. What do you think, darling?'

Alice-Miranda's eyes lit up. 'I'd love to go if you've got time. It doesn't matter about my dress.'

Cecelia glanced at the clock on the dashboard. 'We have got a lot more done than I'd anticipated,' she conceded, 'and it does seem cruel to drive by when we're so close. I've been meaning to invite Lady Tavistock over too – she must think me a dreadful neighbour.' Cecelia bit her lip. 'Perhaps it will take my mind off things for a little while longer.' She nodded firmly. 'Why not?'

'Good decision, Mummy.' Alice-Miranda smiled. 'You'd better let Mr Prigg know we're on our way.'

⋆

Twenty minutes later, and armed with a beautiful bouquet of irises, Cecelia turned down the long driveway into Bedford Manor. Although their properties were adjacent to one another, the entry to the manor was about a fifteen-minute journey on the road to Penberthy Floss. Alice-Miranda had been there on numerous occasions, usually passing through on Bonaparte when she and her father or Aunt Charlotte went riding. Old Lord Tavistock had barely been around in the last few years, preferring to stay in the city. Alice-Miranda had been sad to hear that he'd passed away quite suddenly, especially having seen him not that long ago at Aunty Gee's jubilee celebrations. She'd giggled at his vigorous playing of badminton, but had felt sorry for the man when Aunty Gee had thwacked him in the shin with a boules jack. His wife had died many years before and Alice-Miranda couldn't remember her at all. Their only child, Anthony, was the Lord of Bedford Manor now and had recently married.

They drove through another set of iron gates and up the gravel driveway to the decorative Italianate mansion with its formal border of roses and hedges and sweeping central lawn.

'I think I'd forgotten what a gorgeous estate Bedford Manor is,' Alice-Miranda sighed. 'Do you remember how I used to make up stories about a princess who lived here? At one point I decided she'd been stolen away by a fierce dragon and that it was up to me and Boo to rescue her – except that I was still much too small to ride Boo on my own.'

Cecelia chuckled at the memory. 'Oh yes, it was one of your favourite tales. What was the princess's name again?'

Cecelia hopped out and walked around to help Alice-Miranda from her seat.

'Zinnia,' Alice-Miranda answered as she carefully stepped onto the gravel drive. 'Because Mr Greening had just planted that lovely garden full of zinnias and I thought it was the most perfect name for a princess.'

The front doors swung open and Cedric Prigg strode out.

'Good morning, Ms Highton-Smith,' he said, smiling wryly at Cecelia. 'Lady Tavistock is so pleased that you could come at such short notice.'

'Hello Cedric. We're glad we could too,' Cecelia said, watching as Alice-Miranda wheeled herself around on her crutches. 'I'm only sorry you had to chase me around the entire village. Shilly's a touch distracted at the moment, I'm afraid.'

The man noticed the child was missing a shoe and saw the bandage poking out from the bottom of her trousers. 'Oh dear, what have you done to yourself, miss?' he asked.

'It's not very bad, Mr Prigg,' Alice-Miranda assured him. 'How are you? Are you still enjoying your trainspotting? I wish we could see the rail line from our house. It must be marvellous to watch the carriages rushing to and fro and to be able to judge the time of day from which engine is whooshing by.'

The butler was somewhat taken aback. He'd told the child about his love of trains a couple of years ago, but he never imagined for a second that she would recall their conversation. 'Dear girl, I am as well as can be expected and I'm pleased to report that the morning train to Nibley Green is running on time,' he added with a wink.

Alice-Miranda smiled and hoped he was in good health as his answer seemed rather ominous. She thought he looked a bit pink around the edges, though much better than the last time she'd seen him puffing and panting, having just been in the sack race with Mrs Mudge at the village fair.

'Please, come this way,' Mr Prigg directed, leading them in through the vast foyer.

They passed a grand marble staircase and entered a room on the right, which Alice-Miranda remembered Old Lord Tavistock calling the Great Room. She'd thought it had deserved its name because there were all sorts of interesting things scattered around, such as a stuffed peacock under a dome and a curious cabinet that opened out in all directions and which seemed to contain a never-ending supply of games. When she was very little, Alice-Miranda and Lord Tavistock had played a particularly energetic game of Chinese chequers that he had procured from the cabinet. She wondered if the new Lady Tavistock had discovered its treasures yet.

'Please take a seat while I inform Lady Tavistock of your arrival,' Mr Prigg said. He gave a slight bow then left the room, closing the doors behind him.

Cecelia helped Alice-Miranda onto one of the sofas. She pulled over an ottoman for her daughter to rest her ankle on when the doors opened to reveal a statuesque blonde wearing four-inch heels and a beautifully tailored red dress. It had a fitted bodice and a swishy layered skirt that skimmed the tops of her knees. Her lipstick matched perfectly.

'Hello, you must be Cecelia,' she purred as she stalked over. Lady Tavistock glanced at Alice-Miranda, who was seated on the sofa. 'I didn't realise you'd have your daughter with you. Hello there.'

'It's lovely to meet you, Lady Tavistock,' Cecelia replied, offering her hand and the bouquet of irises. 'Yes, someone had a nasty accident at school last weekend and is now home until next term.'

'Hello Lady Tavistock, it's a pleasure to meet you. My name is Alice-Miranda,' the child said, shaking the woman's hand.

'Do you enjoy it?' Lady Tavistock asked, taking a seat.

Alice-Miranda blinked, then realised the woman was asking about school. 'Oh, yes,' she gushed. 'We have the most amazing lessons at Winchesterfield-Downsfordvale and our teachers are incredible. Recently we had a fantastic week, exploring all manner of scientific and technological things – we had to build towers and solve problems and perform lots of experiments. I can't tell you how many wonderful opportunities I've had since I've been there.'

'How interesting,' Lady Tavistock said, a faraway look in her eyes.

'Lady Tavistock, I do apologise for our appearance too,' Cecelia said, gesturing to their attire. 'We've come straight from running errands in the village and hadn't expected to be calling on you. I hope you'll forgive us.'

Cecelia was dressed in dark jeans and a green silk blouse while Alice-Miranda was in a pair of loose-fitting overalls and a floral shirt. They were hardly what you'd have called shabby, but compared to Lady Tavistock's finery, they both looked a little on the casual side.

Lady Tavistock frowned. 'Please, don't be silly. *I* must apologise for inviting you at such short notice. But it occurred to me this morning that perhaps you might like to pop over and, with Anthony away until tomorrow evening, I'm rather tired of rattling around here on my own.'

Cecelia studied the woman more carefully for a moment. 'Have we met before?'

Jemima swallowed hard. 'No, I'm sure I'd remember. And please, call me Jemima. We're neighbours and I'm certain we're going to be good friends.'

Mr Prigg walked through, carrying a silver tray laden with cups and saucers, a teapot, some fluffy scones and a cake.

Lady Tavistock looked at Alice-Miranda. 'How did you hurt yourself?'

'I fell off my pony, Bonaparte. It was a silly accident,' Alice-Miranda said, glancing at her mother, who was still not feeling overly generous towards the beast.

'We have a lovely stable here,' Jemima said. 'I'm planning to buy some horses soon too. My daugh–' She stopped herself and turned to Cecelia. 'How do you take your tea?'

'Do you have a daughter?' Alice-Miranda asked eagerly, leaning forward in her seat. 'I'd love to meet her.'

Jemima looked away across the room as if she were thinking about something else entirely.

Cecelia smiled at Mr Prigg uncertainly. 'I'll have it white with one sugar, thank you.'

The butler nodded and poured the tea, then offered everyone something to eat before disappearing out the door. Alice-Miranda decided she'd leave it for now. Perhaps there was something the matter and it was none of her business to pry.

'Are you enjoying Bedford Manor?' Cecelia asked between sips.

'It's lovely, but we have major renovations in mind,' Jemima said with a sigh. 'I can't stand the decor. It's so old-fashioned. For a start, I'd like to do something about those ceilings. They're a bit much, aren't they?' Jemima raised her brows skywards at the painted frescos of Greek gods and goddesses.

Cecelia gently put down her teacup, trying to work out the best way to approach the topic. 'I'm afraid I don't think the Heritage Council will allow you to touch them. They're a listed monument. In fact, as far as I understand, the whole house is.'

'What do you mean?' A deep line appeared on the bridge of Jemima's nose. 'It's *our* house. Surely we can decorate it however we like.'

'You would think so, but that's not the way it works with these old places. There are all sorts of restrictions,' Cecelia explained. 'You can't alter any decorative element that's listed other than to restore it to its former glory. We had a devil of a time getting plans approved for our kitchen renovation a few years back. We got there in the end because the original kitchen wasn't practical at all and had been an add-on at some point, but the rest of the house stands pretty much as it was built,' Cecelia explained.

'But I've got inspiration boards! I want to take this house into the twenty-first century and get rid of the fuss and frills,' Jemima griped, as she cut a piece of cake.

Alice-Miranda bit her lip. 'Perhaps you could do something with the gardens,' she suggested. 'There's a lot of room out there.'

Jemima looked up and smiled. 'That silly maze really does have to go. I'll speak to Mr Wilson this afternoon to see if he can call for a bulldozer right away.'

Cecelia and Alice-Miranda looked at each other and Alice-Miranda's stomach sank. Lady Tavistock's idea reminded her of the time one of her parents' business acquaintances, who owned an equally impressive estate, had decided to replace a historic formal rose garden with a go-cart track for his very spoiled son. The man ended up with the head of the planning authority camped out on the property for three whole weeks to put a stop to things.

'I'm sorry to be a stick in the mud,' Cecelia said, 'but you may find that most of the grounds are also listed. I think Alice-Miranda was suggesting you might like to make a new garden elsewhere. I know, years ago, old Lady Tavistock had intended on planting a lot more vegetables, and Mrs Mudge would no doubt enjoy that too. She is such an extraordinary cook.'

Prigg hurried into the room, his feet overtaking the rest of his body. 'I do apologise for interrupting, ma'am, but there is a call for you,' he said. 'The woman was rather insistent that she speak with you immediately.'

'Thank you, Prigg,' Jemima said sweetly. 'I'll call her back after our morning tea.'

'But, ma'am,' the butler replied, lowering his voice, 'someone who identified herself only with the initial M said that she needs to speak with you urgently.'

Alice-Miranda didn't miss the panic that flashed across the woman's face.

'Do excuse me, ladies,' Jemima said, smiling from ear to ear. She rose gracefully, smoothing invisible creases in her dress. 'Please enjoy another cup of tea and I'll be back in a tick.'

Alice-Miranda and Cecelia watched on in bewilderment as the Lady of Bedford Manor practically sprinted the length of the Great Room. She whispered a few words into the hall telephone before racing into her husband's study and locking the door.

Chapter 17

Alice-Miranda and her mother drove back to Highton Hall with Cecelia promising to take her daughter to the stables later in the afternoon. There were some jobs she had to get done at home first and several phone calls to be made. Cecelia headed off to her study while Alice-Miranda hovered in the kitchen, wondering what she could do to be helpful.

She poked her head around the corner into Mrs Oliver's tiny kitchen office only to find the woman asleep on her notepad, snoring gently.

'Poor thing,' Alice-Miranda whispered, and set about making Dolly a strong cup of coffee. The aroma of freshly ground beans soon roused Mrs Oliver from her stupor and she stood up, straightened her skirt and walked out into the kitchen, glancing at the clock.

'Oh, hello, dear,' Dolly said, stifling a yawn and fluffing her hair. 'I'm afraid I nodded off.'

'I can understand why,' Alice-Miranda said as she placed a small plate of biscuits and the coffee onto the pine table. 'You must be exhausted.' She looked at the woman's face and smiled. Alice-Miranda then touched the side of her own cheek and offered Mrs Oliver a tissue from the box on the bench.

'What is it?' Dolly tried to catch her reflection in the glass doors on top of the kitchen cabinets. 'Good heavens! My pen must have leaked.' She licked her finger and wiped the smudge of blue from her powdered face. 'I'm glad you noticed or I might have looked like that for the rest of the day.' She sat down heavily at the table. 'And this,' Dolly said, lifting the cup to her lips, 'is exactly what I needed. Have you only just got back?'

Alice-Miranda nodded. 'Mummy and I had a surprise invitation to morning tea with Lady Tavistock at Bedford Manor.'

'Oh?' Dolly took a sip of her coffee.

Alice-Miranda wriggled into the seat opposite. 'It was lovely. Lady Tavistock is very glamorous and she's certainly full of ideas about how to improve the property. There was something about her that does seem a bit of a mystery, but I'm not quite sure what it is yet. I'll let you know when I figure it out,' Alice-Miranda said. 'Speaking of puzzles, have you made any progress?'

Dolly exhaled loudly and shook her head. 'Nothing. I cannot for the life of me work it out.'

'May I help?' Alice-Miranda asked. 'I could tick off lists and cross-reference ingredients and see if there's anything that jumps out on grocery receipts. And before you tell me that I have other things to do first, I've written all my thank-you letters and made lots of get-well cards for Mummy to send to the hospitals and I'm halfway through the school reading list for next term. I really don't want to sit and watch boring television, especially when I could be doing something much more useful.'

Dolly looked at the child with adoring eyes. 'I wouldn't say no to an extra pair of hands,' she said with a smile. 'But I don't trust myself to help you down the cellar stairs.'

At that moment Alice-Miranda heard a hedge trimmer start up outside. It was very close by. 'Mr Greening could help,' she said, pleased to have found a solution. 'I'm sure I can walk, but if you're really worried about me tripping, then he could hold on to me. My foot doesn't hurt much at all anymore.'

The noise outside stopped and, shortly afterwards, Mr Greening appeared at the back door. He knocked and poked his head around.

Alice-Miranda grinned at him. 'Has anyone ever told you that you have the best timing?'

The old man frowned. 'No, why? Is there cake?'

'We were about to ask you to help me downstairs,' the child replied. 'And of course there's always cake if you're hungry.'

'Well, the trimmer's just run out of fuel and I was going to see if I could catch Max at the stables to bring me a jerry can,' the man said. 'So I'm at your disposal, but I might wash my hands first.'

He ducked into the utility room off the end of the veranda. When he returned, the man insisted on carrying Alice-Miranda down to the cellar, where she was soon perched on a stool at one of the stainless-steel benches. With ruler and pen in hand, the young girl began the exacting task of checking off everything on Mrs Oliver's very long list.

✵

By two o'clock, Jemima Tavistock had asked Mr Prigg to move the irises in the entrance hall three times, before finally settling on the table in the centre, where he'd put them in the first place. She was now wandering through the vast Great Room, with butler in tow, pointing out the various pieces she wanted banished from the house. Her morning tea with Cecelia Highton-Smith and her daughter had proven most disheartening. Anyone would have thought the stupid Heritage Council owned the place. And then there was the phone call. Things were happening much more quickly than she'd anticipated.

'That ghastly thing has just got to go,' Jemima said, shuddering at the peacock under the dome. 'It's hideous. Look at its beady little eyes staring out at me, as if I was the one who put it there.'

Cedric Prigg felt a pang at the thought of how much Lord Tavistock had adored that bird. Dally had once been a much-loved member of the family menagerie. When he had been found dead in the garden, after years of loyal companionship, old Lord Tavistock had insisted they send him off to the taxidermist so he could continue to say hello to his pet every morning, as he'd done for thirteen years. His wife hadn't been quite so keen on the idea, but she understood that her husband's softer side manifested in ways that were somewhat out of the ordinary.

'And that thing there. I don't even know what it is.' Jemima gestured towards a square cabinet on a rotating base.

'I can show you, ma'am,' Prigg offered, walking over to unlatch the mahogany lid. 'It's terribly clever. You might even enjoy it.'

The woman shook her head. 'Don't bother. It's ugly and I won't have anything ugly in my house.'

'Very well,' Prigg agreed, though it went against every fibre of his being. He wouldn't have said that it was unattractive at all. On the contrary, the piece was extremely interesting and one of a kind. He could only imagine what it would fetch in the auction rooms. He had an awful feeling that the new mistress of the house and her lack of sentimentality might see many of the manor's treasures disappear.

Jemima had paused in front of a vase that had been gifted to the family by Queen Georgiana, when her phone rang. She pulled it out of her pocket and looked at the screen. Her body stiffened and a chill entered the air. 'I-I've got a headache,' she stuttered. 'We can sort the rest of this mess later. Thank you, Prigg.'

The butler looked at her curiously. 'Would you like me to bring you something?' he asked. 'A cup of tea? Some aspirin?'

The bleating phone continued.

'No, just leave,' she said curtly. 'Thank you.'

As Prigg marched the length of the room, Jemima took the call. He turned to close the doors behind him but not before catching the look of dismay on Lady Tavistock's face.

Chapter 18

Alice-Miranda hobbled into the stables on her crutches, having spent the past couple of hours helping Mrs Oliver in the lab. Although her cross-checking had been meticulous, the investigations had so far come to nothing, which was disappointing, to say the least. Her head had started to ache when her mother suggested she might like to accompany her to deliver a package to Max at the stables. Alice-Miranda had leapt at the chance to see Bony, and Chops too.

'Darling, do be careful on the cobbles,' Cecelia pleaded, hovering over her daughter.

The child barrelled ahead and greeted the horses in the first two stalls. 'Hello Phinnie! Hello Boo!' she sang.

The Highton Hall stables comprised of an enormous square stone building with a cobbled courtyard and equine accommodation on three sides, accessed via a wide internal passageway. In addition to the large wood-panelled boxes, there were feed and tack rooms and a flat above, where Max resided.

At the sound of Alice-Miranda's voice, Bonaparte stamped his foot and let out an almighty whinny. He thrust his head over the door second from the end of the row and pawed at the ground. Chops, who was in the furthest stall, shook his head and neighed.

'Bony!' Alice-Miranda hurried along to him as fast as she could. It was the first time they'd seen each other since the accident. 'You must have had a terrible shock when I didn't wake up and they took me away in the ambulance. You poor boy.'

Cecelia arched an eyebrow at the pony, wondering if he was truly glad to see her or if he was just hungry.

Max walked out of the feed room further down. 'I think someone's happy to see you on your feet again,' he said, grinning. 'This brute hasn't eaten a thing since I picked him up. I've offered him carrots and apples and, when he rejected those, I tried to woo him with a teensy bit of cabbage, despite knowing I'd suffer the consequences of his noxious wind, but he hasn't touched any of it. If I was any sort of equine psychiatrist, I'd say Bony has had quite a shock. Even old Chops, here, looks worried about him.'

Alice-Miranda leaned on the stable door and rested her head against Bonaparte's neck. He nibbled at her ear and snorted. 'It's all right, Bony. I'm fine. See?'

He raised his head and eyed her as though wanting to be absolutely certain for himself. Alice-Miranda blew softly into the pony's nostrils. He rested his lips on her forehead and it looked for all the world as if he were giving her a kiss.

Cecelia walked across to the feed room and returned with a small bunch of fresh carrots. Bonaparte sniffed the offering, then, with the best manners anyone had ever seen from him, nibbled the tip of the vegetable before he gently took the rest from the woman's outstretched hand.

'Goodness me, your manners *have* improved,' Cecelia said. 'I'd like you to keep this up, young man.'

The others laughed as Bonaparte shook his head up and down as if to agree.

'What are you going to do with him while I'm out of action?' Alice-Miranda asked Max, who had just picked up a curry comb and opened the stable door.

'I thought I'd lunge him for a bit and then take him for a long ride to make sure he's not skittish. He might be a little out of sorts after what happened and you're not getting back on until you're properly healed and he's had some work,' Max said firmly as he combed in circles on the pony's neck.

'I'm almost as good as new,' Alice-Miranda declared. 'In fact, I was hoping Millie and I could go riding next week. If she comes, that is.'

'We'll see,' Cecelia said, shooting Max a knowing look. 'We'd better get back to the house, darling. Daddy should be home by now.'

'I'm so glad. It feels as though he's been away for ages.' Alice-Miranda kissed Bony's nose and said goodbye to Max and Chops. 'I'll see you again tomorrow,' she promised, and gave a wave.

Bonaparte nickered then bared his teeth. If they didn't know any better, they would have thought he was smiling.

Alice-Miranda giggled. 'Now, that's more like it. I knew the real Bony was in there somewhere.'

✷

Francesca Compton-Halls sat on the edge of her bed with Rodney on her lap. She felt a twinge in her tummy. Term was nearly over and the thought of seeing her mother had perked her up considerably – it was probably the closest she'd come to feeling happy since she'd arrived at Bodlington. Her room mates were still at their after-school activities and she'd just about finished her packing.

'What do you think my bedroom will be like?' she asked the tatty toy dog. 'I hope it's lemon-yellow or cauliflower-blue and has a four-poster bed. Do you think there might even be secret passageways in the house? Mummy says it's huge and very beautiful. I can't wait to see it for myself. Do you think there are stables too? Perhaps Mummy will get me a pony and maybe even a real dog – not that *you're* not real, Rodney. You're as real to me as anything else in my life,' the girl prattled.

She wondered if her mother would realise just how much she'd missed Chessie and let her stay. If she insisted on Chessie going back to boarding school, perhaps she could ask to transfer to one a lot closer to home.

The door creaked open and Chessie flinched at the sight of Madagascar Slewt's pinched face. She quickly tucked Rodney under her pillow, hoping the girl hadn't seen him.

'Hello Madagascar,' Chessie said warily.

'You're supposed to be in the sitting room,' the girl snapped. 'Everyone's waiting for you.'

Chessie looked at the clock beside her bed. She was sure Mrs Fairbanks had told them to be in the sitting room at half past five and it was only half past four. 'Really?' she said, her eyes wide.

'Are you calling me a liar?' Madagascar sneered.

Chessie gulped. 'No, I didn't say that.' The last thing she wanted to do was get into an argument with the girl.

'Well, you're late, so hurry up.' Madagascar wrinkled her nose.

Just as she was about to leave, Mrs Fairbanks appeared behind her.

'What are you doing in here, Madagascar? Shouldn't you be packing your things? Your room is a disaster and you've only got another hour before we're going up to the hall. I wouldn't want to be the only girl who's not ready if I was you.'

Madagascar rolled her eyes.

Chessie wondered what the girl was playing at this time.

'Off you go,' Mrs Fairbanks ordered.

Madagascar narrowed her eyes threateningly at Chessie. But this time Chessie had resolved not to cry. She was feeling a whole lot better about everything right at the moment.

'Bye, Madagascar.' Chessie smiled, much to the girl's annoyance. 'See you later.'

'I'm pleased to see you two getting on better,' Mrs Fairbanks said as Madagascar turned and disappeared down the hall.

Chessie nodded. This time tomorrow she'd be home and even the prospect of Madagascar Slewt perpetrating another of her evil deeds couldn't extinguish the flicker of excitement that had ignited in her belly.

Chapter 19

Cecelia drove the short distance back down to the side entrance of Highton Hall. She smiled at the sight of her husband's silver sports car, glad to have him home. Hopefully, they could spend a quiet weekend with Alice-Miranda and their guests. Perhaps they might have lunch over at the Rose and Donkey in Penberthy Floss on Sunday, depending on how Alice-Miranda was feeling. They hadn't been there for ages and a Sunday roast sounded like just the ticket. Dolly could have the day off too. The poor woman had been working herself silly trying to keep up with the house, the preparations for the garden party and the investigations in the lab. Even if things weren't solved by then, Dolly had to take a break or she'd be completely worn out.

Cecelia's brow furrowed then eased as she spotted a black sedan parked beside Hugh's car. She hopped out and handed Alice-Miranda her crutches. The two of them walked onto the veranda and through the side door, where Mrs Shillingsworth was arranging three cups and saucers on a tea tray. The woman turned as she heard them arrive.

'Oh good, you're back,' she said.

Cecelia smiled. 'Where are they?' she whispered.

Alice-Miranda's ears pricked up at the sound of her mother's hushed tones. She wondered if it had something to do with the surprise she'd mentioned earlier.

Shilly frowned. 'Oh no, ma'am. I'm afraid *they* have been delayed.'

'Oh,' Cecelia said, fighting to hide her disappointment. 'So whose black car is outside?'

'I think you should go and join Mr Hugh in his study. He's with Dolly and Marjorie Plunkett,' the woman replied.

'Miss Plunkett!' Alice-Miranda exclaimed. 'Does that mean there's been a breakthrough in the case? Can I come too, Mummy? I'd love to say hello.'

Cecelia sighed. 'Darling, I think you should have a rest. You've had quite a lot of excitement for one day. I'll make sure that Miss Plunkett pops into the sitting room on her way out. You can have a chat to her then.'

Alice-Miranda nodded. 'Mummy, do you promise to tell me what's going on? I'm not silly and I'd rather know than have to imagine all sorts of horrible scenarios.'

Cecelia looked at the child. Silly was definitely not a word she'd ever utter in the same breath as her daughter's name. 'All right, but you must let Daddy and me do the worrying.'

'I'll bring the tea in a few minutes,' Shilly said, fetching three napkins from the drawer. 'And you, young lady, need to do exactly as your mother said and go and have a rest. I'll fix you up a hot chocolate once I've attended to the others.'

Alice-Miranda agreed and took herself off to the sofa, where everything was still set up from the day before. She lay down and arranged herself under the blanket. Ten minutes later, when

Mrs Shillingsworth arrived with her drink, the girl was fast asleep.

✳

Marjorie Plunkett and Dolly Oliver sat side by side in a pair of green leather chairs, an acre of mahogany desk between them and Cecelia, who was in a chair opposite. Hugh was leaning against one of the bookcases, deep in thought. This evening, the room's masculine decor seemed even heavier than usual, weighed down by the worries of its inhabitants.

Marjorie pulled a small notebook from her handbag and flipped it open. 'How many people have fallen ill now?' she asked.

Hugh frowned. 'Last report I heard it was two hundred and forty-three.'

The woman jotted down the number. 'And you're sure they've all shopped at Kennington's?'

Hugh nodded. The skin beneath his tired eyes had creased into several crescent moons. 'Do you think we should close the stores?'

Marjorie's brow puckered. 'I'm not sure. Have you managed to narrow down any possible items?'

'We've examined an extensive range of goods, from the most obvious things, such as bread and milk, to tinned foods and nuts, but there's nothing to report there,' Dolly said. Cecelia couldn't help thinking that the woman's complexion had taken on a concerning grey tinge. She was clearly exhausted. 'And then there are the products that are known to cause salmonella or other bacterial bugs, like chicken or cold meats, but there have been no signs of any problems at all. The food authorities have been testing the same things I have.'

'And what about the processing plants?' Marjorie asked.

Hugh shrugged helplessly. 'The health inspectors have conducted thorough examinations of every plant we own and they're working their way through other suppliers too. It's a jolly nightmare.'

'Darling, if anyone can get to the bottom of this, we know Marjorie can.' Cecelia looked at her husband then at the statuesque woman.

'We'll most certainly do our best,' Marjorie said, snapping her notebook shut and placing it in her handbag. 'Her Majesty has ordered that I put as many resources as necessary into breaking the case.'

'Aunty Gee's a gem – I'll call to thank her later,' Cecelia said.

'I think you'll find she has an ulterior motive,' Marjorie said with a grin. 'Apparently, Dalton has banned all Kennington's products until the case is solved, and you know how much the Queen loves your orange marmalade on her toast in the morning.'

Hugh grimaced. 'Good grief, that's more than I can bear.'

'Don't worry,' Dolly piped up, relieved to finally be able to fix a problem. 'I've got pots of home-made marmalade in the pantry. I'll send some over to the palace immediately. It's the same recipe as the Kennington's brand. We can't have Queen Georgiana missing out.'

Marjorie stood up. 'Right, I should head off and get started.'

Hugh walked around to shake hands with Marjorie as the others rose from their chairs. 'Thank you so much. I really hadn't meant to ruin any weekend plans you might have,' he said.

'Believe me,' the woman replied, smoothing her pencil skirt, 'I wouldn't have been taking the weekend off regardless. I've got another rather perplexing case that I suspect is about to become a whole lot more interesting too.'

'Would you mind doing me a favour on the way out?' Cecelia asked. 'Alice-Miranda was dying to say hello. I told her we'd stop by the sitting room.'

'I saw the news about her accident. Poor darling. I hope she got the flowers I sent. Is she feeling better?' Marjorie asked.

'She's getting stronger every day and, honestly, a bump on the head and a sprained ankle were never going to stop that child of ours. I'm afraid she's bored being a little immobile – I know she'd sooner be back at school,' Cecelia explained.

'I should have her working for me,' Marjorie remarked. 'Alice-Miranda is as good a problem-solver as I've ever seen. In fact, if I didn't think she was destined to take over the family businesses, I'd say she could come and learn the ropes at SPLOD. After Her Majesty told me what happened on the school trip to China, I read the reports filed by the Chinese agents. Your nine-year-old daughter helped to take down a huge criminal network. Elon Fang has been on the international radar for years.'

'We were as surprised as anyone to find out what she'd discovered, but that's our girl – there's never a dull moment with Alice-Miranda around,' Hugh said. 'And really, who knows what she'll do when she grows up. She's certain to have her own ideas.'

Hugh and Dolly farewelled the woman and Cecelia led her back through the house, across the grand foyer with its splendid spiral staircase, through the small dining room and the kitchen into the side sitting room, where Alice-Miranda had woken from her nap and was lying on the couch deep in thought.

She'd had that dream again, although this time it was a little less muddled. She could almost see the person who was standing over her bed, but even though she couldn't recognise them, she somehow knew the words they were saying were spiteful.

'Hello, sweetheart,' Marjorie Plunkett said as she followed Cecelia into the room. 'Were you asleep?'

Alice-Miranda wriggled up into a sitting position. 'I was but I woke up a few minutes ago. I've been having the most confounding dreams ever since the accident.'

'I suppose that's what a concussion might do,' Marjorie said. 'We're all terribly glad you're feeling better. Her Majesty was worried sick and had me call the hospital numerous times for updates.'

'I'm sorry I had everyone so worried. Aunty Gee sent the most wonderful bundle of books for me to read while I'm recovering. There's a beautifully bound copy of *A Little Princess*, which was signed by the author, and another that was inscribed to

Aunty Gee by her father, the King. I'll make sure to return them once I'm finished,' Alice-Miranda said.

'I know she meant for you to keep them,' Marjorie assured her. She'd been at the palace with Her Majesty the morning she was choosing the books from the library.

'Darling, we mustn't keep Marjorie,' Cecelia said. 'She's got a lot on her plate.'

'Has there been a development with the food poisoning?' Alice-Miranda asked.

Marjorie shook her head. 'No, Dolly and your father were just briefing me with the necessary details. SPLOD will be on the case now, so fingers crossed things will come right in a day or so,' the woman said confidently.

'Thank you for coming to say hello and for my gorgeous roses,' Alice-Miranda said. She remembered that she had written Miss Plunkett a card that morning, which hadn't yet been posted. She quickly thumbed through the pile on the coffee table and passed it to her.

Marjorie smiled. 'Oh, that's lovely.'

Suddenly the girl's brow furrowed and she looked as if she were searching for the right words. 'I have been thinking about something, Miss Plunkett . . . Could it be poison?'

Marjorie's eyes widened. 'What do you mean?'

'Last term I was doing some reading for my Science project and there was a section on everyday items that were potentially poisonous. I don't know why, but this evening the thought popped into my head. We were studying *Romeo and Juliet* too and there was poison in that as well. Maybe I've just got poison on the brain,' Alice-Miranda said, shaking her head. 'Sometimes I'm not sure what I'm thinking.'

Marjorie nodded. 'Well, it's certainly an avenue we should explore. I don't know if anyone's considered that yet,' she said, patting the girl's hand. 'We can't leave anything to chance.'

Marjorie then said goodbye and she and Cecelia left Alice-Miranda alone with her thoughts. A face came into focus in her mind for a split second but then it was gone. Alice-Miranda had no idea who the person was and what they had to do with her dream but she wished her mind would stop playing tricks on her so she could work it out.

Chapter 20

'Thank goodness today's over,' Millie sighed as she and Sloane walked into the dining room.

It was already bustling with girls lined up at the servery and carrying trays to tables of chattering friends. The space was looking better than it had in years with Miss Grimm and Charlie recently uncovering an Aladdin's cave of discarded honour boards and portraits that had been abandoned in the cellars under Winchesterfield Manor. Charlie had reinstated them to the walls and Miss Grimm had already had the names of head prefects and duxes from the past thirty years or so added.

'I tell you that assignment on William Shakespeare almost killed me,' Millie groaned. 'He of weirdo language that maketh not much sense to me.'

Sloane giggled. 'I thought *Romeo and Juliet* was kind of charming in a tragic, horrible way.'

'If you like the fact that everyone dies,' Millie said. 'They're so young and in love – it's sickening, if you ask me. Worse than Jacinta and Lucas.'

'Come on, Jacinta and Lucas are cute,' Sloane chuckled. The girl raised her nose in the air and drew in a deep breath. 'At least Mrs Smith's going out on a high for the holidays. It smells like pizza night.'

Sure enough, the servery was crowded with girls eager to get their slices of the home-made ham-and-cheese or supreme pizzas. Unbeknown to the crowd, Mrs Smith had made lots of extras, anticipating the popularity of the treat.

'There's garlic bread too,' Sloane gasped, reaching across to take three pieces, which garnered her a quizzical look from the cook. Her eyes met Mrs Smith's. 'Too many?'

The woman shook her head and smiled. 'There's plenty more. I thought this menu might be a bit of a hit. Besides, you can never have too much garlic bread.'

'That's what I always say, Mrs Smith.' Sloane grinned at her. 'Although I pity whoever has to sit near me tonight with my stinky breath. What are you doing for the holidays?'

'Well, dear, I had a call from Dolly Oliver and it looks like I'll be off to Highton Hall next week to help out there for a little while. They have a big event coming up next weekend and Dolly could do with an extra pair of hands,' the woman explained.

Millie's eyes lit up. 'I'm going to stay with Grandpa for a few days, so I'll be able to visit. Hopefully I'll see you there.'

'You can both say hello to Alice-Miranda from me,' Sloane said.

'Of course,' Mrs Smith replied before scurrying back into the kitchen to fetch some more garlic bread out of the oven.

Millie and Sloane quickly filled their plates and found a table, where they were joined by Sofia Ridout. Millie had just taken a bite of her pizza slice when the dining-room door burst open and Caprice raced into the room huffing and panting. 'They're taking Miss Grimm away in an ambulance!' the girl shouted.

Within seconds, everyone was on their feet, wanting to see the drama for themselves, but Miss Reedy was on to it in a flash. 'Girls, sit down at once,' the teacher commanded. It was fortunate that Benitha Wall was sitting near the door and stood up to block the exit.

The appearance of an ambulance was news to Livinia and the rest of the staff too, who all sported surprised looks. Josiah Plumpton waddled over to his wife and whispered in her ear, then disappeared to investigate.

'Right, Mr Plumpton has gone to see what's happening. For now I'd like you to return to your meals and stop speculating,' the woman ordered. 'Caprice, get something to eat and sit down. NOW!'

'Gosh, Miss Grimm must be really sick,' Sofia said, her voice wavering with concern. 'I hated being in hospital.'

Caprice slotted in beside her, her plate over-flowing with food. 'You only had appendicitis,' she scoffed. 'It's not like you were going to die or anything.'

'No, but it still wasn't much fun and I had to miss the trip to China,' Sofia replied. 'Mummy said that it could have been really serious if we hadn't got there so quickly. There's some awful blood poisoning thing that can happen.'

Caprice rolled her eyes. 'Yes, we know – septicaemia,' she said with her mouth full. 'The golden child told us all about it.'

'Do you really need to be so mean?' Millie said, throwing down her piece of garlic bread.

Caprice wrinkled her nose. 'It's true, isn't it? Everyone knows Alice-Miranda is the golden child around here. I was simply stating a fact,' she said in a menacingly sweet tone.

Millie resisted the urge to pick up one of the pizza slices on her plate and hurl it at Caprice. It would serve the girl right to be slapped on the head with it.

Josiah Plumpton hurried back into the room and skittered along the timber floor to his wife. His cheeks were red and there were two dark patches spreading out from under the arms of his blue shirt. He mopped at his brow as the pair spoke quietly for a few minutes. Miss Reedy then walked to the microphone, which screeched loudly as she switched it back on.

'Seriously!' Caprice bleated, covering her ears.

Miss Wall raced over to the speaker. She fiddled with the dials before the ear-splitting noise thankfully abated and Miss Reedy once again stepped up to speak.

'Apologies for that, girls. It seems that Miss Grimm has indeed been transported to hospital for a suspected gastro bug. Dr Marsh has advised that she be taken in for observation. It's not an emergency, just a precautionary measure. I'm sure you'll all be keeping her in your thoughts and I will update you as any further news comes to hand,' the teacher said.

'Told you,' Caprice sneered.

Millie gripped her pizza slice more tightly, afraid that she wasn't going to be able to stop herself if the girl opened her mouth one more time.

'And girls, please be extra careful about your own hygiene for the remainder of the term. I want to see lots of thorough hand-washing and no sharing of food. The last thing we need is a school-wide outbreak.' Miss Reedy cast a long look over the students before stepping down from the podium.

Caprice poked out her tongue. 'Yuck, I'm glad I'll be in the south of France by Monday.'

'Are you sure about that?' Millie eyeballed the girl. 'Like, really sure?'

Caprice glared at her. 'What are you going on about now?'

'I just want to be certain that you won't be turning up out of the blue at Highton Hall because your mother is catering for the garden party or something,' Millie said.

Caprice flicked her copper-coloured mane. 'Why would she do that?'

Sloane and Sofia giggled. Despite the girl's protests, they knew exactly what Millie was getting at, as Caprice had made a habit of unexpected holiday appearances since joining the school.

Out of the corner of her eye, Millie noticed that Miss Reedy was heading for the door. She jumped up and ran after the woman.

'Excuse me, Miss Reedy, may I speak with you?' Millie quickly wiped her mouth with the back of her hand.

Livinia nodded. 'Of course, Millie. What's the matter?'

'Do you think Miss Grimm's illness could be linked to the Kennington's food-poisoning outbreak?' Millie asked quietly.

'I'm sure that Dr Marsh would have diagnosed that by now,' Livinia said doubtfully.

Millie shrugged. 'I just hate the thought that Miss Grimm might be a victim and I know Alice-Miranda has been worried about her too.'

'You're both very kind. Please say hello to Alice-Miranda next time you're speaking to her. I trust she's feeling much better,' the woman said. 'Mr Plumpton and I are planning to attend the Highton Hall Garden Party in the holidays. Miss Grimm and Mr Grump had expressed an interest in coming along with us, so I hope we still all manage to get there.'

Livinia smiled as she walked to the exit. It was lovely to see how concerned the girls were these days about Ophelia – and rightly so. The woman was almost unrecognisable from the miserable dictator she'd once been. These days, Livinia couldn't imagine the school without her and, truth be told, she hoped the doctors could sort out her health issues sooner rather than later. In all the years Livinia had known her, Ophelia Grimm was as strong as an ox. There was something very off-kilter knowing that she'd been laid so low.

Chapter 21

On Saturday morning Alice-Miranda managed to shower and dress without any assistance at all. She arrived in the kitchen to find her mother at the stove and the smell of sizzling bacon and freshly baked bread filling the air.

'Good morning, Mummy,' she said brightly, easing herself onto a chair at the scrubbed pine table. 'Where's Mrs Oliver?'

'Dolly and Daddy are downstairs in the lab going over some things,' Cecelia said. 'And Shilly's upstairs, I think.'

'I saw her coming out of the blue room. Is someone staying?' Alice-Miranda asked.

'No, she was just tidying up in case Granny decides not to drive home when she's here next week,' Cecelia said. That wasn't exactly true, but Valentina had mentioned on the telephone that she was intending to come and have dinner sometime soon. Cecelia buttered several slices of toast, then filled two bowls of porridge, placing one in front of her daughter and the other opposite.

'Thank you, Mummy,' Alice-Miranda said. She drizzled honey on top of her breakfast, then swirled it about with her spoon.

Cecelia sat down and noticed Alice-Miranda staring into her breakfast bowl. 'Are you all right, darling?' she asked, wondering if the child should be getting more rest. She seemed to be spending an unusually long time focused on her breakfast.

Alice-Miranda looked up. 'Sorry, Mummy. It's just that I've been having some very peculiar dreams recently and I was trying to recall more of the details.'

'Well, you have had a head injury, sweetheart. It's perfectly understandable that your thoughts are a little mixed up.'

'Do you think it could be possible that someone is trying to sabotage Kennington's?' the child asked. 'It just seems strange that no one has found an answer to it yet. Mrs Oliver is so thorough . . . and if there are other scientists as clever as her working on the case, why hasn't anyone found the cause?'

'Sabotage is usually about money and no one has come forward making demands,' Cecelia replied. 'That would be too horrible for words – imagine if all of those people were getting sick on purpose.'

'It's probably my imagination getting the better of me again,' Alice-Miranda said. 'But did you know there are poisons that would be almost impossible to detect, like cyanide and arsenic? Sometimes they make people just a little bit sick. Thankfully, even though there are lots of people in hospital, they've only complained of tummy troubles and disorientation, right?'

Cecelia swallowed a mouthful of porridge and nodded. 'Yes, that's what we've been told. How much study did you do on poisons, exactly?'

Alice-Miranda shrugged. 'I just read a few extra pages for my Science project.'

'You're like a sponge,' her mother marvelled, shaking her head. Do you ever forget anything?'

Alice-Miranda's brows knitted together. 'I don't remember,' she said, bringing a smile to both their faces.

At that moment Dolly and Hugh came in through the back door.

The man walked over and kissed his daughter on top of her head. 'Hello darling.'

'Good morning, Daddy,' she said. 'Mrs Oliver, is that a Post-it note stuck to your forehead?'

Hugh turned and looked at the woman. 'So it is. Sorry, Dolly, I hadn't even noticed,' he said sheepishly.

The woman reached up and pulled the yellow slip from her brow. 'Oh, gracious. I think I must be going mad. What does that say?' Dolly slipped on the glasses hanging by the chain around her neck. 'Poisons. Ah, yes. I want to investigate that option. Marjorie mentioned what you'd said to her last night, Alice-Miranda. Perhaps if you're up to it, you can help me do some more research?'

The girl nodded eagerly. 'Of course.'

Cecelia quickly got her husband and Dolly something to eat.

Hugh picked up a piece of bacon and took a bite. 'Marjorie called to say there are at least a dozen new cases of food poisoning this morning. We've got to do something soon – I just can't have this continue.'

'Is it time?' Cecelia asked.

'Well, if there aren't any developments today, I think we'll have no other choice,' Hugh said.

Chapter 22

Adrienne Treloar yawned widely, then quickly tried to cover it up. She glanced at her watch, realising she should have been off shift hours ago, but with an influx of patients overnight, the hospital was as busy as it had ever been.

'Why don't you go and get some sleep, doctor?' the young nurse beside her suggested.

'I'm fine,' Adrienne snapped. 'I just need a coffee. I'd like a full suite of blood tests on the lad and get an IV line in stat. He needs some fluids.'

The tiny boy on the bed moaned and clutched his stomach before vomiting into the bucket his mother was holding.

'Oh, darling,' she cooed, wiping his mouth. She turned her pleading eyes to Adrienne. 'Doctor, isn't there something else you can give him? He's suffering terribly.'

Adrienne felt a twinge in her chest. They were so dreadfully understaffed and completely unprepared. The ward was almost at capacity with six fresh cases of what looked to be food poisoning presenting that morning. She smiled gently and nodded. 'Let's make him comfortable,' she said to the nurse before hurrying from the room.

The hospital administrator, Edwin Rochester, caught up to the woman as she was making a beeline for the staff lounge. 'Dr Treloar, may I have a word?'

She spun around, surprised to see him at this time of day. He was usually in the coffee shop, eating his body weight in bacon and eggs.

'What is it?' she asked impatiently. Edwin Rochester was one of her least favourite people on the planet, but she was in the unfortunate position of having to be nice to the man, especially since he would be sitting on the panel of her job interview next week.

He ran a hand through his greasy hair and puffed out his chest. 'You've been putting in some big hours lately,' he commented. 'I hope you're not going to be worn out for your interview next week.'

'Someone has to be here,' Adrienne replied, trying to disguise the contempt she felt for the man. 'The Kennington's crisis is showing no signs of abating.'

'Yes, I imagine if you could crack that case, Queen Georgiana would likely make you her own personal physician, never mind the Head of Paediatrics here. You could pick and choose whatever job you wanted.' Edwin raised his bushy eyebrow.

Adrienne blinked. 'Do you really think so?'

'Well, I was joking about Her Majesty, but it would certainly stand anyone in good stead.'

Funnily enough, her husband had said almost the same thing when they'd spoken on the phone last night, except for the nonsense about Queen Georgiana.

'Perhaps if we were properly staffed . . .' Adrienne began.

A sneer crept onto the man's face. 'What are you implying, Dr Treloar?'

Adrienne swallowed the urge to tell him exactly what she was thinking. Ever since the smarmy little man had taken over the staffing, they'd found themselves running on a skeleton medical team at best. His protestations that there was simply no money didn't wash with Adrienne, particularly not when he seemed to be able to find the funds to swan off to several international conferences each year.

'Nothing,' she said firmly.

'Do yourself and everyone else a favour and take a few hours to get some sleep. I don't want you to make any mistakes on my watch,' he said.

She knew immediately that it wasn't a suggestion, it was a threat. 'Thank you for your concern, sir,' Adrienne said. 'I was just on my way to the on-call room.'

That was a lie. She had no intention of sleeping. There was work to be done. Enough was enough – there were far too many people sick. She had to put a stop to things right away.

Chapter 23

Francesca Compton-Halls stared out of the window as the countryside rushed past in a blur. She could hardly believe it when Mrs Fairbanks had delivered the news last night that her mother wouldn't be collecting her from school today. Not only that, Chessie wasn't going home at all. So much for feeling happy about the holidays. She looked at her watch and realised that in just over an hour she would be at her grandmother's house. The first-class carriage was almost empty apart from a man in a suit ahead of them who hadn't looked up from his book once and a lovey-dovey young couple who stared relentlessly into each other's eyes.

To add insult to injury, Chessie was spending the entire journey with Madagascar Slewt. The snooty girl had whinged and griped the whole way, although it hadn't been a surprise to anyone else that she'd been farmed out to her aunt for the holidays. Fortunately, she'd had a selection of students to torment for much of the journey, but after five hours, it had whittled down to just the two of them. Chessie and Madagascar sat opposite one another, wilfully ignoring the other's presence until Madagascar slammed her book shut.

'Why do you always carry that stupid dog around with you?' she demanded, pinching her nose. 'He stinks!'

'My uncle gave him to me when I was a baby,' Chessie murmured.

'When was that? A week ago?' Madagascar chuckled, thinking herself very clever.

Chessie clutched Rodney tighter, her stomach turning loops. In her dreams last night, she had finally worked up the courage to phone her new stepfather to see whether she was right about him not wanting her. But then she woke up and it had never happened. The few times she'd met him before the wedding, he'd seemed rather nice, actually – not an obvious child-hater, at any rate. And to be fair, her mother had never said that about him. Chessie wished she knew why she was being shipped off to her granny. Mrs Fairbanks said that her mother was 'overwhelmed' with a lot on her plate, but what did that even mean? Chessie and her mother had been extremely close – or that's what she'd thought. And now her mother lived in a huge house with a butler and a cook. How could she be so busy that she didn't want to see her only child? None of it made any sense at all – unless of course it was because her stepfather didn't want to have her around and her mother couldn't bring herself to say so.

Thankfully, Madagascar lost interest and returned to her book. Chessie glanced up at the map on the wall at the end of the carriage. This term there had been more than a few times she'd wished she could just run away to a place where no one would ever have to worry about her again. But she hadn't. She wasn't brave enough, for a start.

A young woman with a pile of soft auburn curls pushed a trolley laden with chips and chocolates and an array of soft drinks down the aisle. Her name was Isabella – it said so on her badge.

'Would you like any snacks, girls?' Isabella asked. She had a cheerful voice and kind honey-coloured eyes.

Chessie shook her head. 'No, thank you.'

'Hot chocolate,' Madagascar ordered, not even bothering to say please or look up from her book.

'You must be nearly home,' the woman said as she bent down to get a cup and saucer from the underside of her trolley.

Chessie nodded, smiling shyly. She wasn't exactly sure how much longer it was but she knew she had to get off at Nibley Green, which was the closest station to her grandmother's house.

'I'm on until the end of the line,' Madagascar huffed. 'It's so boring. And make sure you come back again sooner next time. I'm almost dying of thirst here.'

'Oh, I am sorry to hear that,' said Isabella. 'There's a dining car in the middle of the train. You can pop in there anytime if you need something urgently.'

'Yes, but I shouldn't have to get up. It's *your* job to look after us,' Madagascar retorted. 'Clearly, you're not very good at it. Perhaps I'll get my mummy to write to your supervisor, Isabella.'

The way Madagascar said Isabella's name sent a shiver up Chessie's spine. She glanced at the woman, who gulped and brushed at her eyes.

'Are you all right?' Chessie whispered, making sure Madagascar wasn't watching. She handed over a tissue from her pocket.

Isabella took it gratefully and blew her nose. The train slowed to a stop. Chessie had learned that this usually meant the driver was waiting for another train to pass. The young woman poured a large cup of hot chocolate and passed it to Madagascar.

'Oh, look, that's Bedford Manor over there,' she said, doing her best to sound chirpy again. She pointed to a dense grove of trees and hedges across an open field. A huge roof dotted with chimney pots was visible in the distance.

Madagascar rolled her eyes. 'Am I supposed to be impressed? Our house is much bigger than that.'

Chessie slid across and leaned against the window to get a better look. She turned back to the woman. 'Are you sure?' she asked. 'Is that really Bedford Manor?'

Isabella nodded. 'Yes, I know it well. My great-aunt has been Lord Tavistock's cook since forever and I've visited her there lots of times. I think I've explored places in that house I probably shouldn't have. She was terribly sad when the old man passed away, although she said that the new Lord is a lovely fellow.'

As the train resumed its journey, Chessie consulted the map on the wall. The next station was Highton Mill, and she assumed it couldn't possibly be far from there to Bedford Manor.

'Enjoy the rest of your trip,' Isabella said. She mouthed her thanks to Chessie before pushing her trolley forward and moving on to the car ahead.

Green fields flashed by and soon houses began to appear. Chessie's mind was a whirl of thoughts – none of them rational.

The brakes screeched and the train slowed as the guard announced that they were approaching Highton Mill. By Chessie's reckoning, it couldn't have been more than ten minutes since they had stopped near Bedford Manor. She stood up and hurriedly stuffed her book into her backpack, along with Rodney.

Madagascar glared at her. 'Where are you going?'

'Uh . . .' Chessie hesitated. 'It's my stop,' she said, then dashed off to fetch her luggage at the end of the carriage.

As the train ground to a halt, a man helped to lift Chessie's bag down.

'Is someone meeting you?' he asked, and she recognised him as the fellow who had been reading his book.

Chessie's heart thudded in her ears and her mouth felt like a desert. She managed a squeaky yes and a swift nod, which was enough to send the man on his way among the other alighting passengers. Chessie walked along the platform, her pulse racing. What had seemed like a good idea five minutes ago didn't seem even a tiny bit sensible right now.

The whistle blew and the guard called, 'All aboard!'

Chessie turned to run back, but it was too late. The train rolled forward, every revolution of its wheels increasing in speed.

'Oh no, what have I done?' she whispered.

She looked up to see Madagascar at the window, poking out her tongue and making a face. The platform that had been busy with people moments earlier was just about deserted and there was now a chill in the air. On the other side of the platform another train pulled into the station.

Chessie trundled her bag towards the exit, thinking there should be a telephone box nearby.

What she would say to her grandmother, though, she wasn't quite sure. She walked down a small ramp and peered up the street. A woman wearing a dark-brown suit, her arms laden with grocery bags, strode purposefully towards her. Chessie tried to avoid eye contact, but the woman stepped into her path, blocking her way.

'Is someone coming to collect you, dear?' the woman asked.

Chessie gulped and somehow worked a smile onto her face. 'Yes, my mother will be here any minute.'

The woman frowned and looked over the girl's shoulder. 'How old are you?'

'Ten,' Chessie said with as much confidence as she could muster.

The woman exhaled loudly and let her bags drop to the ground. 'I'll wait with you, then. My name is Mrs Bottomley and I'm a teacher at the village school. I think you'll find that I'm perfectly well qualified to supervise you until your mother arrives, though, really, you should know not to talk to strangers.'

Chessie's mind was agog. She needed to find a phone before her grandmother left for Nibley Green station or she'd be in huge trouble. She thought for a second. 'Oh my goodness, I'm so silly. Mummy said that I would have to meet her at the hairdresser. I'd best be going or she'll be wondering where I am,' she said, hurrying off.

'I think you'll find the hairdresser is in the opposite direction,' the woman called after her.

Chessie swiftly turned about face and headed the other way, muttering her thanks.

'What's your name, dear?' the woman asked, but Chessie pretended she hadn't heard and kept on walking. Mrs Bottomley seemed the kind of teacher who liked to know much more than she needed to.

Finally, Chessie spotted a phone box on the next corner and raced over to it. She rummaged around in her wallet for some change, then, with trembling fingers, rang her grandmother's number.

'Hello Granny,' she said cheerily.

Her grandmother was surprised to hear the child on the other end of the line and wasn't the least bit impressed when she was told there'd been a change of plans. She'd had to beg off a trip she'd been looking forward to taking with her sisters when Jemima had asked her to look after Chessie over the holidays. Fortunately, she babbled all about it to her granddaughter.

'Mummy said you should go on your trip and she'll call you when you get back,' the child said shakily. She'd never told so many lies in all her life and half-expected to walk out of the telephone booth with a nose as long as Pinocchio's.

Her grandmother then spent the next couple of minutes ranting and raving about whether there was enough time to get organised, but by the end of the conversation she'd decided that she would throw some clothes in a bag and head off immediately. She told Francesca that she loved her and promptly hung up the telephone.

Chessie looked at the receiver and sighed. She couldn't work out if she was relieved or terrified, though it was most likely a mixture of both. She walked back out along the high street, wondering how on earth she was going to find her way to Bedford Manor. There weren't many people about and she was beginning to think this was probably the worst idea she'd ever had. Her mother would be furious and her grandmother would never trust her again. But another part of her thought that, surely, her mother would be so excited to see her that she'd overlook Chessie's disobedience. This was the new Chessie, the brave one who wouldn't put up with being sent away to boarding school. Well, that's what she'd told herself yesterday when she was feeling a whole lot better about life.

Chessie was debating whether to go into one of the shops and ask for help when she spotted a man in the distance she thought looked vaguely familiar. Come to think of it, she'd just seen him getting off the train from the city. He was tall and slim with a shock of dark hair. And then she realised – he was her mother's new husband, Anthony Tavistock. Chessie's stomach felt as if a swarm of butterflies had hatched inside it. She walked as close as she dared, dragging her noisy suitcase along the footpath.

Chessie was only a few metres away when she heard his phone ring. He pulled it out of his suit pocket and answered. He turned around and, for absolutely no reason at all, Chessie ducked into the open shopfront of the greengrocer, pretending to examine a bunch of bananas.

'Anthony Tavistock speaking,' the man answered.

At least she had the right person, Chessie thought. It would have been embarrassing to ask a perfect stranger if he was her stepfather.

'Look,' he said sharply, 'my wife is extremely competent and, no, she doesn't have any other commitments or distractions at the moment.'

Tears pricked at Chessie's eyes. Is that what she was? A commitment? A distraction?

'Are you going to buy those, sweetheart?' asked a round man wearing a long apron over shorts and a singlet.

Chessie leapt into the air. She shook her head and dropped the bananas back onto the display before she turned and ran up the street as fast as she could. She wiped her face on her sleeve and tried with all her might not to cry, but this time there was no stopping the flood. She ran past the butcher and the patisserie, charging along the street until the shops disappeared and there were only houses and a park. Chessie dashed into the empty playground and fell to her knees behind a bush, where, for the next hour, she sobbed her aching heart out.

Chapter 24

Cecelia Highton-Smith straightened her husband's tie, then turned her attention to Alice-Miranda. She tucked a rogue ringlet behind the girl's ear.

Marjorie Plunkett smiled at the family. 'The press is ready when you are,' she said.

'I just wish we had some good news to tell them,' Hugh said. Things had gone from bad to worse in the past twenty-four hours. There were many more reports of food poisoning and Marjorie hadn't made any headway. This left

Hugh with no other choice than the one he was about to announce.

Alice-Miranda slipped her tiny hand into her father's. 'You're doing the right thing, Daddy,' she said gently, looking up at him with her brown eyes as big as saucers.

Hugh sighed. 'Let's just hope we can get this solved sooner rather than later.'

Marjorie led the way into the Kennington's foyer to the waiting media.

'Good morning, everyone,' Hugh said, walking to the microphone that had been set up for the press conference. 'I think you all know my wife, Cecelia, and our daughter, Alice-Miranda. And of course, Marjorie Plunkett, Head of the Secret Protection League of Defence.'

Alice-Miranda gave a wave and smiled at the sea of journalists, cameramen and sound recordists. Cecelia managed a tight smile, but Marjorie gave nothing away. Several flashes went off as the photographers got shots of the group.

Hugh explained that, until the source of the contamination was found and dealt with, all Kennington's stores would be closed immediately and there would be a complete recall of products purchased in the past ten days with full refunds. He promised that every employee would continue to be paid as per usual and he would be working with his suppliers to ensure that they weren't out of pocket either. His first responsibilities were to his customers and staff. Marjorie then spoke for several minutes about the reason for SPLOD's involvement – that this was an unprecedented situation and, due to the number of people ill and the extent of the apparent contamination, it was only proper that the investigations be carried out by a national agency with a wide range of resources at hand. Then it was over to the journalists for questions. The first few were directed at Hugh and Marjorie, but then a young woman with a dazzling set of white teeth put up her hand.

'My question is for Alice-Miranda,' she said loudly. 'You've recently had a stay in hospital too. Can you confirm the rumours that you were actually a victim of the food-poisoning outbreak and that the story about the horseriding accident was just a cover-up?'

Alice-Miranda's eyes widened in surprise. She stepped forward. 'Oh my goodness, no. I can assure you I fell off my pony, Bonaparte, while on my way back from visiting Mr Frost and his daughter at Wood End. I have my best friend, Millie, to thank for being so brave in the heat of the moment, as well as the wonderful staff at the children's hospital in Chattering for looking after me so very well. Especially Mrs Tigwell – that woman makes the best hot chocolate. My face is still a little colourful and so's my ankle, but apart from that I'm almost completely better.' Alice-Miranda's forehead puckered. 'I can't imagine why anyone would spread a rumour like that. It's simply not true.'

The woman who asked the question suddenly looked sheepish.

'But as lovely as you are to ask after my health, this press conference isn't about me,' Alice-Miranda pointed out. 'This is about making sure we get to the bottom of this situation. Everyone is working very hard to find answers and I'm sure that, with the help of the best minds in the country, it will only be a matter of time until things are sorted.'

'Mr Kennington-Jones, have you thought about having your daughter handle all your public relations in future?' a young fellow piped up. Alice-Miranda had seen him on the television before. 'She's got a high believability factor.'

Everyone in the room laughed, including Marjorie, who usually remained impassive at press conferences.

'She sure has,' one man agreed.

'She's adorable,' gushed the ladies.

'I'd swap her for my daughter any day,' confessed a woman with flaming-red hair. When all eyes turned to her, her face swiftly took on the same hue as her locks. 'Sorry, I didn't mean to say that out loud. My daughter is just going through a bad stage,' she mumbled.

The briefing concluded with a further short statement from Marjorie before the four of them walked back out to Hugh's office.

'Well, that wasn't nearly as awful as I'd been anticipating,' Hugh said with a smile.

Marjorie grinned. 'That fellow was right, you know. Next time you have to address the media, send Alice-Miranda. She'll have them charmed and thinking about everything but the problem at hand before you know it.'

Chapter 25

Anthony Tavistock walked out of the florist with an armful of white roses. He'd finished his meetings earlier than expected and was planning to surprise Jemima, although the call he'd just received had come as a bit of a surprise too. Apparently, Mr Prigg had been making some enquiries about purchasing several horses. The breeder had phoned Anthony to check that the property had the right facilities and that his wife would be completely committed, as he didn't sell his stock to just anyone. Anthony had almost choked when the chap had mentioned the cost of the animals. He couldn't imagine Jemima was going to be happy when he put a dampener on her plans and, even worse, when he told her that, instead of renovating Bedford Manor and filling the stables, she might need to think about what she could do to contribute to the household income. Perhaps he could break the news to her gently during a nice lunch tomorrow.

He hopped into his battered Landrover and within a few minutes was on the road to Penberthy Floss. He'd always loved that stretch of road with its stone walls and rolling green fields. He was about to turn into the driveway when a shiny red sports car zoomed around him at high speed. He laughed when he realised it was Violet Appleby. The woman had a terrible reputation for her lead foot.

Anthony continued along the tree-lined drive to the house. He parked outside the garage and walked across the courtyard to the kitchen door.

'Something smells delicious,' he said, entering the warm room. 'Hello Mrs Mudge.'

Beverley Mudge turned from where she was stirring a bubbling pot on the stove. 'Good evening, sir. I thought I'd make your favourite.'

Anthony's eyes lit up. 'Don't tell me. Coq au vin?'

She shrugged, her eyes glimmering. 'There's no putting anything past you.'

'Lucky me,' he said, drawing in a deep breath. 'I'll look forward to it. Is Jemima around?'

'I think Lady Tavistock is upstairs, sir,' Mrs Mudge replied.

In truth, she didn't know where the woman was, nor did she care. Jemima Tavistock was a cagey one at best, always on the telephone and skulking around corners, trying not to be heard. Beverley Mudge wondered what sort of secrets the new Lady Tavistock had. She was hiding something, that was for sure. With each passing day, Beverley was more and more convinced of it.

✷

Jemima Tavistock had likely broken every road rule to get to her destination in the time she had. She'd just about stood on the brakes when she thought she saw a police car lurking in the bushes on the side of the motorway. Fortunately, she'd been wrong, although she'd come close to being rear-ended by the car behind her.

She pulled into the car park and switched off the ignition, then opened the glove box and retrieved a brown wig. She quickly put it on and checked that it was secure, tucking her own hair tightly underneath. Jemima felt around for the sunglasses she had hidden before taking a few deep breaths. She hopped out of the car and walked around the corner to the bus stop, where she waited just a few minutes before jumping on the number 16 that would take her where she needed to go.

Chapter 26

After the press conference, the Highton-Smith-Kennington-Joneses stopped off at Highton Mill to pick up some supplies. While Cecelia paid a visit to the butcher, Alice-Miranda and her father sat in the car, completely lost in their own thoughts. Hugh couldn't remember ever having felt so utterly helpless, except perhaps the night that his mother had died and his brother disappeared from his life for nearly forty years. Even then, this was not the same. He'd been a tiny boy, just five years of age, and now he was a man, responsible for the livelihoods and wellbeing of tens of thousands of employees. He couldn't fail them.

Alice-Miranda's thoughts wandered to Miss Grimm. Millie had called that morning to relay the worrisome news. She hoped that the poor woman was feeling better and made a mental note to call the hospital when she got home. During her musings, Alice-Miranda's eyes fell upon a young girl trundling a small black suitcase behind her. She was carrying a blue backpack and clutching a toy dog and looked rather upset. Alice-Miranda wondered if she should go and see if she was all right. She was just about to step out of the car when her mother returned.

'Well, I'm not sure what Dolly's ordered, but from the weight of it, this piece of meat is big enough to feed an army,' Cecelia said as she slid into the front passenger seat. She hefted the oversized brown paper bag to a spot by her feet.

'Mummy,' Alice-Miranda said, 'should we see if that girl across the road is all right?' She pointed out the window.

'Which girl, darling?' Cecelia craned her neck to see.

Alice-Miranda looked up and down the street, but there was no sign of the girl or her suitcase. 'Oh, she's disappeared.'

Alice-Miranda shook her head. She was sure there had been a girl. In fact, there was something about her that had given Alice-Miranda a strange feeling and now she most likely would never know why.

✳

Francesca Compton-Halls stood in the telephone box with the last of her change. She felt crushed with exhaustion and paused, her hand hovering above the coin slot. It was getting late and Chessie needed to talk to her mother, but she was scared. She took a deep breath and dialled the number, listening to it ring until Jemima finally answered.

'Hello Mummy,' Chessie said, mustering as much enthusiasm as she could.

Her mother's response was terribly confusing. She seemed excited to hear from her yet, when Chessie asked why she had to spend the break with Granny, the reply she got was unexpected, to say the least – particularly after Chessie's earlier conversation with her grandmother. Her mother explained that Granny had begged to have her and, as Jemima was so busy, it had worked out perfectly. Jemima said she would try to visit Chessie next week when she wasn't so stressed and frantic with the house. She was in a dreadful rush to get somewhere and would speak to her again later. Chessie thought on her feet, though, and told her mother that Granny's phone was on the blink again, so they would call her instead.

When she hung up the phone, she felt completely betrayed. She had no idea where she would go, but it was clear that Bedford Manor was definitely not an option. Perhaps the best thing was to go to her grandmother's house. She had a vague recollection of a spare key hidden inside a cast-iron frog in the garden. She could stay there until school started up again. She retraced her steps to the train station and looked up at the timetable to see when the next train was due.

'Excuse me,' Chessie said to a young railway guard. 'Can you tell me what time the next train to Nibley Green will be coming?'

The lad shook his head. 'I'm afraid you've missed it. The last one came an hour ago. There's only another train due from the city and then I'm off for the night. There'll be one through at nine in the morning for Nibley Green, but that's it for the day, being Sunday and all.'

Chessie gulped and clutched Rodney to her. Where would they sleep? She probably had enough money to go to a hotel, but people would ask questions about a ten-year-old girl on her own. She had to find somewhere else. There were always empty farm buildings on the edge of villages like this. At school they had several and sometimes when girls were upset or wanted to bunk off lessons they'd run away and hide in one of them.

Chessie trundled her bag behind her, her stomach grumbling loudly. She told herself she'd be fine once she got to Granny's. The woman had enough tinned food to survive a war.

There was a sweet-looking French patisserie, but after a quick peek through the window, Chessie couldn't see any bread left on the shelves. She would have loved a cupcake, but the man inside looked much too friendly. He might ask her questions she wasn't prepared for. At the end of the row of shops she found a small general store. A pimply young lad stood behind the counter, flicking through a magazine. He didn't even look up when she entered. She hurried through the aisles, picking up a loaf of bread, the smallest container of butter she could find and a tiny jar of jam, then walked to the counter. Now all she had to do was find somewhere warm and dry for the night.

Chapter 27

Alice-Miranda knew immediately whose four-wheel drive was parked by the kitchen door when they returned from the village. Before her parents could say a word, she was out of the car and inside in a flash. Shilly was holding court with Millie and her mother at the kitchen table. Alice-Miranda dropped her crutches and hobbled over to greet her friend.

'This is the best surprise ever!' Alice-Miranda exclaimed as the two girls hugged each other tightly.

Millie beamed. 'You can't imagine how much I've missed you.'

Pippa smiled at the child. 'You're looking almost as good as new – well, apart from that black eye.'

'At least it's only the one colour now,' Alice-Miranda replied, taking a seat. 'It was purple and yellow and green before yesterday. Mummy said it resembled the make-up at one of her favourite designers' fashion shows last year, which I guess is perfectly all right if I were going for a "just gone ten rounds with the world boxing champion" effect. I feel absolutely fine now and even better because you're both here. I'm planning to give up the crutches for good tomorrow.'

Cecelia and Hugh entered the kitchen and Pippa hugged both of them, whispering some quiet words of comfort.

'We'll be fine, Pip,' Hugh said. 'Now that the stores are closed, no one else can get sick, and Marjorie is confident they'll have some leads soon.'

Mrs Shillingsworth hopped up and bustled over to the stove to make a fresh pot of tea while Cecelia invited Pippa and Millie to take a seat.

'That cake's impressive, Shilly,' Alice-Miranda said, spying the lemon-iced confection sitting under the large glass dome on the bench. 'When did you find time to bake it?'

The woman arched an eyebrow in the child's direction. 'You can thank Mrs Greening for that. She's decided to bake her way out of the blues and assures me that she'll keep up the morning and afternoon tea supplies so Dolly and I don't have to worry – not that I'd have been worried, mind you. I'm sure I could source a packet of biscuits in the pantry.'

'Her cakes are the best!' Alice-Miranda grinned, then quickly added, 'Hers *and* Mrs Oliver's, and you do always find the best biscuits, Shilly.'

Cecelia finished unpacking the meat from the butcher and popped her head around the fridge door. 'How are things coming along with the preparations for the garden party?'

Shilly grimaced. 'It's going to be a race to the finish, but I've got Mrs Greening and Lily coming up tomorrow. Daisy too, although she might have to mind the Treloar children again so she'll only be able to do short days. Dolly's arranged for Doreen Smith to come and give us a hand with the cooking, which is marvellous as it frees up Dolly's time to work in the lab.'

'Do you mean Bentley Treloar's children?' Hugh asked.

'I'm not sure,' Shilly said. She lifted the whistling kettle off the stove. 'They live on the other side of the village. Daisy said their regular nanny has fallen ill and the poor man was in a bit of a bind. She's been taking care of the children while he works nights and I understand his wife works away during the week.'

'Yes, that sounds like our Bentley. He's on the night shift at the Kennington's packaging factory,' Hugh said. 'Lovely chap – smart as a whip but not terribly sociable. He never comes to any of the staff celebrations, though I'm not sure why, and he certainly hasn't brought the children to the Christmas party. I'll have to get on to him about that this year. Anyway, for some time now he's been working on a project that could potentially revolutionise the way we dispose of plastic containers.'

'Wow,' Millie said. 'I've just done an assignment on the impact of plastic on marine life and it's seriously bad. It would be amazing if someone could fix that problem.'

Hugh nodded. 'I couldn't agree more, Millie. I've got a deal in place with him – if this invention of his works, we'll co-patent and I'll wear all the costs.

It could prove extremely lucrative for both of us in the long run.'

The mention of the packaging factory triggered a thought in Alice-Miranda's mind. 'Has the factory been checked for contamination, Daddy?' she asked.

Hugh paused. 'I'm sure it would have been, but I'll speak with the food authorities and make sure they've been around.'

Mrs Shillingsworth carried the teapot back to the table and Cecelia offered everyone cake.

'Can Millie stay?' Alice-Miranda asked.

The flame-haired girl looked hopefully at her mother. 'I was going to stay with Grandpa but he's come down with a cold.'

Pippa eyeballed her daughter and shook her head. 'Oh, I think you've all got far too much on your plates and we *weren't* going to mention that, were we?'

'But Millie's no trouble at all,' Alice-Miranda insisted.

'I promise I'm not,' Millie chimed in, fluttering her eyelashes innocently and smiling like a manic Cheshire cat. 'And I could check on Grandpa and make sure that he's okay.'

Hugh laughed.

'We can help with the preparations for the garden party,' Alice-Miranda added. 'And we won't get in the way and Millie is a *really* hard worker.'

Millie nodded eagerly. 'I'm quite good at polishing silver.'

Cecelia glanced at her husband and then at Pippa. 'You know we'd love to have her. As long as you don't mind being without her another week.'

'Yes!' Millie and Alice-Miranda turned and hugged each other fiercely.

Pippa hesitated. 'Are you sure?'

Hugh nodded. 'She's no problem at all and, if she is, we'll just pack her off and she can walk home,' he teased.

Millie pulled a face and Hugh wrinkled his nose, the two of them fast dissolving into a fit of giggles.

It occurred to Alice-Miranda that she and Millie could make Daisy's life easier too. After all, they both liked little children and Daisy would be much better at polishing the silver than either of them would be.

★

Adrienne Treloar could barely keep her eyes open. She had just come off another double shift and was sitting in front of the television in her tiny flat. She'd called and said goodnight to the children as soon as she'd got in and now there were other things to do before she could get some much-needed sleep.

Bentley had been keen to chat, asking her lots of questions about how she was getting on with the food-poisoning case. They'd had quite a good conversation, actually, and he'd given her several interesting ideas for her to research. Sometimes it was useful having a husband who was clever, despite the infuriating fact that he didn't employ any of his talents.

Adrienne watched the news bulletin flash onto the screen. She turned up the sound.

'This is Simon Brent reporting from Kennington's HQ, where Hugh Kennington-Jones has just told the assembled media that all of their stores would be closed until further notice while the source of the recent food-poisoning outbreak that has now affected hundreds across the country is thoroughly investigated.'

A picture of Hugh with his wife, Cecelia, and their tiny daughter beside him flashed onto the screen.

'How does it feel, Hugh? For once in your perfect life, there's a bump in the road,' Adrienne hissed. If only they knew the man had no integrity whatsoever.

Exasperated, she turned off the television then walked to the table and opened her laptop. There were things to be done – things that simply couldn't wait.

Chapter 28

Francesca Compton-Halls had wheeled her bag past the shops and a row of houses before reaching the edge of the village. So far she hadn't seen one shed or building that looked like a place where she could take shelter for the night. And now it was almost dark. Chessie shivered as a car started up on the road behind her. Why hadn't she just stayed on the train and gone to her grandmother's house? This was surely the most stupid idea she'd ever had.

She clutched her toy dog. He looked back at her with his amber eyes. 'I know, Rodney. I'm scared too.' She stroked the toy's furry head. 'Where do you think we should go?'

Chessie walked on until there was no longer a footpath at all, just the road. She had no idea how far she'd gone. A dog barked somewhere in the distance, causing Chessie to jump. She forced her way through a hedge and pulled her bag behind her but it got wedged. She yanked hard but it was stuck fast. With one last almighty wrench, the bag tumbled through, and Chessie along with it, rolling backwards down a small embankment and landing in a muddy puddle at the bottom. Chessie could feel something prickling her arm and there was a rustle in the bushes. Her heart was pounding so hard she thought it was about to beat right through her chest.

She began to cry, but what was the point? Mrs Fairbanks wasn't there to give her a hug. There was no one Chessie could rely on except herself. She sniffled and wiped her eyes, then flicked a glob of mud from Rodney's face.

'Come on, Rodney,' she sighed, grabbing the handle of her grubby case.

Chessie squinted into the fading light. Finally, there were some buildings – a row of sheds and, on the other side of the laneway, she glimpsed a cottage hidden behind a hedge and a tangle of vines. A light flickered in the windows. Someone was home, but the barn opposite was quiet. Chessie undid the bolt on the door as quietly as she could and dug around for the little torch in her backpack. The girls all had torches at school in case of an emergency and Chessie had become particularly attached to hers. She'd had a lot of emergencies last term.

She shone the light around the building. There was a rusted tractor with a flat tyre. That was a good sign – it probably wasn't going to be used any time soon. At the rear of the building there was a small enclosure lined with straw. It wasn't exactly fresh but it didn't smell as if there had been any animals using it recently. Chessie pulled her bag inside and plonked down with her back against the wall. She sat Rodney beside her. She pulled the loaf from her pack and suddenly realised the butter and jam weren't much use without a knife.

'Looks like it's dry bread for us tonight, Rodney.' She broke off a piece and offered it to the toy as she'd done a million times before. Chessie ate several slices before she packed it away and laid her bag under her head as a pillow. She covered herself with some straw, clutched Rodney to her chest and minutes later was fast asleep, dreaming of the big house she'd seen from the train and the mother who no longer wanted her.

✳

Desmond Berwick lay back on the thin mattress and shivered beneath the even thinner standard-issue blanket. Above him, on the top bunk, Jezza began to snore. Thank heavens this would be the last night he'd have to put up with the clattering tractor sounds of his cellmate.

Tomorrow, he'd set the wheels in motion that would put everything to rights. He couldn't wait to see Chessie and hoped that Jemima would bring her to meet him. Although he'd asked her several times, she was cagey. She'd been that way ever since this had happened. But at least she hadn't abandoned him.

He just needed to see Chessie – she was the key to everything.

Chapter 29

Chessie rolled over and felt something stiff poke the side of her head. Her eyelids were as heavy as lead and for a few moments she wondered where she was. Then, like the opening of a dam wall, it all came flooding back to her. She sat up, blinking in the grey morning light, and pulled a piece of straw from her hair.

'How did *you* sleep?' she asked her cuddly companion. 'I was out cold. Maybe that's what a whole term of crying does to a person. But there's no point crying anymore, is there?'

The girl stood up and brushed the straw from her clothes. She walked out of the stall and surveyed the barn properly. It was smaller than she'd thought when she'd arrived last night. The rusty tractor with the flat tyre sat in the middle of the floor and there were actually three barn stalls side by side at the rear. The one adjacent to where she'd camped housed some rusty farm equipment and in the last one there was a newish-looking ride-on mower.

Outside, an engine sputtered to life and the girl almost leapt through the roof. She scampered to the door and peered through a hole, blinking to adjust her eyes to the brilliant sunshine. A bearded man with a generous head of blond hair sat atop a large green tractor. He turned and waved to someone behind him.

'Hurry up, Jasper. Are you coming or not?' he shouted in a thick German accent.

Chessie saw a young boy run towards the machine and leap onto the trailer at the back. 'Poppy's staying with Mum,' the lad yelled over the noise.

The vehicle lurched forward and Chessie ducked away from the peephole, terrified they would see her. She slowly stood up again and watched the pair putter off down the lane.

She had to get out of there. Although the train wasn't due for another couple of hours, she didn't want to risk missing it. She was also increasingly desperate to find a toilet. Chessie rushed to the rear of the building and quickly packed her things into her bag, then grabbed Rodney and stuffed him inside her jacket. She picked up the case and her backpack and carried them to the door.

Outside, a gaggle of geese honked loudly as they waddled past. They weren't Chessie's favourite of animals, having suffered the wrath of a particularly feisty creature called Beatrice at school last term. That grumpy goose loved nipping bottoms and for whatever reason picked her targets early on. Chessie couldn't ever get from one side of school to the other without the bully giving chase.

She reached through the hole in the door and slowly undid the bolt. It screeched a little but fortunately the geese did too. Chessie was about to push it open when she heard a woman's voice.

'Poppy, have you got the eggs yet?' the woman called. 'I've got to look for the signboards for the garden party. I think they're in the barn.'

Chessie looked around and spotted a sign that read 'Garden party this way' resting against the far wall.

And *this way* was exactly where that woman was heading.

The child grabbed her bag and raced back into the stall, covering herself with straw. She nestled down and held her breath.

The metal door scraped open on the concrete floor.

'Ah, perfect. They're in here,' she heard the woman say to herself. 'Mmm, where did you come from?'

'There were fifteen eggs, Mummy,' a little girl replied.

'That's good. The girls are in excellent form,' the woman said. 'Is this yours?'

Chessie suddenly felt a tickle in her nose. She scrunched up her face, trying with all her might not to let the sneeze escape.

'No, but it's very cute. Can I keep him?' the little girl asked.

'Let's see if he belongs to Alice-Miranda. Put him on the sideboard in the kitchen with the eggs,' the woman replied.

'Can we go and see her this morning?' the little girl asked.

'I have to let Max know that I've found the signs so he and Mr Greening can collect them this afternoon,' the woman said. 'We'll pop into the Hall then.'

'Is Alice-Miranda better?' the little girl asked.

'I think so. Although she's still sporting a black eye,' the woman replied. 'Come on, let's get moving then.'

The sneeze teased and taunted Chessie's nostrils but she managed to hold it in as the barn door scraped closed and the bolt slid across. She waited as long as she possibly could until the voices disappeared. It was lucky the little girl was a bit of a chatterbox.

Suddenly, Chessie sneezed so loudly she was sure they would double-back to investigate. She held her breath, waiting to be found, but no one came.

After several minutes she emerged from her hiding spot, covered in more straw than she had been earlier. She did her best to get as much off as she could, then carried her bags to the door. She had a niggling feeling that she was missing something – and then it hit her. Chessie reached inside her jacket, but there was nothing there. Rodney was gone! She ran back to the stall and dug around in the straw, but he wasn't anywhere to be found.

'That's what the woman was talking about,' she whimpered, tears flooding her eyes. 'Rodney.'

She simply couldn't go anywhere until she had him back. The pair had been inseparable since Chessie was a tiny girl. She had to find out who this Alice-Miranda was and where she lived right away.

Chapter 30

Jemima Tavistock felt as if her life was unravelling at a rate of knots. Her outing the previous afternoon had been far more difficult than she'd hoped and now Anthony had just dropped his own bombshell of sorts. Apparently, old Lord Tavistock hadn't been as good with his money as everyone had thought and had left a trail of debts that needed to be paid from the estate. It seemed that the upkeep of Bedford Manor had put a serious drain on the family finances and, coupled with a rather abysmal few years on the stock market, cash was in perilously short supply.

'What about Chessie's school?' Jemima looked at her husband as they crossed the main road into the village. It was such a lovely day that Anthony had insisted they walk to Penberthy Floss for lunch at the local pub. But now she felt like turning around and going straight home again.

'Darling, I'm sure that we can manage it. We're not broke yet, but I do need to work out the most prudent way to pay down the debts and whether it might be best to put Bedford Manor up for sale.'

'You can't do that!' Jemima sputtered. 'It's your home. It's been in your family for generations and we were going to raise our family there too.'

'Living there has been a privilege,' Anthony said, slipping his hand into hers, 'but it's going to continue to cost a fortune to maintain. I don't want to reach a point where the place is falling down around our ears and we're sitting in one wretched room in front of a bar heater while the rest of the place is freezing. We've also got to think about Mr Prigg and Mrs Mudge.'

Jemima's face paled. 'What about them?'

'We can't manage the house on our own and my wages won't cover anywhere near to even a quarter of our expenses,' Anthony said. There was an uncomfortable silence between them.

'I know you'll work things out,' Jemima said quietly. 'Surely there's a way we can keep Bedford Manor and have the life we wanted in the country.'

Anthony nodded. 'I've got some valuers coming tomorrow to go through the house. There might be some things we can sell.'

'I can tell you *some things* to get rid of,' Jemima huffed. 'Starting with that beady-eyed peacock under the dome.'

Anthony sighed. Poor old Dally wasn't going to put any sort of dent in the tax bill – that he knew for sure.

The pair walked past the church and rectory, and the recently rebuilt village hall to the pub around the corner. The Rose and Donkey was a pretty building with a red door and painted brick facade. Its white walls were draped with a clematis vine in full flower, like the sweep of a veil on a race-day hat. Anthony led Jemima through the cosy front bar and out into a sun-drenched courtyard filled with families and couples enjoying the glorious day. A young woman showed them to a table in a quiet corner and handed them each a menu.

'Sunday roast today is pork with crackling, Yorkshire pudding, spring vegetables, baked potatoes and home-made apple sauce. I'll be back to take your orders soon,' she trilled, then danced away to another table.

'I'd forgotten how charming it is back here,' Anthony said, looking out across the low wall to the green fields beyond. 'Penberthy Floss is such a quaint village.'

Jemima felt the sun on her cheeks and wished that what he'd said earlier had been a bad dream. But it wasn't and now they had to devise a plan. It was just that coming on top of everything else, she really felt quite hopeless.

Anthony peered over his wife's shoulder. 'Oh, there's Hugh Kennington-Jones,' he commented. The man was being guided to an adjacent table with his wife and two girls. Anthony stood up as he and Hugh made eye contact. 'Hello old boy, long time no see,' Anthony said, grinning as they shook hands warmly.

Alice-Miranda glided along on her crutches, accompanied by another child with flaming-red hair and a sprinkling of freckles across her nose.

'Hello Lord Tavistock.' Alice-Miranda beamed up at him, then looked over at Jemima, who had jumped to her feet. 'It's lovely to see you again, Lady Tavistock. This is my friend Millie.'

The woman smiled tentatively. 'It's a pleasure to meet you, Millie.'

'Goodness, that looks nasty,' Anthony said, motioning to Alice-Miranda's leg.

'I'm fine. Just a little riding accident,' the child replied cheerfully. It was true; she felt better every day and was pleased when her father had suggested they lunch out in spite of the fact that she knew both her parents were still worrying about the case.

'Oh, what a pity Chessie isn't here,' Anthony said.

'Yes,' Jemima said quickly. 'But she's having a lovely time with her grandmother.'

Alice-Miranda frowned. She wondered why Jemima hadn't mentioned that on Friday.

'Darling, I don't believe you've met Hugh yet,' Anthony said, and swiftly introduced the pair.

Hugh shook Jemima's hand, then leaned forward and kissed each of her cheeks. 'We've been looking forward to having permanent neighbours again. Your father-in-law wasn't about much in the past few years.'

Cecelia kissed Anthony, then turned to Jemima. 'Fancy seeing you again so soon,' she said. 'It's very fortuitous as I wanted to ask whether you'd like to come along to the garden party. It's on next weekend and I realised after we'd left yesterday that it would be the most wonderful introduction to the village. This year we're relaunching the Paper Moon charity for the children's hospitals.'

Jemima inhaled sharply.

'It was such a pity about that dreadful man who ran off with all the money. What was his name, Hugh?' Cecelia looked to her husband.

'Berwick,' Hugh said disdainfully.

'Yes, that's right. Desmond Berwick,' Anthony confirmed.

'What a shocking swindler he turned out to be. I'm just glad he got his comeuppance in the end. I hear he's being detained at Her Majesty's pleasure,' Hugh said.

'Who was he?' Millie asked, intrigued.

'He was in charge of the Paper Moon Foundation, working across all the major children's hospitals,' Cecelia explained. 'It was a magnificent organisation until he made off with millions. The charity went into liquidation, but we're thrilled to be relaunching it with Aunty Gee's help at the garden party.'

Jemima Tavistock fidgeted with the rings on her left hand and stared vacantly into the distance.

'Is Chessie your daughter, Lady Tavistock?' Alice-Miranda asked.

'Yes,' Anthony said, leaping in, 'she's probably a year or so older than you and she just started at Bodlington last term.'

'Oh, my cousin goes there,' Millie said. 'She loves it. Maybe she and Chessie are friends. Her name is –'

'Yes, perhaps they are,' Jemima said, earning a confused look from Millie, who had been cut off before revealing her cousin's identity.

'That's a long way away,' Cecelia said. 'It must be tricky to get up there during the term.'

'Yes, but you understand – family tradition and all that,' Jemima said.

Cecelia nodded. 'Of course. Alice-Miranda had absolutely no say about where she was heading for her primary years, although I didn't expect her to make arrangements to start quite as early as she did. Now that her school has expanded into secondary I think we'd have to drag her out of there kicking and screaming.'

'You're right about that, Mummy,' Alice-Miranda said. 'I don't fancy moving one little bit.'

'Me either,' Millie agreed.

'What a pity Chessie's not here for the holidays,' Alice-Miranda said. 'I could have introduced her to Jasper and Poppy. They live on the farm at Highton Hall and we always have the best adventures when we get together.'

'Anyway, we should leave you two lovebirds to have your lunch,' Hugh said. 'I imagine you're still on your honeymoon.'

'Why don't you join us?' Anthony suggested. He looked at his wife, who smiled blankly.

'Oh no, we don't want to intrude,' Hugh said.

'Trust me, it's so good to see you and we hardly ever get to catch up. Besides, Jemima and Cee can chat about the garden party and there are a couple of things I'd like to run by you, if I may?' Anthony realised that if anyone could give him sound financial advice it would be Hugh.

The decision was made and the waitress, who had been hovering with a slightly tense look on her face, quickly joined another table to the one the Tavistocks were sitting at. More menus were distributed and the group sat down.

Anthony Tavistock suddenly remembered that Hugh and Cecelia had some rather large problems of their own at the moment. 'So where are things up to with the . . . incident?' he asked.

'Miss Plunkett has taken over the investigation,' Alice-Miranda said, and noted how Jemima's eyes widened at the mention of the woman's name.

Anthony frowned. 'Oh, you mean the Head of SPLOD. Wasn't that a curious thing when she and Queen Georgiana went on television to reveal all about the organisation? Talk about going from a closed shop to a totally transparent operation.'

'She's so clever,' Alice-Miranda said, earning a nod from Millie. 'They both are.'

'Well, that's very good news,' Anthony said. 'Don't you think, darling?'

But Jemima was a world away. Alice-Miranda couldn't help but notice that her sparkle seemed to have dimmed. She worried that it was perhaps her and her mother's fault for telling Lady Tavistock all the things the Heritage Council wouldn't allow her to do with Bedford Manor. She hoped that wasn't the case, although Jemima couldn't seem to get rid of her visitors fast enough after her phone call the other day.

Orders were taken and it wasn't long before plates of food were delivered. It was Sunday roasts for everyone except for Jemima, who had opted for a poached fish dish.

'So what did you want to discuss?' Hugh asked quietly.

Cecelia and Alice-Miranda were in the middle of an animated discussion about the arrangements for the garden party, regaling Jemima with how it all worked and who was involved. Millie listened intently, having never been before either.

'It's about the estate,' Anthony said in hushed tones. 'Perhaps I should come to see you at home some time and we can talk privately, when you don't have so much on your plate.'

Hugh chewed his pork slowly and looked over at his friend with concern. 'Not good?'

Anthony shook his head. 'Worse than I ever imagined.'

'Why don't you pop over this evening?' Hugh suggested. 'Bring Jemima, and Cee can give her a tour of the house.'

'Are you sure?' Anthony asked.

Hugh nodded. 'Absolutely.'

'Great, that would be great.' Anthony smiled. If anyone knew the best way to get out of the mess they were in, it was Hugh Kennington-Jones.

Chapter 31

After their lunch at the Rose and Donkey, Hugh and Cecelia and the girls headed back to Highton Hall. Alice-Miranda and Millie planned to visit Bony and Chops at the stables then make some signs for Mrs Oliver's garden-party tea tent.

'I wonder why Lady Tavistock didn't tell us about her daughter yesterday,' Alice-Miranda pondered aloud.

'Maybe she doesn't like her,' Millie said. 'She wouldn't be the first parent we've known who isn't fond of their own children.'

Alice-Miranda grinned. 'She hardly seems evil to me.'

'Perhaps Jemima didn't hear you properly, darling,' Cecelia said. Her phone buzzed and she reached into her handbag to check the message. Alice-Miranda didn't miss the smile on her mother's face.

'What was that, Mummy?' Alice-Miranda asked.

'Oh, just Granny with a silly question about the garden party,' Cecelia replied.

'I didn't think Granny knew how to do anything on her phone except make calls and even then she's pretty hopeless,' Alice-Miranda said. The last time she'd seen her grandmother, the woman was bemoaning people's inability to pick up a phone and dial their friends these days. Her mother's answer sounded a bit fishy.

'She's been practising,' Cecelia said, the fib sitting uneasily on her tongue.

'Well, she's doing better than my grandpa,' Millie said. 'He ended up calling the Lost Dogs Home to make an appointment for a check-up when he was meant to call his doctor. They couldn't work out what he was on about when he said that he needed someone to take his temperature and his blood pressure and the like. When he was telling

Mummy what he'd done, she said she was sure he wouldn't have wanted them to take his temperature at all.'

Alice-Miranda giggled into her hands.

'There's no arguing with that,' Hugh laughed.

He turned into the long driveway at Highton Hall and into the path of Heinrich, who was driving the tractor and towing a trailer laden with straw bales. He brought the vehicle to a clattering halt beside the car.

Hugh put down his window and Alice-Miranda lowered hers too.

'Hi there,' Heinrich called, giving them a wave. 'How are you feeling, Alice-Miranda?'

'Very well, thank you. Can Poppy and Jasper come up to play tomorrow?' Alice-Miranda asked.

'Lily and Poppy dropped in today but you had gone out. She left a toy she thought might be yours with Mrs Shillingsworth,' the man said.

Alice-Miranda frowned. She couldn't remember losing any toys last time she came home and wondered where Lily would have found it.

'Perhaps the children will see you in the morning, but I think you are going to be very busy with your –' He stopped suddenly when he caught sight of Cecelia's face. 'I will see you all later. Got to get this unloaded into the hay shed,' the man said, and put his foot down, the tractor exhaust billowing smoke as it lurched forward.

'That was strange. Heinrich didn't even finish what he was going to say,' Alice-Miranda said, putting up her window.

Shilly greeted the family on the veranda and helped Alice-Miranda inside. 'How was your lunch?' she asked.

'Lovely, thanks,' Cecelia said with a smile. 'But I think someone needs to head upstairs and have a rest.'

'I'm fine, Mummy,' Alice-Miranda protested. 'I'm not a baby and I don't need a sleep. Millie and I can play cards in the sitting room.'

'I'm not playing cards with you,' Millie said. 'You always beat me. Besides, when your parents said I could stay, I promised I wouldn't tire you out.'

Alice-Miranda wrinkled her nose. 'I'm fine, really. Can we lay on my bed and read, Mummy?'

'All right.' Cecelia gave her daughter a look that said this was not negotiable. The child flew through the kitchen and up the back stairs, eager to show her parents and Millie that her sprained ankle wasn't slowing her down at all. She reached the top landing and stopped.

'Did you hear that noise?' She turned to Millie, who had charged up behind her. Her father had followed them up as well.

Millie looked at her quizically.

'Daddy, can you hear giggling?'

Hugh shook his head, the corners of his mouth lifting. 'What noise? I can't hear a thing.'

'It's coming from the blue room.' Alice-Miranda turned back to her father, her brown eyes huge. 'Are they here? Are they really here?'

Cecelia had crept up the stairs too and watched as her daughter opened the bedroom door to the delighted squeals of her twin toddler cousins and Aunt Charlotte.

Chapter 32

That evening, Highton Hall was a hive of activity. Alice-Miranda and Millie played games with Marcus and Imogen until the toddlers could no longer keep their eyes open. Millie carried Imogen upstairs and Charlotte carried Marcus, while Alice-Miranda brought up the rear, treading carefully without her crutches. They put the twins to bed, with Imogen in the cot that had once belonged to her mother and aunt and Alice-Miranda after that, and Marcus in an almost identical one that Cecelia had especially built when she found out her sister was having twins.

Although Marcus objected when his mother laid him down, he squawked for mere seconds before falling fast asleep. Imogen didn't even try to resist.

'Goodness me, I think I need to have you two around all the time. They're completely worn out. I don't remember them ever having gone to sleep so quickly,' Charlotte whispered as the trio prepared to exit the room. She checked the baby monitor and slipped the remote unit into her pocket.

As they wandered along the hallway to the back stairs, the kitchen doorbell rang.

'That must be Lord and Lady Tavistock,' Alice-Miranda said.

'Surely your mother didn't invite them to dinner,' Charlotte berated. 'She's got quite enough on her plate at the moment.'

'No, I think Daddy and Lord Tavistock had some business to talk over and Mummy's going to show Lady Tavistock around the house,' Alice-Miranda replied.

'Well, I hope no one's expecting me to be sociable. I'm exhausted. I was hoping for dinner in front of the telly and time to watch a movie.'

Charlotte smiled. 'Although, knowing me, I'll be asleep before the first ad break.'

The girls and Charlotte made their way down to the kitchen, where Cecelia and Hugh were holding court with Anthony and Jemima Tavistock.

'Charlotte, darling, come and meet Jemima,' Cecelia said.

'Hello.' Charlotte offered her hand. She looked into Jemima's eyes and for a moment was completely taken in.

'It's a pleasure to meet you,' Jemima replied.

Charlotte finally found her voice. 'Your eyes are the most extraordinary colour.'

'Aren't they just?' Anthony said, giving Charlotte a kiss on either cheek.

'Mesmerising,' Charlotte agreed, lost in her thoughts.

'We might leave you ladies to it,' Hugh said, as he and Anthony headed off to the study.

Cecelia turned to Jemima. 'Are you still up for a tour?'

The woman nodded, although she didn't look particularly excited at the prospect.

'Would you like me to whip up something for dinner?' Charlotte asked.

'No need – there's soup on the stove. It's a bit of a help yourself affair tonight, I'm afraid,' Cecelia said. 'Perhaps you can take something down to Dolly. She was supposed to have today off, but the cheeky thing is downstairs working.'

'Millie and I can take it,' Alice-Miranda offered. She walked over to the sideboard to get some bowls and spotted a rather ratty toy dog. 'Oh, this must be the toy Heinrich was talking about.'

'Where did you get that?' Jemima gasped, the colour draining from her face.

'Lily found it at the farm and thought it belonged to me,' Alice-Miranda said, passing it to the woman.

'My daughter has one just like it,' Jemima said, turning it over in her hands. 'I suppose toys like this can't be especially rare. Chessie never goes anywhere without hers. It's a silly thing, really. His name's Rodney.'

'He's very cute. I wonder if this fellow has a name too,' Alice-Miranda said, as Jemima passed it back to her. She sat it on the sideboard and vowed to return it to Lily tomorrow.

'Why don't we start the tour?' Cecelia suggested. 'There's quite a lot to see.'

Mrs Shillingsworth bustled down the back stairs just as the ladies set off. 'Goodness,' she puffed, wiping her brow with the back of her hand.

'Are you all right, Shilly?' Alice-Miranda looked at the woman, whose face was bright red. 'Would you like me to pour you a cool drink?'

'I won't mind if I don't change another set of sheets for a month, I know that much.' The woman exhaled loudly.

Millie pulled out one of the kitchen chairs for Shilly to sit down while Alice-Miranda placed a glass of iced water on the table in front of her.

'Ooh, I could get used to this,' Mrs Shillingsworth said gratefully. 'Thank you, dears.'

But the second she'd begun to relax, Mrs Greening's voice floated through the back door.

'Hello,' the woman called, walking inside. She was carrying two large cake boxes.

Alice-Miranda hurried to help her. 'Have you made more treats for us? We'll be looking like whales by the end of the week.'

'Yes, I have, but I think Betsy must have got to the chicken-and-leek pie I made this afternoon. It was the strangest thing. I set it down on the windowsill to cool and when I came back it was gone. She doesn't usually steal food. That dog is the best fed creature around here. I even smelt her breath and it didn't tell me anything other than she needs her teeth cleaned.' The woman shook her head.

Millie pulled a face.

'That's not like Betsy at all,' Shilly said, frowning.

'You're right,' Charlotte agreed. 'She's got better manners than the twins, especially when it comes to food.'

'Never mind, I still have a heaven cake and a devil's food cake too – at least they didn't disappear.' Mrs Shillingsworth unpacked the desserts and placed them under two free domes on the bench.

'Yum!' Alice-Miranda licked her lips. 'My favourites.'

Harold Greening appeared at the back door.

'Hello Mr Greening,' Alice-Miranda said. 'How are you?'

'I could do with a good night's sleep, because, quite frankly, I think I'm losing my marbles,' the man said, scratching his head.

'Why do you say that?' Millie asked.

'Well, today I've managed to misplace a bucket, a tarpaulin and the old rug I keep inside the utility so Betsy doesn't drop hairs all over the place,' he replied.

'You have been terribly busy,' Alice-Miranda said. 'I'm sure they'll turn up somewhere.'

'I don't know,' the man replied. 'Perhaps one of the young fellows from the village who's been helping with all the extra jobs moved things.'

'Never mind, Harold. Let's just get home, shall we? I'll fix you up a nice cup of tea.' Mrs Greening gave a wave and walked out the back door. 'See you all tomorrow.'

'Bye,' the others chorused.

Charlotte filled a soup bowl for Mrs Oliver and organised some warm bread and salted butter as well. 'Girls, are you sure you wouldn't like me to take that downstairs?' she asked, setting it on a tray.

'No, I'm fine,' Millie said. 'Besides, I promised my mother I'd make myself useful.'

Charlotte smiled as Alice-Miranda opened the back door, and she and Millie ventured onto the veranda.

Millie met Mrs Oliver at the bottom of the stairs just inside the lab.

'Thank you so much, darling girl,' the woman said, taking the tray from her. 'I'm famished.'

'I bet you're not eating any of that,' Millie said, eyeing the array of Kennington's products lined up on the benches.

The woman grinned. 'Too right I'm not.'

Meanwhile, Alice-Miranda was waiting on the veranda when she heard a noise out in the garden. It sounded like footsteps and she turned around to see if there was anyone there.

'Hello,' she called. 'Is that you, Max?'

But there was no reply.

✳

On the other side of the hedge, Francesca Compton-Halls crouched down as low as she could. She had spent the entire day searching the property for her Rodney. He hadn't been at the cottage across from the barn nor at the gatehouse, where she'd helped herself to the most delicious chicken-and-leek pie. Although, she'd had to share half of it with the labrador to stop it from barking.

And now she'd finally got herself to the main house. It was huge, like something from a fairytale but even more beautiful. Rodney must be inside, but there were so many people about. There was a dark-haired girl on the veranda and another with red hair, who had just gone down a flight of steps, which Chessie assumed led to a cellar. Why she would have been carrying a tray of food down there was anyone's guess. Perhaps they kept someone prisoner or that's where the servants lived. Chessie gulped at the thought.

'What are you looking at?' Millie asked as she bounded up the stairs.

'I thought I heard something out there,' Alice-Miranda replied with a shrug. 'Ever since the accident I've been dreaming about weird things – I think my brain is quite muddled.'

'What do you mean?' Millie asked.

'I've been having this dream about someone standing over my hospital bed and they aren't very nice,' Alice-Miranda said.

'Like a werewolf?' Millie grinned.

Alice-Miranda giggled. 'No. They don't really have a face, but all these words spill out of their mouth. I have no idea what they're saying but I'm pretty sure it's mean.'

'You did have a concussion, remember.' Millie raised her eyebrows. All of a sudden there was a rustling in the garden again. Millie leapt off the veranda and ran towards the source. 'Who's there?' she demanded, brandishing her arm in the air like a sword.

'I'm sure it's just a breeze,' Alice-Miranda said.

Millie spun around, popping her finger into her mouth and raising it skywards to check the direction of the wind. 'Except that there isn't any.'

Chessie wished the girls would hurry up and go back inside. She held her breath and squirmed beneath a bush.

Millie started running all over the lawn, leaping like a gazelle. 'I think there must be someone over there,' she yelled, scurrying like a mouse on the balls of her feet, 'behind Bess!' She darted towards one of the three topiary horses that took pride of place in the garden.

'You're mad, Millie,' Alice-Miranda chuckled, shaking her head. 'But I'm so glad you're here.'

'Of course you are,' Millie said. 'Who else makes you laugh as much as I do?'

Millie made another run and tripped over, sprawling on the grass.

'What did you do?' Alice-Miranda said, rising on her tippy-toes.

'Someone tripped me. I swear there was a foot,' Millie said crankily.

Chessie could hardly breathe. She was about to be found for sure and then who knew what was going to happen. One thing was certain, though. She wasn't going home to her mother or stepfather. She'd go anywhere but there.

'Come on, Millie. I'm starving,' Alice-Miranda called.

Millie had almost reached the hedge when she made an abrupt about face. 'All right, but I'm telling you there's someone out here.'

She looped her arm into Alice-Miranda's and the pair walked back inside.

Chapter 33

Alice-Miranda was just beginning to stir when she felt something tugging at her bedclothes. She rolled over to see Marcus's big brown eyes staring at her. 'Up,' he said, then gave a clap.

'What are you doing in here, mister?' Alice-Miranda leaned over to help the wriggling toddler climb onto the bed. He jumped under the covers and snuggled down beside her with his head on the pillow.

'Where's your sister?' Alice-Miranda wondered if Aunt Charlotte knew that Marcus was missing.

She was also worried about how he had come to be in her room. The house wasn't exactly toddler-friendly with all those stairs.

Millie poked her head around the bathroom door. 'I thought I heard something,' she said, racing over and climbing into the other side of Alice-Miranda's enormous bed.

There was a noise at the door followed by the sound of tiny feet thudding across the floorboards. Imogen appeared and looked at the trio, eager to join them. She clambered up and snuggled in between Millie and Alice-Miranda. The two toddlers babbled away, telling the girls all sorts of things they couldn't quite decipher.

Millie decided to try to teach them her name. Marcus managed 'me' but couldn't get his tongue around the rest of the sounds. Alice-Miranda had a little more success with Marcus calling her 'Anda', which the girls giggled at.

The four children lay under the covers for quite some time, chatting and playing games. The twins particularly liked 'Where's your?' followed by the naming of some or other facial feature. They were both surprisingly good at it too, although Marcus thought it was hysterical to stick his finger up Alice-Miranda's nose instead of pointing at his own.

'Do you ever wish you had a brother or sister?' Millie asked.

'I used to want that more than anything, but then I got a big sister, anyway.' Alice-Miranda turned to look at Millie, whose red curls were spread out all over the pillow.

Millie smiled. 'And I got the best big little sister I could ever have hoped for.'

The bedroom door opened and Charlotte poked her head around. On seeing their mother, the twins dove under the covers and started giggling loudly.

'Good morning. I hope those cheeky monkeys didn't spoil your sleep,' Charlotte said as she sat down on the edge of the bed. Imogen jumped up and headed to her mother for a cuddle.

'Not exactly,' Alice-Miranda said.

'We've been teaching Imogen and Marcus how to say our names,' Millie said.

'Then you're doing better than me. I can't get them to say anything close to Mummy or Daddy,' Charlotte said. 'What shall we do today?'

'Maybe we can look in on the lambs at the farm?' Alice-Miranda suggested. 'And the chickens. Would you like that?' She turned to Marcus, who had crawled up into the crook of her arm and was leaning against her shoulder.

Imogen clucked like a hen and the boy let out a loud bleating sound.

'We'll have to ask Heinrich where Ramon is – he's the daddy and he's a bit tricky,' Alice-Miranda said.

'That sounds like a plan,' said Charlotte. 'We'd better get dressed and hop to it, then.'

Imogen and Marcus slipped down from the bed and pretended to be bunny rabbits as they ran out the door with their mother right behind.

Chapter 34

The twins' first visit to the farm was a resounding success. Imogen developed an instant love affair with the lambs, who she decided were her babies, while Marcus took on the role of chicken wrangler. At one stage the boy had a hen under each arm, triumphantly carting them around the coop. It was fortunate the fowls were all good-natured creatures and used to the attention. Heinrich then capped off a wonderful morning when he sat the giddy pair on his lap on the tractor and fired up the engine.

'All right, we'll see you later then!' Charlotte called as she hopped into the driver's seat of her car.

'Bye!' the toddlers chorused, waving their hands like windscreen wipers. Marcus was blowing kisses too – something he'd only recently learned to do.

'I swear that boy is going to be even more charming than his father.' Lily grinned, holding the little bouquet of dandelions he'd picked for her.

'And his big brother, although I don't think Jacinta would say that,' Millie said, chuckling to herself. 'I miss her and Lucas.'

'Me too. I hope Jacinta and Ambrosia are having a lovely holiday. I think Jacinta was planning to spend time with Lucinda in New York and maybe even convince Mr Finkelstein to let her come to Winchesterfield-Downsfordvale on exchange soon.'

'That would be great,' Millie replied. 'Will they get to catch up with Lucas while he's staying with his mother in LA?' Millie said.

'I suspect Kitty is planning to keep him all to herself,' Lily said, referring to her sister. 'I'm so thrilled that they're spending the holidays together.'

Alice-Miranda nodded. It had been a tough time for Lucas the past couple of years, not only finding out who his father was but gaining a stepmother and the twins too. Fortunately, they all got on brilliantly, but the revelation had initially put a strain on things with his mother. It was good to see their relationship had improved.

Heinrich and Lily decided to walk back to the farmhouse to prepare some sandwiches for an al fresco lunch. The children huddled together, deciding what game to play.

'I vote skipping,' Poppy said.

'No way!' Jasper shook his head vigorously. 'Alice-Miranda still has a sore ankle and you're hopeless at turning the rope.'

Poppy scrunched her nose up at her brother.

'You stink!' the little girl growled.

'Poppy,' Alice-Miranda chided. 'It's probably best if I don't go overboard just for another day or so.'

'No, I didn't mean it like that. He really does stink.' Poppy flapped a hand in front of her nose and pointed at the stain on the back of the boy's trousers. At the height of the morning's excitement, Jasper had leapt onto one of the calves, pretending to be a bull rider, which had made the twins squeal and giggle. Unfortunately, his antics hadn't ended well when he was dumped into a pile of steaming manure.

'It's not that bad,' Jasper protested.

Millie gave the lad a sideways glance and sniffed the air.

'Come on, I don't really smell, do I?' Jasper pouted.

The girls shook their heads.

'What about we play I-spy?' Millie said half-heartedly. She wasn't especially keen on the game, but it was all she could think of that didn't involve much physical activity.

'I think I could manage hide-and-seek,' Alice-Miranda suggested. 'But instead of having to run back to bar, you're automatically in when spotted.'

'Sounds fair,' Jasper said. A smug smile crept onto his face. 'You'll never find me. I know the best hiding spots.'

'That's why you're in first,' Millie said.

Jasper poked out his tongue and Millie tried to pinch it.

'Fine then,' he said. 'I'll count to one hundred, but you're not allowed to go anywhere together, okay? And if I can't find anyone after ten minutes, you have to come out. I'm not going to look for you *all* day.'

The three girls nodded and hurried off to the other side of the front garden.

'And you can't go past Rose Cottage and you're not allowed in the field on the other side of our house,' Jasper shouted. He buried his face in his hands and began to count loudly.

Millie indicated that she was going around the back to the chicken coop.

Poppy ran off towards the stone wall and promptly ducked down behind it while Alice-Miranda decided on the old barn opposite Rose Cottage. She remembered there were stalls right at the back, where no one ever went.

✷

Chessie heard the bolt on the barn door slide open. Her heart pounded and she burrowed beneath the straw, trying to stay as still as she could. She held her breath as footsteps skittered closer and closer.

'Oh, hello. Are you all right? Surely it's hard to breathe under there,' the girl said. 'There's no need to be afraid.'

Chessie froze, wondering what to do. Her lungs felt as if they were about to explode and she couldn't stand it any longer. She burst out of the straw, coughing and spluttering.

'Goodness, you poor thing.' The girl's eyes fell upon Chessie's black suitcase and the empty bread bag beside her. 'Have you run away?'

There was a long pause before Chessie finally spoke. 'I didn't mean to,' she said, her eyes filling with tears. Chessie wiped at them angrily, determined not to cry again. 'It just sort of happened and now I can't go back.'

'Of course not,' the tiny child said. 'I'm Alice-Miranda Highton-Smith-Kennington-Jones and I live here. Well, not here exactly but in the house on the hill. I am very pleased to make your acquaintance, especially as I wasn't expecting to find anyone in here at all. I thought it would be the perfect hiding place.' Alice-Miranda smiled. 'I suppose we both had the same idea, which means I'm sure we'll get on famously. What's your name?'

Chessie gulped. 'I'd rather not say.'

Alice-Miranda caught sight of the tag on the girl's bag. It had a swirly B and the name Francesca written in large letters underneath. Alice-Miranda's forehead puckered as she tried to think of a school starting with the letter B.

'Bodlington?' she wondered aloud. 'But that's hours away.' Her eyes widened and she hesitated for a few seconds. 'Oh my goodness, I know *exactly* who you are. You're Lady Tavistock's daughter. Your mother must be worried sick about you,' she blurted. But then she remembered that Lady Tavistock had been at Highton Hall last night and hadn't mentioned a thing about Francesca.

Chessie shook her head miserably. 'I'm quite sure she's not.'

Alice-Miranda knelt down beside her. 'How did you get here?'

Chessie's eyes filled with tears again.

'Please don't be afraid.' Alice-Miranda gently placed her hand on the girl's shoulder. 'I promise I'll do whatever I can to help – I just need to understand a few things.'

Chessie sighed. There was something about this girl with cascading chocolate curls and big brown eyes that made her want to tell her everything. She soon found that once she'd started speaking, the words tumbled out like a waterfall and she couldn't stop until she had reached the very end.

Alice-Miranda hugged her tightly. 'Try not to worry. I'm sure we can sort things out.'

'Do you really think so?'

Alice-Miranda nodded. 'Did you enjoy Mrs Greening's chicken-and-leek pie?'

Chessie looked sheepish. 'I swear I don't usually go around stealing things, but it was delicious and I was starving.'

Alice-Miranda grinned. 'Just wait until you taste her heaven cake – it's beyond scrumptious.'

Outside, Jasper could be heard yelling for everyone to come out of their hiding spots. 'It's been ages,' he moaned. 'You're all too hard to find.'

Chessie gasped and grabbed Alice-Miranda's hands. 'Promise me you won't tell anyone,' she begged.

Alice-Miranda looked into the girl's terrified eyes. 'I promise,' she replied. 'But no more running away. Please stay here and I'll be back as soon as I can.'

And with that, Alice-Miranda hurried from the barn, taking extra care to bolt the door on her way out.

Chapter 35

Jemima Tavistock's stomach was in knots. Having spent the morning supervising the appraisers, she had finally got away just after midday. She pulled into a side street and donned her wig and glasses before driving to the edge of the village and finding a parking spot in a back lane. Then she walked the short distance to the Goose and Gander, where there was a larger than expected lunch crowd. Jemima hoped the presence of so many people hadn't put him off. But as she walked through the room, she spotted him in one of the booths with just the top of his head visible. She slipped into the seat opposite and allowed herself to breathe.

'You took your time,' he said, passing her a menu.

'Sorry – there was some business at home I had to attend to. I'm glad you didn't decide to go anywhere,' she replied.

'Oh, but I have,' he said, smiling. 'I've found a lovely little cottage not too far from you, actually. It's in a sweet village called Penberthy Floss, right next door to the general store.'

'You can't live there.' The words flew out of Jemima's mouth before she had time to check herself.

'Really.' He picked up his glass of mineral water and took a sip. 'Well, I'm sorry to disappoint you, dear sister, but I've already agreed. I'll be moving in this afternoon, and I expect you to bring Chessie around this evening – she is home for the holidays, I presume.'

Jemima wrung her hands beneath the table. She wanted to run and never come back, but she couldn't. The damage he could do was irreparable. 'Chessie's on holiday with our mother at the moment. Perhaps there'll be time for her to visit before she returns to boarding school.'

He frowned. 'Well, I'll need some money.'

Jemima glanced up from the menu.

'Just until I get back on my feet,' he added, looking dolefully into her eyes. 'You know that I'm going to sort everything out.'

Jemima wanted to believe him with all her heart. She pulled some notes from her wallet and passed them over. 'That's all I've got,' she said. She wasn't about to tell him that things weren't exactly rosy in her world at the moment.

He laughed. 'I meant real money, Jem, not a grocery allowance.'

'I don't have anything more,' she said, on the verge of tears.

He leaned in, over the table. 'But you can get it,' he said, lowering his voice. 'You're a . . . *Lady* now.'

'That doesn't mean anything,' she snapped.

He sat back, his mouth set in a grim line. 'How is darling Chessie?'

'She's fine,' Jemima said quietly.

'I have to say I am a bit surprised, Jem. Boarding school and holidays with our mother?' he said, arching an eyebrow. 'What happened? The two of you were so close.'

Jemima looked at him fiercely. *He* had happened. *He* was the one to blame for all this. She took a deep breath to calm herself before speaking. 'Mother wanted to take her on a special trip. Just the two of them. Make some memories,' she lied.

'Yes, clearly the old bird's memory isn't too good these days. She's forgotten how to use the telephone or drive a car since I changed address,' he spat.

Jemima sighed. 'You can't blame her for that.'

'No, but I'm sure she'll feel terrible once she realises that it was all a big mistake,' he said.

'Let's just prove that, shall we?' Jemima tucked a strand of brown hair behind her ear.

'Perhaps we should make a move then?' he suggested.

'What?'

'You can drop me off at the new place and arrange to get me some things,' he said.

'N-no, I can't.' She shook her head. 'People know my car.'

'Then you'd better hand over your credit card, my dear. I'm afraid it's going to be a very expensive taxi ride,' he said.

Jemima bit her lip. This was proving to be even more difficult than she'd anticipated.

Chapter 36

Alice-Miranda's mind was in overdrive as she raced down the lane towards Jasper.

'Where are the others?' she asked, spinning the lad around.

'You're not supposed to be running,' Jasper said as they charged back towards the house.

'I'm okay. My ankle doesn't hurt at all,' Alice-Miranda assured him. She ignored the tiny twinge that had started up, eager to get the lad as far from the barn as possible.

Millie came careering around the back of the Bauers' farmhouse and Poppy sprung up from the other side of the stone wall.

'You were so close to me, Jas,' his sister said. 'I had to hold my breath for *hours*.'

'I thought you were going to get me too,' Millie said. 'That stupid hen wouldn't stop clucking. It was like she was trying to tell you exactly where I was.'

'Let's play something different,' Jasper said, just as Lily called out from the front veranda that lunch was ready.

'Great! I'm starving,' Millie said.

Lily had set up a picnic in the sun-drenched courtyard. There was a huge platter of sandwiches, a Greek salad and a tin of chocolate brownies. She poured the children cups of home-made lemonade.

'I have to go back to the hall as soon as you've finished lunch,' Lily informed them. 'Mrs Shillingsworth has a rather ambitious roster for the next six days.'

'Is Daisy up there too?' Alice-Miranda asked.

'Yes, but she's nannying for the Treloar children as well. I'm not sure how that's going to work alongside her garden-party duties,' Lily said with a shrug.

Poppy looked up from where she was arranging her sandwiches in a neat row on her plate. 'Dottie goes to our school.'

'Weren't you going to offer for us to mind them?' Millie said to Alice-Miranda, while picking out the olives from her serving of salad.

Alice-Miranda nodded absently. She felt terrible keeping Chessie a secret, especially from Millie, but she decided it would only be for a little while. At least until Chessie felt brave enough. For now, Alice-Miranda had to gather some supplies for the runaway girl and come up with a plan.

'Lily, can we go back to the Hall with you?' Alice-Miranda asked.

Jasper and Poppy groaned. 'Ohhh, do you have to go home?'

'That works out well, actually,' Lily replied. 'These two have a visit to the dentist this afternoon.'

'You didn't tell us that,' Jasper said, a note of betrayal in his voice. 'I hate going to the dentist.'

'And now you know why I left it until this minute to say something,' their mother said with a grin.

'I love the dentist,' Poppy declared. 'He always gives us a lollipop if we're brave and we get to choose the flavour and everything.'

'Your dentist sounds really smart,' Millie said.

'Why?' Poppy asked. She'd never thought about him like that before.

'If he gives his patients lollipops, he's pretty much ensuring future business,' the girl replied, taking another bite of her sandwich.

Lily laughed. 'Mmm, I think you're on to something there, Millie.'

Alice-Miranda placed two sandwiches and a brownie on a white paper napkin in front of her. The children were chatting and laughing when she suddenly dusted her hands and stood up. 'Oh bother, I must have left my hat in my hiding spot,' she said with a frown, before quickly wrapping the food. 'I'll go and check while you're all finishing lunch.'

'I'll come,' Millie offered.

'It's okay. I'll be back soon,' Alice-Miranda replied. She picked up her parcel, then hurried around the side of the house.

★

Millie glanced at the clock on the kitchen wall. Alice-Miranda had been gone for ages. She and Lily had cleared the lunch plates, and Heinrich had already left with Jasper and Poppy for the dentist.

'I won't be long,' Lily called from the utility room, where she was finishing up a load of washing before heading up to the Hall. 'Is Alice-Miranda back?'

'Not yet. I'll go and look for her. I hope she hasn't hurt her ankle again,' Millie said. She hopped off the kitchen stool. 'We'll meet you at the car.'

Millie raced outside and realised that she didn't actually know where Alice-Miranda had been hiding during their game. She and Jasper were already in the garden when Millie had emerged from her spot. She shot up the lane calling her friend's name.

'Alice-Miranda!' she shouted as she neared the old barn. 'Are you here?'

'Coming,' came the child's muffled reply.

Sunbeams poured into the dreary building as Millie unbolted the door. She wondered why Alice-Miranda would have bothered to latch it.

'Alice-Miranda!' she called out. 'Did you find your . . .?' She thought she saw a silhouette of a figure duck down out of sight near the back of the building. She was just about to say something when Alice-Miranda appeared beside her.

'No luck, I'm afraid,' Alice-Miranda said with a hapless shrug.

'Who's hiding there?' Millie demanded.

She charged past Alice-Miranda to the stall where Francesca Compton-Halls was lying facedown in the straw. Millie tilted her head to the side to better appraise the ridiculous scene.

'You do know I can see you,' Millie said, her hands on her hips.

Chessie slowly rose to her knees and turned around. She looked as if she had the weight of the world on her shoulders – in addition to a thick layer of straw. Chessie was about to say hello when her nose twitched and she let out an enormous sneeze. A plume of dust and straw shook out of her hair.

Alice-Miranda hurried over to the girl and handed her a tissue. 'Chessie, this is my best friend, Millie. I promise you she's very good at keeping secrets,' Alice-Miranda said. 'Millie, meet Francesca Compton-Halls. She needs our help.'

Millie frowned. 'Well, you'd better start talking. Lily's almost ready to go.'

Chapter 37

Lily drove Alice-Miranda and Millie back to
Highton Hall, where the garden now resembled
an ants' nest. A team of men and women were
busily pruning the hedges, stringing fairy lights
in the trees and marking out the areas for the
various stalls on the front lawn. Mr Greening was
in the middle of the chaos, directing everyone this
way and that like a traffic warden. Lily checked
Mrs Shillingsworth's extensive list of jobs, grabbed
her bucket full of cloths and polishes and scurried

away to the dining room to make a start on the furniture.

'So that poor girl has been hiding in the barn for two whole nights?' Millie said. 'And all because of her toy dog?'

Alice-Miranda had relayed the entire story as she'd heard it as soon as the two of them were safely within the four walls of bedroom.

Alice-Miranda nodded. 'Rodney. At least we know where he is. I'll get him as soon as I can.'

'I'm so sorry about jumping in with the baby-sitting offer earlier,' Millie said, shaking her head at herself. 'Daisy looked so frantic. It wasn't until after I opened my big mouth that I realised we had to think about Chessie first.'

The girls had met Daisy on the back stairs on their way up to Alice-Miranda's bedroom and before Millie even realised it, she'd offered for them to look after the Trealoar children so Daisy could work into the evening. The young woman had seized upon the idea and had raced off to make the arrangements.

'Don't worry,' Alice-Miranda said. 'It might even work in our favour. We could bring Chessie here before the Treloar kids arrive.'

'But there are so many people around, outside and inside the house,' Millie said, biting her lip.

Alice-Miranda grinned. '*Exactly*. Chessie's less likely to be noticed that way. We could say she's with the Treloar kids if anyone see her.'

Millie's eyes lit up. 'You're a genius! Where should we put her?'

Alice-Miranda tapped her finger to her chin as her mind swam with possibilities. 'What about here?' she said. 'It's perfect. No one's going to clean the upstairs bedrooms because this floor isn't open to the public, and they'll be much too busy fussing over the rest of the house to notice. We can keep the Treloar children downstairs. We've got the bathroom as an escape route between us too.'

Millie looked at Alice-Miranda and slowly nodded her head. 'I think we might just have a plan.'

✶

Jemima Tavistock walked through the kitchen to the laundry room at the rear of Bedford Manor. Although it had been updated over the years with modern washers and dryers, the old boilers and wringers still took up much of the floor space along with a whole row of stone tubs and racks of timber airers in the centre. There must once have been a small army of staff to warrant such an extravagant facility, but these days Jemima begrudgingly changed her own sheets and towels.

Mrs Mudge had the afternoon off and Jemima had got rid of Prigg by sending the man on a wild goose chase. After hearing that the Kennington's supermarkets had closed indefinitely, she handed him a haphazard list of the most obscure items and was counting on the fact he would have to travel all the way to the Wandsworths in Ashwood Grove.

Through another door was a gigantic linen press with sheets and towels stacked high. The smell of starch filled the air. Jemima closed her eyes for a second and was transported back to the old laundromat her mother used to run when she was a little girl. How life had changed over the years.

She had already filled a box with some cutlery and crockery from the kitchen and various other household odds and sods she hoped no one would miss. She pulled down two sets of sheets and towels, then spotted a couple of duvets tucked into the far corner of the shelf. Jemima retrieved the stepladder from behind the door and climbed up the rickety thing. She found herself hefting and heaving before the first quilt tumbled to the ground, swiftly followed by the second. She quickly refolded them and carried the lot to the car.

As she was stuffing the goods into the boot, she heard the unmistakable clatter of Anthony's old Landrover. Her heart almost stopped on the spot. What on earth was he doing here? Jemima thought to herself. He wasn't due back until tomorrow.

Jemima hastily loaded the last of her supplies and gently pushed down on the boot lid until she heard a soft click. She waited for the sound of the kitchen door opening and closing before she jumped into her car and roared off, hoping to goodness he hadn't noticed.

Chapter 38

'What if I run down and get Chessie?' Millie said. 'You can stay here and wait for the Treloar children and I'll take her straight up to your room.'

Alice-Miranda thought for a moment. Her ankle was still a little sore and she didn't want to push her luck. 'You'll have to come back through the field and the long-walled garden,' she advised. 'Just wave to any passers-by and make sure to act normal. I'll unlock the conservatory door and meet you there.' She paused. 'You know how to get there, don't you?'

Millie nodded. 'I think so – it's around the same side of the house as the big dining room, isn't it?'

'That's right.' Alice-Miranda opened one of her armoires and dug around in the bottom drawer. She pulled out a backpack and passed it to Mille. 'Transfer Chessie's belongings into this as it'll be easier to manage than her suitcase. Probably best if you hide that under the straw and we can collect it later.'

'Brilliant,' Millie agreed. While she had her reservations about the new girl, she was rather excited to be conducting a clandestine mission.

There was a knock on the door and Cecelia Highton-Smith poked her head in. Millie dropped the backpack to the floor and kicked it under Alice-Miranda's bed in one seamless movement.

'Hello darlings, how is everything?' Cecelia asked.

Alice-Miranda skipped over to her mother and gave her a hug. 'We're having a delightfully eventful day. How are you and Daddy?'

'Sadly, we have no news to report,' Cecelia replied, kissing the top of her daughter's head. 'I thought I'd better come home and see if Shilly needed a hand. And Mrs Smith's just arrived too.'

'Did she mention if Miss Grimm is better?' Millie asked.

'Apparently, she's still in hospital but they have ruled out food poisoning,' Cecelia said.

Alice-Miranda sighed. 'That's a relief.'

'But if she's still sick, that's not so good at all,' Millie said.

'True.' Alice-Miranda bit her lip. 'Let's hope the doctors work out what it is very soon.'

'I heard that you're going to be running a crèche this afternoon. Sorry, girls. I should have postponed the garden party. I don't know what I was thinking and now it's far too late to cancel.' Cecelia looked the most downcast Alice-Miranda had ever seen her.

'We're happy to help, Mummy,' Alice-Miranda said. 'And I think it's important that we carry on with the garden party. Fundraising for the children's hospitals is a very noble cause and a wonderful way to do some good for those affected with food poisoning. And look how well I was cared for at Chattering – everyone was so kind.'

'You know, you're absolutely right, darling,' Cecelia said, brightening. She pushed the sleeves of her crisp white shirt to her elbows. 'It is a welcome distraction from everything else that's going on. I'll be in the dining room if you need me.'

'Perfect!' Millie said excitedly. 'You don't need to come near us for the rest of the week, really,' she added. 'We'll look after ourselves.'

Alice-Miranda grimaced at her friend.

'Um, I mean, don't worry about us,' Millie said, her face growing red. 'Just worry about everything else.'

Cecelia eyed the girl warily. 'Are you all right, Millie? Is there something the matter?'

Millie shook her head a little too emphatically. 'Of course not. I'm fine. You're fine too, aren't you, Alice-Miranda? We're both fine.'

'If you say so,' Cecelia said, looking far from convinced as she pulled the door shut behind her.

'What was *that*?' Millie huffed. 'I might as well have come out and told your mother that we're about to smuggle her neighbour's daughter from the barn to the house and we have to keep her a secret because her mother is an evil witch and her stepfather doesn't want to know her.'

'Shhh!' Alice-Miranda put her finger to her lips. 'Millie, pull yourself together or I'll have to fetch Chessie myself. If you carry on like that, the poor girl will be terrified.'

'Sorry. I think it must be the excitement of knowing that we're helping a fugitive,' Millie said.

'She's not a fugitive,' Alice-Miranda said. 'She's run away, and at the moment it sounds like she has every reason to. But we're going to get to the bottom of things and soon.'

Millie took a deep breath. 'I think I need to do some yoga and practise mindful breathing. Maybe meditate for a minute to calm myself down.'

A smile tickled Alice-Miranda's lips. 'You do know you're getting more and more crazy as you get older,' she said.

Millie nodded and pulled the backpack out from under the bed. 'Yes, and that's exactly why we're best friends.'

✱

Adrienne Treloar picked up the telephone on her desk and dialled the number, marvelling at how easy it was these days to get hold of the direct line for SPLOD.

'I'd like to speak with Marjorie Plunkett, please,' she said. 'I have some information about the Kennington's case.'

She'd imagined she'd be put through to an underling and was stunned when the woman herself answered.

'My name is Adrienne Treloar and I'm a doctor and researcher at the children's hospital in Chattering. We've had forty-three children present with symptoms that would suggest they have been caught up in the Kennington's food-poisoning incident. I believe I have the answer everyone's been searching for – the answer that should bring an end to all this.'

Adrienne listened intently as the woman spoke.

'Yes, of course I'll be here at the hospital,' she said, and hung up the phone.

She smiled to herself as she imagined the look on Edwin Rochester's face when Marjorie Plunkett arrived by helicopter, wanting to speak with her. Adrienne's fate was about to be sealed. The Head of Paediatrics position couldn't possibly go to anyone else now.

Chapter 39

Once Millie had departed, Alice-Miranda had gone in search of Rodney, but the toy was nowhere to be found. Shilly said she hadn't seen him either and suggested that Dolly may have put him somewhere for safekeeping. Alice-Miranda hurried back to her bedroom window and kept an eye out for Millie and their stowaway.

Suddenly, there was a flash of colour among the greenery. Alice-Miranda smiled and gave a thumbs up as Millie and Chessie dashed along the inside of the wall. Her eyes, however, also stumbled upon Mr Greening, who was heading their way on the ride-on mower. Alice-Miranda quickly unlatched the window, pushed the pane upwards and leaned outside.

'Hello Mr Greening,' she shouted, waving her arms wildly.

The man stopped the mower and waved back. 'How are you today?' he cried out. He almost seemed to startle himself, having forgotten that he'd cut the engine. 'Sorry, Alice-Miranda, I didn't mean to yell.'

Alice-Miranda grinned down at him. 'I am feeling much better, thank you. Please tell Mrs Greening we've been enjoying her cakes,' she said. Her eyes wandered over to Millie and Chessie. She hoped they were about to make a run for the side of the house. 'Did you find your things?' Alice-Miranda asked, knowing exactly where his missing bucket and blanket were.

The old man shook his head. 'Still a mystery.'

All of a sudden, Betsy bounded over to the wall and began to bark. She charged through the hedge.

'Betsy, girl, what have you found in there?' Mr Greening called, squinting at the bush.

Alice-Miranda gasped. She held her breath until the labrador charged out of the hedge with a large bone gripped between her jaws.

'Where did you get that?' the man said, scratching his head.

Alice-Miranda laughed with relief and snuck a look sideways, where she saw Millie and Chessie heading for the conservatory. 'She probably buried it there. Well, I best be off to help with the preparations. Have a lovely day, Mr Greening!'

She slammed the window shut and raced out into the hallway, skidding around the corner on the polished wooden floors. The tiny child leapt onto the banister rail and whizzed to the bottom, where she pulled up short of doing her usual jump to the ground below. Her dismount was tame, to say the least.

She scurried past the dining room, where it looked as though the entire household had taken up residence. Shilly was working away at the sideboard while Cecelia was up a ladder, dusting picture frames. Lily was polishing the solid brass dinner gong and Daisy was cleaning the windows.

The windows!

Alice-Miranda screeched to a halt and raced back to the doorway. 'Daisy,' she shouted, louder than was necessary.

The woman spun around, as did everyone else in the room.

Alice-Miranda scrambled for something to say. 'Um, what time are the Treloar children due?' she asked.

Daisy checked her watch. 'Fifteen minutes. Have you changed your mind about looking after them?' she asked anxiously.

'Oh, not at all. I was just checking,' Alice-Miranda said, flashing a reassuring smile.

Once she saw Millie and Chessie had flown past, she threw the group a wave and hurried down the hallway, past an assortment of clocks and antiques, to the conservatory. Crowded with ferns and potted palms, magnificent tubs of orchids, as well as several settings of elegant rattan furniture, the space was a tropical oasis. Cecelia had been working on the renovation all year, having taken inspiration from Prince Shivaji's magnificent room in the palace at Jaipur, with a mind to reveal the finished masterpiece at the annual garden party. Alice-Miranda couldn't help thinking her mother had done a wonderful job.

She met Millie and Chessie at the conservatory door. It was going to be much too hard to navigate the foyer without being spotted, but there was another way to get to her bedroom. A secret staircase in Hugh's study led directly to her parents' bedroom.

Alice-Miranda hugged Chessie. 'I'm so glad you came,' she said. 'Follow me. It may be a little tricky, but we'll be fine once we get to Daddy's study.'

Millie frowned. She had no idea why they were going there.

Alice-Miranda led the girls down the passageway as quickly and as quietly as she could. She pressed her ear to the study door, then pushed it open. She beckoned for Chessie and Millie to go through.

'What are we doing in here?' Millie asked, still at a loss.

Alice-Miranda walked over to the bookshelf and pulled on a copy of *War and Peace*. There was a loud click before the shelf came to life before their very eyes, pivoting to reveal a spiral staircase.

'Whoa!' Millie's jaw dropped. 'This house is the coolest.'

Chessie's eyes almost popped out of her head. 'Where does it go?' she asked.

'It's perfectly safe. Just follow me.' The girls did as they were bid and Alice-Miranda pulled the case closed from the other side, listening for the click. A dim yellow light illuminated the space and she led the way upstairs, emerging into her father's walnut-panelled walk-in-wardrobe. There was a mile of shirts arranged by colour on the top rail, and racks of trousers below.

'Is this a shop?' Chessie whispered.

'You should see her mother's wardrobe,' Millie whispered. 'It's *twice* as big.'

Alice-Miranda poked her head out of the room to check the coast was clear. The only person she was worried about now was her Aunt Charlotte.

The girls sped along the landing, trying their best to avoid the squeakiest floorboards. They were almost at her bedroom door when Aunt Charlotte emerged from the blue room. Alice-Miranda shook her head and pointed to another door, which Millie hurriedly opened and shoved Chessie through before jumping in herself.

Charlotte heard the kerfuffle and turned around. 'Hello sweetheart,' she said, smiling at her niece. 'I was just on my way to the kitchen to warm up some bottles for the twins.'

'Would you like me to watch them?' Alice-Miranda offered.

'That would be great. They'd love that,' Charlotte said, and headed to the back stairs.

Alice-Miranda waited until her aunt had disappeared before she tapped on the door Millie and Chessie were hiding behind.

'That was close,' Millie said, as the girls scooted around to Alice-Miranda's bedroom.

'I'm going to watch the twins. Be back as soon as Aunt Charlotte is,' Alice-Miranda said.

Millie led Chessie inside Alice-Miranda's room and the girls dumped their bags onto the floor.

Chessie was grinning from ear to ear. 'I've never done anything even remotely rebellious in my whole life until the past couple of days. Now look at me. I don't even know who I am.'

Millie grinned back at her. 'Well, I don't think I've harboured too many escapees before either.'

Chessie wandered around the room, taking it all in. 'This doll's house is incredible.'

Millie walked over to join her. 'It's an exact replica of this house. We could probably find that secret staircase in Hugh's study.'

'I've dreamed about a beautiful room like this,' Chessie said wistfully. 'I'd hoped there might be one at my mother's new house, but I don't imagine I'll ever get to see it even if there is.' The smile slipped from her face.

'You can't be sure of that. It's probably just a big misunderstanding.' Millie reached out and patted the girl on the back.

Chessie sniffed. 'Thank you for being so kind to me. I hope you and Alice-Miranda don't get into trouble for housing a fugitive.'

'You're not really a fugitive,' Millie reasoned. 'It's not as if you've committed a crime or anything. Technically, you're a runaway.'

'You know,' Chessie said, sitting down on the edge of Alice-Miranda's bed, 'I am really quite tired of running.' She yawned and laid her head on a pillow and within a minute or two was fast asleep.

Chapter 40

Millie met Alice-Miranda outside her bedroom.

'Chessie fell asleep almost straight away,' Millie said quietly, as they headed downstairs, 'so I tucked her under the duvet and made it look as if it was you – at least you have the same colour hair.'

Cecelia Highton-Smith appeared at the end of the hallway carrying a towering stack of newspapers. The top section began to totter and sway before the entire thing came crashing down.

Alice-Miranda and Millie raced over to help her.

'Oh, silly me,' Cecelia sighed. 'I thought I'd fetch some old newspapers from the cellar to clean the windows, but it seems I've just created more mess.'

'It's all right, Mummy, we'll give you a hand,' Alice-Miranda said as she and Millie set about picking up the pages.

Cecelia and Millie each carried a smaller pile into the dining room. While Alice-Miranda gathered the last of the pages from the floor, a photograph caught her eye. It was of her grand-mother at a charity ball. She was standing next to a very handsome man, whom the caption revealed to be Desmond Berwick, CEO of the Paper Moon Foundation. But even more troubling was the other woman by his side. Her name was Jemima Berwick and, if Alice-Miranda wasn't mistaken, she looked strikingly similar to Jemima Tavistock albeit with a slightly different nose. A thousand questions were running through Alice-Miranda's mind but there was no time to raise them right now. She tore out the page and tucked it into her pocket.

Cecelia reappeared with Millie, and Alice-Miranda passed her mother the last little stack of papers just as the front doorbells chimed.

'We'll get it,' Millie volunteered.

The two girls, wearing only their socks, skidded on the polished floor across the entrance hall. Alice-Miranda fished around in the antique bureau and pulled out an oversized iron key on a long red tassel. She turned the lock and opened the front door.

Standing on the veranda were the Treloars. The smallest girl was perched on her father's hip while the other two, a boy and girl, were holding hands.

The little boy's jaw dropped open. 'Are you a princess?' he asked.

Alice-Miranda laughed. 'Not at all.'

'But this is a palace,' the boy said, craning his neck to see inside.

'Welcome to Highton Hall,' Alice-Miranda said warmly. She extended her hand to Bentley, who gave it an awkward shake. 'You must be Mr Treloar. I'm Alice-Miranda Highton-Smith-Kennington-Jones and this is my friend, Millie. We've been looking forward to your visit all day.'

The man's face quickly turned the colour of his hair. 'I'm sorry. I wasn't sure where we should go.'

'We tend to use the side entrance by the kitchen,' Alice-Miranda told him, 'but of course you weren't to know. Mummy should really put up a sign, especially because the bells on this door can be a bit hit and miss at times. You could have wound up standing out here for ages if they were having an off day!'

The ginger-haired family blinked in response, quite taken aback by the charming child.

'You must be Dottie,' Alice-Miranda said. She offered her hand to the older girl, who reminded her of Millie but with strawberry-blonde curls and fewer freckles. Dottie grinned shyly and shook her hand. Alice-Miranda turned to the boy. 'And you're Leo?'

'Like a lion,' he growled, and Millie recoiled in mock horror.

'Leo, stop that,' his father chided. But the boy continued to bare his teeth.

'And this must be Martha.' Alice-Miranda tickled the little girl's chubby bare leg. The toddler giggled.

Daisy scampered down the hall and out onto the veranda, tucking her dusting cloth into the back pocket of her jeans and wiping her brow. Martha's eyes lit up as soon as she spotted her. She released the grip on her father's neck and leaned out, eager to be in the young woman's arms.

'Thank you so much for bringing the children over, Mr Treloar,' Daisy said. 'I hope it wasn't too much of an inconvenience.'

'Not at all,' the man replied, his eyes sweeping the entrance foyer. 'I'm just thankful you can look after them. I hope you won't be too tired. It's a lot to manage.'

'I'm fine. It's a busy time, that's all,' Daisy said. 'And Alice-Miranda and Millie have everything worked out. They've got games for the children to play in the side sitting room and plenty of toys.'

Martha clapped her hands at the mention of toys.

'Can we go exploring?' Leo asked.

'Yes, of course,' Alice-Miranda said. 'There are lots of secret places and maybe we can go to the treehouse too. It's not dangerous, I promise.'

The little boy's smile couldn't have been any wider.

A clock struck somewhere inside the house, reminding Bentley to get a move on. He leaned down to give Leo and Dottie hugs and kisses then Martha too. 'I'll see you at home in the morning,' he said and gave a wave as he walked back to the car.

'Okay, you lot, Alice-Miranda and Millie are in charge. I want you to be on your best behaviour and do as they say,' Daisy instructed, leading the troupe into the entrance hall.

Leo smiled and pointed at Alice-Miranda. 'She's pretty,' he said.

'Thank you, Leo,' Alice-Miranda said with a grin. 'And I think you make a very handsome young lion.'

The little boy beamed and raced to grab her hand.

'The house is beautiful,' Dottie breathed.

'I think so too,' Millie agreed.

'We're very lucky to live here,' Alice-Miranda said.

'You *are* a princess,' Leo gasped, and pointed at a shiny coat of armour that stood guard in an alcove under the staircase.

Alice-Miranda laughed. 'I do know some princesses but I am definitely not one of them. Is anyone hungry?'

The three children nodded.

'Perfect,' she said. 'Mrs Greening made a heaven cake. I can't wait for you to try it. It tastes like clouds and has cream frosting that tingles on your tongue. It's my favourite – along with devil's food cake, which is the best chocolate cake in the whole wide world.'

'She's right,' Millie jumped in. 'It's not like anything you've ever tasted.'

The group made their way to the kitchen, where Millie poured milk for the children and helped Alice-Miranda to cut some slices of heaven cake.

'It's not usually so busy,' Alice-Miranda explained as they sat around the kitchen table. 'It's just that we have a big garden party and open house event next weekend and Mrs Shillingsworth likes everything to be spick and span from top to bottom.'

The children relished their first afternoon tea at the Hall. Martha stuffed her chubby fingers into her mouth, licking every last morsel, although her tongue wasn't quite long enough to reach all of the places on her face where she'd left crumbs.

Alice-Miranda cleared the plates and glasses, stacking everything neatly into one of two dish-washers while Millie grabbed a packet of wet wipes and she and Dottie washed the children's hands and faces before they headed into the side sitting room. Alice-Miranda was about to join them when she spotted something poking out from behind the biscuit jar on the bench. She smiled and picked up the furry creature. 'I don't know where you've been hiding but I know someone who will be very glad to see you when she wakes up.'

Alice-Miranda hadn't noticed that Aunt Charlotte had arrived in the kitchen with Imogen in her arms. Imogen reached out and grabbed the dog from her cousin's hand.

'Mine,' she declared.

Alice-Miranda shook her head. 'I'm afraid this little dog belongs to someone else,' she said, trying to prise the soft toy from the toddler's grasp.

Imogen's lip began to wobble and her face scrunched up.

'Please don't cry, darling,' Charlotte cooed. She turned to Alice-Miranda with a desperate look in her eyes. 'Can Imogen keep him for now? I'll get it back to you as soon as she forgets.'

Alice-Miranda nodded. 'Of course.'

'Would you mind watching her for a few minutes while I go and get Marcus?' Charlotte asked. 'That boy is so patient. He never complains when I take bossy boots here first.'

Alice-Miranda cuddled her cousin and took her through to the sitting room. Millie had the children involved in a great game of cubby building with sheets and pillows everywhere.

'This is Imogen,' Alice-Miranda said, introducing the toddler.

Martha eyed her warily for a few seconds before thumping over and grabbing her hand.

'Would you like me to take your dog for you?' Alice-Miranda asked Imogen, eager to separate the two as quickly as possible.

'No!' Imogen clutched the creature ever more tightly. 'Mine.'

Alice-Miranda looked at Millie, then at the dog. Millie's mouth formed a perfect 'O' when she realised what her friend was getting at.

'Don't worry,' Millie said with a grin. 'As soon as she puts him down, I'm on it.'

Trouble was, Imogen had no intention of being parted from her new friend – no matter what.

Chapter 41

Marjorie Plunkett felt a wave of relief wash over her. Dr Treloar's investigations had resulted in the most extraordinary revelations. It had transpired that it was just as Alice-Miranda had suspected – a mild poison, the culprit being cyanide. Now all that was left to do was to locate the source of the contamination and neutralise it. She'd called Hugh, who was eager to consult with his team on the next step in the process. Hopefully, they would be able to isolate the cause and have the shops reopened within a matter of days.

The chopper hovered over the moonlit field beyond the front lawn of Highton Hall. Marjorie could see that preparations for the garden party were well underway. Fingers crossed it would be an occasion to celebrate, after all.

As the helicopter came in to land, its headlights shone on to the front of the house, illuminating a child's face. She could only assume it was Alice-Miranda's, although it was difficult to tell.

Marjorie's phone buzzed in her pocket. She took it out and looked at the screen, and decided she'd have to call back later. Juggling two major investigations always kept things interesting. The Kennington's case had taken up most of her time lately due to the urgency of the situation, but things were also beginning to gain traction on the other matter. Marjorie would certainly have her hands full for a while yet.

✫

It was just after seven o'clock when Daisy took the Treloar children home and Aunt Charlotte put the twins to bed. Alice-Miranda had hoped to have retrieved Rodney by now, but there was no way Imogen was going to be parted from her new love. Millie and Alice-Miranda were on their way downstairs to tidy up the sitting room when they heard the aircraft approach.

'Is that Birdy?' Alice-Miranda asked her mother.

Cecelia shook her head. 'It shouldn't be. Cyril's taken her away for servicing. I'm not sure who that is.'

Alice-Miranda and Millie dashed back into the kitchen, out the side door and around to the front of the house. They waved wildly as they leapt off the veranda and onto the lawn.

As the rotors shuddered to a stop, Marjorie Plunkett emerged from the helicopter. She grinned and waved back to the pair when something caught her eye. She looked to a second-floor window. The curtains billowed and she could have sworn she saw a child duck down out of sight.

Just as Marjorie reached the girls, Hugh Kennington-Jones pulled up outside the kitchen door.

'Daddy's home!' Alice-Miranda sang out and raced to the driver's door.

'Hello darling,' he said, giving her a huge hug. 'I've missed you.'

Alice-Miranda beamed up at him. 'Miss Plunkett's here,' she said excitedly.

'Ah, yes, so I see.' Hugh walked over to greet the woman, with his daughter in tow. 'Marjorie. Well done, my dear.'

The woman shrugged. 'It had nothing to do with me. You have a very clever doctor to thank for blowing this case wide open.'

Alice-Miranda gasped.

'Have you solved the case?' Millie asked, and the two girls danced about on the spot.

Hugh smiled. 'We're close. At least we know where to look now.'

Cecelia rushed out of the house and embraced her husband. 'Hello darling.'

'That's the best news ever!' Alice-Miranda exclaimed. She hugged her father again and then her mother.

Marjorie considered the two girls in front of her and cocked her head to the side. 'Who was that in the window upstairs?' she asked.

Hugh frowned, wondering what the woman was talking about.

Alice-Miranda and Millie exchanged knowing looks, which Marjorie Plunkett didn't fail to miss.

'There's only these two down here.' Cecelia grinned. 'Unless they're hiding someone.'

Millie laughed nervously. 'No, of course not. Why would we do that? That's just silly.'

Alice-Miranda grabbed Millie's arm, hoping it would cause her to close her mouth.

Fortunately, the group walked into the kitchen, where the smell of garlic and tomato sauce filled the air and turned the conversation to food.

'Marjorie, you'll join us for something to eat, won't you?' Cecelia asked, already pulling out an extra bowl from the cupboard.

Marjorie collapsed into a chair and sighed. 'Actually, that would be lovely. I'm famished,' she replied gratefully. She put her phone on silent mode and placed it on the tabletop.

Alice-Miranda snuck into the pantry, trying not to draw attention to herself.

'What are you after, dear?' Mrs Smith called as she dished up three bowls of spaghetti for Hugh, Cecelia and Marjorie.

Alice-Miranda grimaced. Squirrelling away food for Chessie was proving harder than she'd anticipated. 'Oh, nothing,' she replied. 'I was just . . . looking.'

She grabbed a paper napkin and walked back to the bench, where she wrapped up several slices of garlic bread and popped them inside her jacket. What she didn't realise was that Marjorie Plunkett had been watching her the whole time.

'So, who is this clever doctor to whom I owe a huge debt of gratitude?' Hugh asked, sprinkling a generous helping of parmesan over his pasta.

Marjorie tore her gaze away from Alice-Miranda and smiled. 'Her name is Adrienne Treloar. She's over at the children's hospital in Chattering.'

'Treloar?' Millie repeated. 'We had the Treloar children here this afternoon. Their mother is a doctor.'

'You're quite right, Millie. Is her husband Bentley Treloar?' Hugh asked.

Marjorie Plunkett looked at them in surprise. 'What a coincidence. Adrienne didn't mention that she knew you.'

'Bentley's worked for Kennington's for years,' Hugh explained. 'He's a very clever fellow – does a bit of research and development at the packaging factory on the edge of the village, but he mostly works the night shift now. He could run the place but prefers not to. Didn't you say the contamination most likely came from plastic containers?'

Marjorie nodded. 'No wonder Dr Treloar has been able to figure out what's been making everyone sick. Apparently, the woman's been toiling day and night, going through every possible option on top of her regular duties. It all makes sense, really. Dr Treloar would have a far greater awareness of the ingredients in plastic if her husband works in the factory.'

Mrs Oliver walked in through the kitchen door and greeted the group.

'Oh, Dolly, you look dead on your feet.' Cecelia stood up and raced to pull out a chair for the woman. Alice-Miranda was standing beside her, waiting for the right time to dash upstairs.

'You smell good enough to eat, young lady,' Dolly quipped, and her stomach let out a loud growl in agreement. 'Did you work your way through a whole loaf of garlic bread?'

Mrs Smith chuckled and immediately set about preparing a serving of dinner for the woman.

'I'll be back in a minute,' Alice-Miranda said, and darted away. She needed to get upstairs and talk to Chessie. She'd barely had a minute to herself all afternoon and only got to look at the newspaper article when she'd locked herself in the loo for five minutes.

Alice-Miranda opened her bedroom door and walked inside to find Chessie sitting on the bed reading.

'Oh, thank goodness it's you,' Chessie exhaled. She placed the book facedown on the duvet. 'For a second I thought I was a goner.'

'I've brought you some garlic bread, but I'm afraid that's all I can get for now.' Alice-Miranda produced the napkin from her pocket. 'Sorry, it's a bit squashed.'

'I don't mind,' Chessie said happily. She took the slices and piled them on the bedside table.

'Chessie, there's something I need to ask you,' Alice-Miranda said, pulling the article from her other pocket. She handed it to the girl. 'Who is that man?'

Chessie examined the black-and-white photo and gasped. 'That's Mummy's brother. Uncle Desmond lives overseas now and I haven't seen him for ages. Why do you ask?'

Alice-Miranda bit her lip. There was no easy way to say this. 'Chessie, I think your uncle might be the reason your mother sent you so far away to school,' she said.

Chessie's eyes widened. 'What do you mean?'

Alice-Miranda sat on the bed and invited Chessie to sit beside her. Then she told the girl everything she knew about the Paper Moon Foundation and what Desmond Berwick had done. Chessie listened to the story without once interrupting. She was shocked to learn that the man she thought she knew was someone entirely different.

'Please let me tell Mummy you're here?' Alice-Miranda implored.

Chessie stared at the pattern on the duvet cover, missing Rodney more than ever. She still didn't understand why her mother hadn't wanted her home for the holidays, especially if her uncle was now in jail. It was fair enough to be sent away to a school where no one would know about him, but the rest of it really didn't add up.

'Not yet,' she said, shaking her head. 'I'm not ready.'

★

Meanwhile, downstairs, Doreen Smith attended to the washing-up. Shilly was still cleaning in the dining room and had vowed not to go to bed until she could cross it off her list. Lily had gone home to her family over an hour ago.

'I've been doing some research on plastics contamination ever since you called, Hugh,' Dolly said, dabbing at her mouth with a napkin. 'You need to do a thorough check of all the factories that supply packaging for any of the Kennington's goods. And as for it being an accident, I'm not so sure about that.'

Hugh frowned. 'Do you really think it could have been deliberate?'

'It's a very odd thing,' Dolly said. 'To create a poison, you'd need to have some fairly accurate quantities and compounds and know exactly how to release it.'

Hugh sighed. 'Golly, Alice-Miranda could have been right all along.'

'I've got teams on it now and I'm hoping they'll have the checks done by tomorrow,' Marjorie said, her eyes flicking to her buzzing phone. She excused herself to take the call and headed out of the kitchen. She charged through the small dining room and into a larger drawing room. To say the woman on the end of the line was hysterical was something of an understatement. But the revelation that her daughter had been missing now for three days was even more shocking. It took her several minutes to explain how she had been able to disappear for that long, but Marjorie Plunkett had an inkling she might be able to solve the mystery far more quickly than the Kennington's affair. She told the woman she'd call her back shortly, then added that she might need to come over to Highton Hall.

Marjorie trotted up the staircase in the entry foyer and waited. Two minutes later, a door opened and Alice-Miranda stepped out. With the stealth of a lioness hunting its prey, Marjorie was beside the girl before she had time to pull the door shut.

'I need to talk to you, young lady,' Marjorie said.

Alice-Miranda smiled and ducked under the woman's arm. 'Of course, Miss Plunkett. Shall we go downstairs?'

'No, I think we'll go in here,' Marjorie said, pushing open the girl's bedroom door.

Alice-Miranda gulped and raced ahead of her into the room, but it was no use.

'Francesca Compton-Halls?' Marjorie looked at the dark-haired girl who was sitting in the middle of the giant four-poster bed, munching on some garlic bread.

The girl coughed and sputtered, almost choking on the crumbs.

'Miss Plunkett, I can explain,' Alice-Miranda said. 'Chessie didn't mean to do anything wrong. And we were going to tell Mummy and Daddy as soon as she felt up to it.'

'Francesca, I need to call your mother right away to let her know you're safe. The poor woman is beside herself,' Marjorie said, already dialling the number.

Fat tears spilled onto Chessie's cheeks. 'I'm sorry. It's all my fault. Alice-Miranda and Millie were only trying to help,' the girl sobbed.

Marjorie got off the phone and regarded the pair. 'Chessie, I'm Marjorie Plunkett. I know this year has been hard for you, but trust me when I say that it's been hard for your mother too.'

'I don't understand. Who are you and how do you know my mother?' Chessie peered at the woman through her wet lashes.

'I'll explain everything when she gets here,' Marjorie said as the door opened.

Millie stepped into the room and her jaw almost hit the floor when she realised that Miss Plunkett was there too. 'Um, what's going on?' she asked.

Alice-Miranda shrugged.

'In view of something your mother told me today, I think this might actually be the best thing, Chessie,' Marjorie said.

The girls looked at one another, wondering what this was all about.

Marjorie walked over and rested her hand on Chessie's shoulder. 'Go and wash your face. Then how about we get you something a bit more nutritious to eat?'

'I'll organise it,' Millie offered.

'And can you let Hugh and Cee know that Lady Tavistock will be arriving soon?' Marjorie instructed. 'When she gets here, I need them all to come upstairs.'

Millie returned a few minutes later with a bowl of bolognaise, which Chessie practically inhaled. She hadn't realised just how hungry she'd been and was feeling quite a lot better with something in her stomach.

Not twenty minutes later, Hugh led Lady Tavistock into the room. Jemima pounced on Chessie, hugging her as if there was no tomorrow. Between the two of them, there were more tears than a cinema full of women watching a Lawrence Ridley romantic comedy.

'Oh, darling, I am so sorry,' Jemima sobbed, her shoulders heaving. 'This is all my fault.'

'No, Chessie. Your mother's wrong about that. If anyone's to blame it's me,' Marjorie said.

Hugh and Cecelia were both completely confounded by the scene in front of them and were at a loss as to how Lady Tavistock's daughter happened to be in Alice-Miranda's bedroom.

'What's going on?' Hugh said, scratching his head.

With the rest of the group spread around the room, Marjorie and Jemima took turns telling them everything about Jemima's brother, Desmond Berwick. Although the man had protested his innocence throughout the whole sordid Paper Moon affair, Jemima had always harboured the suspicion that he had no intentions of clearing his name when he got out of jail. Apparently, he'd been boasting to his cellmate that he had enough money to live like a king – something the man had been kind enough to pass on to Jemima during one of her regular visits.

Since then, Jemima had known it would be up to her to stop him. He'd ruined not only his own life and reputation but hers and their mother's as well. As Queen Georgiana had been a patron of the Paper Moon Foundation, Jemima had written to Her Majesty to say that she wanted to do everything possible to not only bring her brother to justice but to recover the missing funds. That was when Jemima had begun working with Marjorie.

When Jemima had fallen in love with Anthony, she'd been terrified he would break things off with her once he'd learned of her brother. In hindsight, she probably should have let him in on things before now. She resolved to tell him that very night, no matter the consequences. Hugh and Cecelia assured the woman that she had absolutely nothing to worry about. Anthony was an honourable man and it was clear he was madly in love with her. Jemima had sent Chessie away to school to protect her and to give her time to continue her investigations. She needed her brother to think that she was still on his side so that he would lead her to the money.

'So we have met before, haven't we?' Cecelia said. 'At a charity ball. But there's something different about you . . .'

'Oh, I know what it is!' Chessie jumped in. 'Mummy had her nose fixed after an accident and her eyes changed colour, which was a bit weird.'

'Something like that,' Jemima said, nodding sheepishly.

Millie raised an eyebrow. Now wasn't the time to delve any deeper, but she did have many questions.

Jemima also revealed she was concerned about how Desmond was continually asking to see his niece and, now that he had been released from prison, kept harping on about it day and night. Everyone agreed that the best thing was for Chessie to stay on at Highton Hall. If Jemima's assessment was correct, her brother would stop at nothing to see the girl and they needed to work out why. He surely had some ulterior motive, but what that was still remained a mystery.

Chapter 42

The three girls lay side by side in Alice-Miranda's giant bed, exhausted from a night of revelations.

'Well, that was unexpected,' Millie said, staring at the canopy above them.

'I can't believe the lengths my mother has gone to in order to get to the truth,' Chessie said, shaking her head. 'And I can't believe my uncle is such a horrible rogue.'

Alice-Miranda gave her a playful nudge. 'At least we get to be together until the weekend.'

'Do you think I'll really be able to get it out of him?' Chessie asked, turning to look at her new friends.

'Miss Plunkett seemed to think so.' Millie rolled onto her side and propped her head on her hand. 'I like that woman. She's an awesome spy. Maybe that's what I'll be when I grow up.'

Chessie pushed back the covers. 'If you don't mind, I think I'll sleep in the other room. I'm an awful snorer and I don't want to keep you up.'

Millie smiled and waved her hand. 'You are free to go.'

'I wish I had Rodney with me,' Chessie said, hopping onto the plush carpet. It felt odd making friends without him.

Alice-Miranda smacked her head and sat bolt upright. 'I'd completely forgotten to tell you – I know where he is. It's a long story, but he's found his way into Imogen's hot little hands and I'm afraid she's quite attached to the fellow already.'

Chessie felt a pang of jealousy. 'That's okay,' she said. 'It helps to know he's just next door and, seriously, I should be able to go to bed without a stuffed toy at my age.'

'Do you want me to try to rescue him now?' Millie offered. 'I'm sure with my new stealth skills

I could be in and out without Imogen so much as stirring.'

'I wouldn't risk it,' Alice-Miranda said. 'Aunt Charlotte may kill you if you wake them up.'

'Don't worry. We can get him in the morning,' Chessie said. She padded over to the connecting bathroom when she paused and turned around. 'Thank you both for everything. Just when I'd forgotten what it was like to have a real friend, the two of you showed up and I couldn't be happier.'

Alice-Miranda and Millie jumped down from the four-poster bed and hugged the girl.

'Sleep well,' Alice-Miranda said.

Chessie grinned. 'Sweet dreams,' she replied, and disappeared through the bathroom door and into the room beyond.

Chapter 43

The rest of the week zoomed by. Alice-Miranda, Millie and Chessie had the most marvellous time, playing on the farm with Poppy and Jasper in the mornings, and looking after the Treloar children and the twins in the afternoons. Despite numerous attempts to wrestle Rodney back from Imogen, the toddler steadfastly refused to give him up. Chessie was terribly gracious about letting the little girl keep him – for now. She spoke to her mother on the phone at least twice a day, and Jemima and Anthony visited each night too. Anthony had been shocked to learn his wife's secret but was relieved to find out there was a reason why she'd been so cagey about having Chessie come to stay.

Alice-Miranda's dreams, however, had been far from sweet. For almost a week she'd woken up in the most befuddled state, having had the same nightmare over and over again. But she decided not to worry anyone and carried on through the days with a smile on her face.

Kennington's was back in business after every factory and plant had been declared safe. It transpired that an odd computer glitch had caused a mix-up with the formulas at the local packaging factory. Thankfully, it was easily fixed, and Hugh had a team of engineers install fail-safe mechanisms to ensure it would never happen again. To everyone's great relief, all patients had now been discharged from hospital and it seemed, at last, that the horror was over.

✭

Adrienne Treloar's interview on Wednesday afternoon had gone even better than she could have hoped and she'd been offered the job as Head of Paediatrics the following morning. Bentley sent her a huge bouquet of flowers and the most beautiful card telling her how proud he was. The best part was knowing that it was killing Edwin Rochester to have to put her in charge. The man had never liked her and the feeling was absolutely mutual.

She arrived home on Friday night and was surprised to find the house empty until the children burst through the back door with Daisy Rumble close behind.

'Mama!' Martha squealed, racing to her mother, who scooped her up. She nuzzled the toddler's clean little body, taking in the powdery baby smell that she hadn't quite outgrown.

'Where have you lot been?' she asked, as Daisy led the children into the house.

'We've been at Alice-Miranda's,' Leo said. 'She's a princess and she lives in a palace and I'm making her a special drawing.'

Daisy laughed. 'No, she's not, but I think someone's got a big crush on her.'

'I don't crush her. I love her,' the boy insisted. 'And I need some paper.' Leo disappeared to search for some.

Adrienne smiled in mild bewilderment. She could never get over the mixture of joy and guilt at seeing her beautiful children.

They entered the kitchen and Daisy flicked on the kettle. 'I wasn't sure if you'd be home tonight, but I'm glad you are. I have to be up at the crack of dawn for the garden party tomorrow.'

'What garden party?' Adrienne asked, stifling a yawn.

'The one at Alice-Miranda's house,' Dottie piped up. 'Daddy's taking us and you have to come too because her mummy and daddy have bought you a special present.'

Adrienne blinked, then it dawned on her – the Kennington-Jones child.

'How do you have your tea, Dr Treloar?' Daisy asked. 'I'll make you a cup and then put the children to bed.'

'Milk, no sugar,' the woman said absently. She put Martha down on the floor and the little girl ran into the sitting room to play. 'So where have you all been *exactly*?'

'I've been helping out at the Hall to get ready for tomorrow,' Daisy explained. 'Alice-Miranda and two of her friends and Dottie have been watching the children for a couple of hours in the crossover time between when Bentley – I mean, Mr Treloar – had to leave for work and I finished up. We've got loads done and the children have had the most wonderful time.' Daisy smiled and handed the woman her tea.

'I see,' Adrienne said, taking it all in. 'And no one thought to ask me how I felt about that arrangement? I'm paying *you* to look after the children, Daisy, not a bunch of nine-year-olds.'

Daisy looked at the woman in surprise. 'I – I'm sorry, Dr Treloar. I had assumed your husband had told you. I assure you the girls have done a brilliant job and the children have been so happy.'

'Of course they're happy,' Adrienne retorted. 'They've been playing in a mansion with a little girl who lives like a princess, no less, having ridiculous thoughts put into their heads.' She picked up her cup and stared into her tea.

'Would you like me to put the children to bed?' Daisy asked after a while. The woman was obviously tired and out of sorts.

'No, I'll do it,' Adrienne said frostily.

'Well, I'll see you tomorrow at the party. It's going to be lots of fun – especially now that everything is back to normal with Kennington's and all those poor people are better,' Daisy said.

Adrienne slammed down her teacup impatiently, causing Daisy to jump. 'We won't be going tomorrow.'

'But we have to!' Leo protested. He had wandered into the kitchen, clutching a ragged sheet of paper, and heard what his mother said. 'Alice-Miranda is taking me on a hay ride, and Daddy said that we could go.' The boy stamped his foot and his bottom lip began to tremble.

'Stop that nonsense, Leo,' Adrienne ordered. 'Daddy had no business taking you there this week. He should have told me and I would have arranged someone more reliable to look after you.' She shot Daisy a glare.

Daisy trembled. 'I think that's a little unfair, Dr Treloar. Your husband has been working very long hours to make sure that the factory was clear of any contamination. And I had to help out. Highton Hall – well, Rose Cottage, which is on the estate – is my home.'

Adrienne rolled her eyes and scoffed. 'What do you think I've been doing? Did you know that *I* was the one who cracked the case? If it wasn't for *my* research, they might never have found the solution. And I don't know why you'd want to live there with that lot. Hugh Kennington-Jones is nothing but a double-dealing swindler.'

Daisy was at a loss as to what to say. Never in her life had she thought she'd hear anyone utter such words about Hugh Kennington-Jones. 'I'd better get going,' she said, hastily picking up her things. 'Goodnight, kids. See you in the morning.' She prised Martha's tiny fingers from around her waist and knelt down to wipe Leo's tears.

'Kiss?' he said.

Daisy pecked the boy's cheek, avoiding his mother's piercing gaze.

'I love you, Daisy.' Leo reached out and hugged her tightly around the neck.

'I have to go, sweetheart,' Daisy said, and hurried out the door, not daring to look back.

Chapter 44

The morning of the garden party couldn't have been more glorious nor any busier. The girls were up early and, along with the rest of the adults, were allocated a final range of jobs by Shilly to make sure that everything was in order. Alice-Miranda, Millie and Chessie were to double-check that the upstairs bedroom doors were locked and the rope barriers were all in place.

'Now, I'm going to put you in charge of the keys,' Shilly said to Alice-Miranda. Hanging from a round metal ring, this particular bundle was just for the bedrooms on the second and third floors. 'But I think Charlotte will likely need the twins' room kept open, as they'll be up for their nap time later in the day.'

'I'll put them back into the cabinet once we're all done,' Alice-Miranda promised, taking them from Shilly.

'Good girl.' The woman gave a smile, which was a rare sight from her during the past few days.

'At least the weather has been kind to us this year,' Alice-Miranda said brightly.

'Thank heavens I won't be cleaning mud out of the carpets for months.' Shilly winked. 'And I think that staircase could do with one final polish, if you know what I mean.'

Millie gasped and her eyes lit up. 'Can we borrow your stopwatch?' she asked.

Shilly nodded and reached into her apron pocket. She handed over the stopwatch as well as a folded piece of paper. 'You'll be needing this too. But no riding the banister for you, Alice-Miranda. This is Millie and Chessie's race.'

'Too late, Shilly – I've already been on there twice this week.' Alice-Miranda grinned. 'I've totally regained my balance, although I'm being very careful on the dismount.'

Shilly shook her head. 'You'll be the death of me one day, young lady.'

The girls giggled and one by one leapt onto the banister, timing each other as they whizzed down the rail. Millie was the fastest and even beat Jacinta's record, which she couldn't wait to announce the minute they got back to school. The trio then charged up the stairs to Alice-Miranda's room to get ready for the big day.

Cecelia had arranged three beautiful dresses, each of them white with different coloured sashes and trims. Alice-Miranda's had mid-length sleeves, a green bow around the middle and pretty pink flowers that danced along the hem. Millie's dress was a sleeveless design with a pattern of broderie anglaise all over, and Chessie's had full-length sleeves and a trimming of pink satin ribbon. They helped one another into their outfits and slipped into their matching ballet flats, before Cecelia styled their hair. Her own dress was a gorgeous floral frock with a cinched waist and full skirt.

'Perfect.' Cecelia smiled as she placed the last of the three floral garlands on top of Millie's flame-red hair. 'Chessie, I've got to get my hat, but I'll be back in a few minutes to take you downstairs to meet Miss Plunkett in Hugh's study.'

'And Millie and I will finish checking things up here,' Alice-Miranda added.

Cecelia gave a wave and dashed out the door.

Alice-Miranda took Chessie's hands into her own and gave them a squeeze. 'How are you feeling?'

'Fine, I think. I just don't know what I'm supposed to say to my uncle if I see him,' the girl confessed.

'He'll hopefully do most of the talking,' Millie said, trying to make her feel better. 'If he comes, that is.'

Chessie nodded. She wished the butterflies in her stomach would settle down. 'I can hardly believe it was only a week ago when I was hiding out in the barn and planning to never see my mother again. She's been through so much and I was such a wimp.'

'No, you weren't,' Alice-Miranda said. 'It was a horrible situation and I think you were very brave.'

'Well, I feel a lot braver now, especially since I have two amazing new friends.' Chessie hugged the girls.

Cecelia poked her head around the door. 'Ready?'

Chessie took a deep breath and hurried out to join her.

✶

Marjorie Plunkett arrived at the house just after nine. She and Jemima were confident they'd laid a good-enough trail for the man. One of Marjorie's agents was stationed in Penberthy Floss and had been instructed to follow Desmond and there were others ready for when he arrived. To err on the side of caution, Marjorie had decided to fit Chessie with a tiny microphone beneath her clothes.

'Do you really think he's going to come looking for me?' Chessie asked nervously.

Jemima nodded, biting a nail. 'He's been asking about you every day. I keep wondering what you could possibly have that he's after.'

Chessie couldn't think of anything either. The last time she'd seen her uncle, he hadn't given her any presents.

Hugh and Anthony walked into the room as Marjorie was finishing up.

'Are you sure Chessie's going to be safe?' Anthony asked, frowning with concern. In the few days he'd got to know his stepdaughter, he'd already grown very fond of her.

'I've got agents crawling all over the garden and there'll be some in the house too,' Marjorie assured him. 'If and when he approaches Chessie, we'll have eyes and ears on both of them.'

There was a knock on the door, and Alice-Miranda poked her head in and smiled. She and Millie had left them to it while they'd done a last-minute check upstairs. 'Is everything all right?' she asked.

'Chessie, why don't you go with the girls and have a look around outside?' Marjorie suggested.

Chessie turned to her mother, who hugged the child tightly.

'We'll come too,' Jemima said, 'but don't worry, we'll keep a safe distance.'

Anthony and Jemima exited the room with Chessie and the girls, leaving Hugh and Marjorie alone.

'Do you really think Berwick's likely to give up any of his secrets to Chessie today?' Hugh asked.

Marjorie's mouth was set in a grim line. She wasn't entirely sure, but it was all they had. 'We can only hope. Jemima has risked a lot the past year. I really want her to feel as if it was all worthwhile.'

Outside, the garden party was in full swing. A jazz band struck up on the front lawn and there were men and women arriving in their Sunday best, armed with hats and gloves and parasols. Little did they know the drama that was about to unfold.

✶

Meanwhile, at the Treloar residence, Bentley's plans to take the children to Highton Hall weren't shaping up as well as he'd hoped. When he'd arrived home from work that morning, his wife had been full of accusations. For the life of him, Bentley couldn't understand why she was so upset. She'd got her promotion, which had been the most important thing in the world to her. Adrienne should have been happy but she wasn't at all.

'Adie, please, I promised the children we'd take them, and Hugh has asked to have a quiet meeting with you as well,' Bentley begged.

His wife glared at him. 'Why? Because he's finally realised that at least one of us in this family is a genius?'

Bentley could feel his resentment rising. 'What? You think it was all your own idea?' he muttered.

'Well, I didn't see you working around the clock to get to the bottom of it,' Adrienne retorted. 'If your venture hadn't been such a spectacular failure then I wouldn't have to work so hard.'

Bentley exhaled. He didn't want to say something he'd regret, but his wife was pushing all of his buttons. He was also worried he'd misplaced a page of his notes. He knew he'd brought it home and he thought he'd put it in the shed, but the piece of paper wasn't there.

'No, of course you're right,' he said.

'And if Hugh Kennington-Jones hadn't diddled you out of what you were due, maybe I could spend more time at home with the children,' she added.

'I sold him that concept for a good price, Adie. I wasn't to know that his team would improve it and be able to get a worldwide patent,' Bentley said, as he had done many times before. 'And he gave me a job.'

'You were sold up the river!' she hissed. 'And now you want to attend the scoundrel's garden party.'

In the kitchen the children were all wailing and sobbing. Adrienne tried to hold on to her resolve, but she couldn't stand it another minute.

'Fine!' she shouted. 'Let's go.'

Within seconds Bentley had the kids in the car. 'We don't have to stay long,' he said, patting his wife's leg.

She flinched as if he'd just poked her with a cattle prod.

In the back seat, Dottie gulped. She hated it when her parents fought. And she hated that she liked it much better when her mother was away for work.

'Let's go and have a lovely day,' Bentley said, mustering all the cheer he could.

'Yeah, lovely day!' Leo parroted, quickly followed by Martha. The boy scrunched up his nose and patted his jacket pocket. 'And I've got a present for Alice-Miranda.'

Chapter 45

Desmond Berwick smoothed the moustache onto the top of his lip and checked that his hairpiece was secure. He placed the glasses on the tip of his nose and turned sideways in the mirror before scanning the full-page advertisement for this year's garden party event. So many waiters, so much tea to be served. So fortunate that he'd learned a trick or two during his recent time away.

He peered through the gap in the curtains. The car out the front had been sitting there for the past three days. If that fellow worked for him, he'd have been sacked a long time ago. Bentley had walked past the vehicle twice yesterday and the dopey chap hadn't even glanced up from his magazine. Talk about making yourself conspicuous.

Desmond strode out the back door and around to the carport. Dear Mrs Mogg, the woman who owned the shop next door, was such a kind soul. When he'd mentioned that he had got a job working at the garden party but no way of getting there, the sweet lady had offered to loan him her husband's old banger. Clyde was minding the shop for the day while Mrs Mogg was leaving early to help out at the Hall, so he was welcome to it. Mustard-brown wasn't exactly Desmond's colour of choice, but as long as he could get where he needed to go, he didn't care.

Desmond puttered out of the Moggs' driveway and nodded to the chap out the front. The man looked up from his newspaper and nodded back.

It didn't take long to reach Highton Hall and it certainly wasn't hard to find. Desmond flashed his ID and was directed to park in an area cordoned off for staff.

'You'll need to report to Mrs Oliver. She's in the marquee on the front lawn and will point you to whichever team you're part of,' a fellow advised.

Desmond drove through and parked the car. He hopped out and stood there for a moment, taking in his new surroundings. A chirpy young woman got out of the car beside him and smiled.

'Hi there,' she said. 'Beautiful day for it.'

'It certainly is,' Desmond replied, grinning. In just a few hours, he would have what he needed and be gone. His silly sister could weep all she wanted, but he hadn't worked this hard for this long to end up broke and slaving away at some dead-end job for the rest of his life.

Desmond followed a trail of workers to the marquee, where a sturdy woman with a lilting Irish accent was giving instructions, and soon found himself setting tables. He hoped he would be able to get out of there and find a way into the main house. Chessie could have been anywhere, but her belongings were bound to be inside. It was fortunate Mrs Mogg had mentioned having met the girl at Highton Hall, where she was staying with some brat called Alice-Miranda for the weekend. He wondered what Jemima was playing at, keeping Chessie away from him. As luck would have it, it wasn't long before the Irish woman asked him to fetch some more cakes from the kitchen.

✶

'Have you seen anyone that looks like your uncle?' Millie asked as the girls wandered about the stalls.

Chessie shook her head. 'Maybe he's not coming. Mummy and Miss Plunkett might've got it wrong.'

'Why don't we just have a lovely time?' Alice-Miranda suggested. 'Granny's due soon with Aunty Gee, who's coming especially for the relaunching of the foundation. I can't wait to see them both.'

Millie turned to Chessie. 'Don't worry, Aunty Gee's the best. She's really funny and she loves to dress up too. And she sent me this beautiful bracelet for helping Alice-Miranda when she had her accident.' Millie held out her arm, showing off the little gold band.

Chessie wondered why Millie was cautioning her about the old woman and, on the contrary, felt slightly alarmed.

'There's Aunt Charlotte and the twins,' Alice-Miranda said, leading the way over to them.

'Asmanda!' Imogen bleated. She had Rodney clamped under one arm in a headlock.

Chessie looked at the toy and felt a pang in her chest.

'I am so sorry, sweetheart,' Charlotte apologised. 'I have tried to get her to give him up, but she has a complete meltdown each time. I've never known her to be so attached to anything. I promise he won't be coming with us when we leave tomorrow. Alice-Miranda told me Rodney is yours and I feel terrible that my little monster has hijacked him.'

Chessie smiled graciously. 'I should be able to cope for another few hours, although I must admit I've rarely been apart from him since I was about Imogen's age. My uncle gave him to me and he's the thing I've always loved best in the world.'

An idea sparked in Alice-Miranda's mind. Could that possibly be it?

'We're on our way to get ice-cream. Do you want to come?' Charlotte asked.

'I'll pass this time,' Millie said. 'We just had some a while ago.'

'Have fun, girls. I think these two will be needing a nap soon,' Charlotte said, then headed off in search of the icy treats.

Alice-Miranda could see Daisy Rumble walking towards them and gave a small wave.

'Hi there, girls,' Daisy said. 'Are you enjoying yourselves?'

'Oh, yes,' the trio chorused. For a moment, they had almost forgotten about SPLOD and Chessie's uncle.

In the distance Millie spotted Dottie Treloar. She was holding Leo's hand while Mr Treloar was carrying Martha. The children were in high spirits, but Mr Treloar and the woman beside him looked as if they'd stepped out of the car and into something unpleasant.

'Whoa,' Millie whispered. 'Did they just lose the lottery?'

Chessie bit her lip. She had been thinking the same thing herself.

'What are you talking about?' Daisy spun around. 'Oh, Dr Treloar was in an awful mood when I saw her last night. I have to say I wasn't impressed with some of the things she was saying about your father, Alice-Miranda.'

Alice-Miranda frowned and wondered how Dr Treloar would even know her father.

Daisy eyed the crowd swarming in front of the pancake stand and hoped they hadn't run out of maple syrup already. 'Sorry, girls, I'd better get back to it,' she said, and hurried away before Alice-Miranda could ask her what she'd meant.

'Mayday, mayday,' Millie mumbled under her breath. 'Grumpy parents incoming.' She motioned to the Treloars, who were headed their way.

'Hello Mr Treloar.' Alice-Miranda grinned at the man, then turned to his wife. 'You must be Dr Treloar. I've been looking forward to meeting you very much, not only because of your delightful children but because you solved the problem with the Kennington's plant and you have made Mummy and Daddy so happy.'

Alice-Miranda held out her hand, but the woman simply stared at it. Bentley, in turn, glared at his wife.

'Alice-Miranda, I've got a present for you!' Leo rushed forward and handed her a piece of paper, which was folded in a very four-and-a-half-year-old way.

'For me?' She opened the page and smiled at the drawing.

'That's you and that's me and that's the palace where you live,' he said proudly, pointing at each one of the figures on the piece of paper.

Alice-Miranda gave the boy a hug. 'It's gorgeous, Leo. I love it. Thank you.'

'L-Leo, where did you get that piece of paper?' his father asked. Small beads of perspiration peppered the man's brow.

'The shed,' the boy replied.

'But you're not allowed in there,' Bentley said through gritted teeth. 'I've told you a hundred times before.'

Leo's bottom lip trembled and tears started to well in his eyes.

The man turned to Alice-Miranda and smiled. 'It's a lovely picture, but I'm sure you wouldn't mind if I took that back. It's a rather important document,' he said, reaching for it.

Adrienne pushed away her husband's hand as Leo began to wail. 'For goodness sake, Bentley, let the girl have it. It can't be anything of vital significance.'

Alice-Miranda felt a strange stab of familiarity. 'Have we met before, Dr Treloar? I'm usually quite good at recalling acquaintances, but I've recently suffered a bump on the head and I'm afraid my memory may be letting me down . . .' She peered up at the woman. 'Perhaps we met at the children's hospital in Chattering.'

Adrienne shook her head firmly. 'I am one-hundred-per-cent certain we haven't. I would remember. It was lovely to meet you, but I think we'd best be going. Dottie wants an ice-cream.'

The man hesitated, then reluctantly scurried away after his wife.

'Well, that was weird,' Millie said, wrinkling her nose.

Chessie nodded in agreement. 'No wonder those kids loved coming here all week.'

'Let's go and find Jasper and Poppy,' Millie suggested, heading off in their direction. 'I think they're helping Heinrich with the farmyard in the walled garden.'

'Okay,' Chessie said, scratching at the microphone. It was awfully itchy for such a tiny thing.

Alice-Miranda turned Leo's drawing over in her hand. On the other side was what looked to be scrawls of chemical symbols and scientific formulas. The piece of paper must have belonged to Bentley Treloar. She was happy to return it to him when she could catch him on his own. Alice-Miranda began to fold Leo's drawing when she noticed some words at the bottom of the page. She studied them for a moment, a shiver running down her spine.

'Alice-Miranda, are you coming?' Millie called.

'I'll meet you there,' she shouted back.

Millie shrugged and carried on with Chessie by her side. They made their way to the farmyard, where Jasper and Poppy were busy looking after a menagerie of animals. There were lambs, chicks, rabbits and ducklings. Poppy's friend Clementine Rose was there too. Millie introduced her to Chessie and then to the girl's great-aunt Violet, who was fascinated to hear that Chessie's mother was the new Lady Tavistock. Millie soon found herself rescuing an embattled hen that was almost being loved to death by an overly enthusiastic toddler.

'It's been lovely to meet you,' Chessie said to Clementine and her great-aunt, 'but please excuse me. I need to go to the toilet.'

'You'll be waiting a while, my dear.' Aunt Violet nodded towards the long line at the portable loos that had been installed at the bottom of the garden.

Chessie grimaced. 'Oh, I don't think I can hold on that long. I'll just run back to the house.' She deposited a bunny over the fence and into the pen.

'I'll only be a few minutes, Millie,' she called, and hurried out of the enclosure.

✫

'Hello Chessie, what are you doing back here?' Alice-Miranda asked as the girl flew into the kitchen.

Upon hearing the name, Desmond Berwick looked up from the bench. The sweet little girl had grown. But of course children have a habit of doing that.

Chessie grinned and waved hello without stopping. 'Need the toilet and the lines were crazy,' she explained, rushing to the downstairs loo.

Chessie quickly went about her business, then adjusted her dress. She realised that the microphone Miss Plunkett had stuck to her chest had come loose. She'd have to get some more tape and ask Alice-Miranda to help put it back on.

Inside Hugh's study, an agent winced as the microphone screeched in his ear. 'Kids,' he groaned, 'should not wear wires.'

As Chessie exited the powder room, she noticed a waiter hovering at the end of the hallway. He probably had to use the bathroom too. The sound

339

of people echoed from somewhere in the house and she realised that Cecelia must have started the tours.

Chessie walked back down the hallway and, as she passed the man, she felt a frisson between them. He grabbed her arm and the tiny microphone fell to the floor.

'Hello Francesca,' he whispered in her ear. 'Come with me.'

Chapter 46

Alice-Miranda hadn't been able to find Marjorie Plunkett anywhere in the house. She was on her way back to the garden when she suddenly remembered the parasols her mother had organised to complete the girls' outfits. It was getting warm outside and they *were*, after all, supposed to look like ladies, not sweaty ragamuffins, especially in Aunty Gee's presence.

She bounded up the stairs and caught a glimpse of the door to the blue room closing. Aunt Charlotte must have been quick with the ice-creams, Alice-Miranda thought to herself. As she walked past the room, she heard a scuffle and loud whispering. She wondered if some of the visitors had got lost.

'Excuse me,' Alice-Miranda said as she walked in. 'I'm afraid this room is private.'

A man who was standing on the other side of the bed turned around in surprise. He had a bushy moustache and was dressed as one of the waitstaff.

'Oh, I'm terribly sorry,' he said. 'I was sent to fetch some towels for a spillage and I somehow ended up in here.'

'Not to worry,' Alice-Miranda assured him. 'It happens all the time. I'd be more than happy to show you where they're kept. You weren't too far off, actually.'

'That would be lovely, thank you,' he said gratefully. His eyes darted towards Marcus's cot. 'Would you mind if I use the bathroom and meet you outside?'

Alice-Miranda hesitated. There was something rather familiar about the fellow, but she couldn't quite put her finger on it. What was more alarming was that the corners of the man's moustache seemed to be working free of his face.

'Alice-Miranda!' Chessie called out, popping up from the other side of the bed. '*He's* my uncle!'

'Oh!' Alice-Miranda gasped, then turned to face the man. 'Mr Berwick, what are you doing here?'

Desmond tensed at the sound of his name. He paced back and forth along the small silk rug on the floor. 'Look, I needed to speak to my niece alone,' he said. 'If you'd just give us a minute, I'll be gone and you can return to your precious party.'

Alice-Miranda couldn't understand why half of SPLOD hadn't yet descended on the room. She motioned to Chessie's microphone, but the girl shook her head.

'Now, Francesca,' the man growled, 'give me what I came for and I'll be on my way.'

Chessie's face crumpled. 'But I don't have anything that belongs to you.'

Desmond glared at her. 'Don't play dumb with me, Francesca. Where is he?'

Suddenly, Alice-Miranda realised exactly what the man was after. They had to get out of there and fast. She looked at Chessie and motioned to the rug. Chessie shrugged and Alice-Miranda gripped her fists and pulled them towards her. Chessie's eyes lit up and she nodded.

'Run!' Alice-Miranda yelled. She opened the door and Chessie sprinted towards her. Desmond Berwick stuck out his foot just as Alice-Miranda pulled hard on the edge of the rug. He lost his balance as the carpet slid from underneath him. With his arms fanning like a windmill, he flew backwards and hit the deck with an almighty thud.

The girls fled along the landing to the back stairs, taking two at a time.

'Francesca!' Desmond yelled from above.

He raced after the girls into the kitchen, where several waiters were collecting cakes for the tea tent. Desmond shoved the smiling young woman, whose cake box flew out of her arms, splattering its contents all over the kitchen floor.

'Hey, what do you think you're doing?' she cried out as he charged through the door.

Marjorie Plunkett had just completed another sweep of the grounds and was eager to return to the house for a quiet cup of tea. Twenty minutes hearing about the benefits of eating organic sugar snaps had been quite enough.

Alice-Miranda hoped like mad that Charlotte and the twins were still among the crowd.

'Where are we going?' Chessie panted.

'To find Aunt Charlotte,' Alice-Miranda said, scanning the grounds. 'And keep a lookout for Miss Plunkett too.'

Chessie was confused. 'Why do we need to find Charlotte?'

'Because I'm almost certain that Imogen has exactly what your uncle is looking for and if we don't find them before he does, he'll be gone and Rodney along with him,' Alice-Miranda explained.

Chessie frowned. 'Rodney? What's he got to do with all this?'

'I'm not exactly sure, but let's hope we find him before your uncle does.' Alice-Miranda held Chessie's hand as the girls wove through the crowd, which seemed to be moving towards the stage. Surely if Desmond Berwick caught up to them there were enough people to pounce on him and, besides, the place was supposed to be crawling with SPLOD agents.

Granny Valentina and Aunty Gee had arrived and Alice-Miranda spotted her father on the little podium in the middle of the front lawn. The official launching of the foundation was to happen at midday, in five minutes' time.

There was still no sign of Charlotte and the twins anywhere.

Desmond Berwick was right behind them but had slowed his pace so that no one would take any notice of him.

Cecelia appeared on the stage beside her husband and Aunty Gee, flanked by Marjorie Plunkett, who still hadn't made it back to the house for her cup of tea.

Alice-Miranda and Chessie wriggled to the front of the throng, knowing that Desmond Berwick would be watching their every move from somewhere close by. A child began to cry and Alice-Miranda hoped that it was Marcus or Imogen, but it was Martha Treloar, who looked as if most of her ice-cream had ended up on her face. Alice-Miranda continued to scan the crowd and saw Millie, who gave a wave and hurried towards them.

'He's here,' Chessie whispered, her eyes everywhere.

'Your uncle?' Millie whispered back.

'Have you seen Aunt Charlotte?' Alice-Miranda asked. 'We need to find her.'

Millie pointed at Charlotte pushing the stroller from the side of the stage area and parking it in front. Imogen was still clinging to Rodney.

'Don't all stare at them, or he'll realise,' Alice-Miranda ordered.

The girls smiled up at Alice-Miranda's parents, Granny Valentina and Aunty Gee, who waved from the stage.

Chessie looked at Millie. 'Is that who I think it is?'

Millie grinned and nodded. 'I told you Aunty Gee was fabulous.'

Chapter 47

'Welcome, everyone,' Hugh said into the microphone. 'Thank you for joining us on this beautiful day. We'd like to especially welcome our guest of honour, Her Majesty, Queen Georgiana.'

The crowd clapped and cheered just as Alice-Miranda felt a hand grip her arm.

'What do you think you're doing, little girl?' the man hissed in her ear. 'Where is it?'

'And without further ado, Her Majesty would like to speak about a charity very close to her heart, the Paper Moon Foundation.'

'What?' Desmond looked up at the podium. He released his hold of Alice-Miranda's arm and began to shrink backwards into the mass of people.

Aunty Gee spoke for several minutes about the important work the foundation did with the children's hospitals and how incredible the doctors were. 'And Hugh tells me that one of those very clever doctors is actually here today. I'd personally like to pay tribute to Dr Adrienne Treloar, who has just been announced as the new Head of Paediatrics for the children's hospital in Chattering, and whose brilliance also put a stop to the recent Kennington's strife. I'd like Dr Treloar to come to the stage and accept this token of our great appreciation.'

Adrienne Treloar was in no mood for this. Had she known she was going to be paraded about like a show pony, there was no way she would have agreed to come to this silly garden party. She reluctantly walked onto the stage.

Alice-Miranda glanced back at Imogen and was ready to pounce as soon as the formalities were over. She'd tried to catch Marjorie's gaze several times, but the woman seemed to be watching everywhere else.

Hugh handed Adrienne an enormous bunch of flowers and Queen Georgiana presented her with a small parcel.

'Would you like to say a few words, Dr Treloar?' Hugh asked.

'Not especially,' she mumbled, trying to hide behind the blooms.

'Oh, now is not time for modesty. You've solved a very perplexing mystery and I'm sure we'd all love to know how you did it,' Queen Georgiana cajoled the woman.

'Your Majesty, I was just doing my job,' Adrienne said curtly.

Alice-Miranda's eyes widened. That was it – the voice! The one in her dreams. She pulled Leo's drawing from her pocket and stepped forward.

'It was you,' she said loudly. 'You were in my room in the hospital and you were saying lots of mean things about Daddy and how it served him right that something terrible should happen. It wasn't a dream, it was real.'

Adrienne Treloar looked at the child as if she were mad. 'No, of course I didn't. I've never met you before today. You're lying.'

Cecelia Highton-Smith jumped up. 'No, I saw you too. You came into Alice-Miranda's room the first night she was in hospital.'

'Liars, all of you,' Adrienne snapped. She had bottled up her feelings about Hugh Kennington-Jones for years and right now her own internal Mount Vesuvius was set to explode. 'You,' she said, pointing at Hugh. 'If you hadn't stolen my husband's work, things would be very different for us.'

Hugh held up his hands. 'Steady on, Dr Treloar. I paid your husband well for his invention. And when he came back to me after his own research failed, I was happy to take him on and go fifty-fifty in any new discoveries he makes.'

'Are you lying about that too?' Adrienne's face crumpled.

Bentley was shaking his head. 'I didn't tell you – I wanted to make something happen and then you could be proud of me.'

Alice-Miranda looked at Bentley. 'But it wasn't just Dr Treloar, was it? It was you too.'

'What are you talking about, you ridiculous child?' Adrienne was getting up a right head of steam.

'Miss Plunkett, you need to see this.' Alice-Miranda held out the paper and the woman hurried over to take it.

From the look on Bentley's face, he knew exactly what Alice-Miranda was about to show her.

'I'm afraid I don't understand. Dolly, are you out there?' Marjorie called, scanning the crowd.

Mrs Oliver charged towards the stage. 'Here I am, dear. What is it?' She studied the page. 'Good heavens. It's a very clever formula for cyanide poisoning – and if I'm not mistaken, it's the poison that was created at the local packaging plant. Where did you get this?'

Alice-Miranda pointed at Bentley Treloar.

The crowd gasped.

'I think Mr Treloar and his wife poisoned all those people,' Alice-Miranda said.

'We most certainly did not!' Adrienne shouted. 'How dare you accuse us of such a thing? It's true I don't like your father, but I'd never do anything like that. I'm a doctor! I make people *better*, not worse. I solved the case.'

Adrienne looked at her husband, whose face was the colour of his hair. He hung his head.

'Bentley?' The woman was incredulous. 'Oh no, it can't be true.'

'I . . . I just wanted you to get what you deserved and I knew that if you solved something huge, they'd have to give you the job. After what happened last time, when Desmond Berwick ruined everything, I couldn't stand it any longer. I'm a failure and you're a star and you deserve to be recognised.' Tears streamed down the man's cheeks. 'I didn't realise how bad it would be. I didn't mean to make all those people so sick. I was a fool.'

'You're hardly a failure, Treloar,' Hugh said.

'My research – it's rubbish. I can't make it work. I'm at a dead end,' the man sobbed.

Adrienne shook her head, fighting back tears. 'But this? People were sick, Bentley. Horribly sick and *you* caused it.'

Alice-Miranda looked around for Desmond. For a moment, he'd completely slipped her mind, but she was sure he was still there, watching her every move.

She glanced at her cousins and saw Marcus reach out and grab the toy his sister was holding and fling it across the front of the stage. Imogen began to bawl. Alice-Miranda had seen it and so had Desmond. He practically launched himself through the crowd and onto the toy dog.

'Good grief! What are you doing, man?' Aunty Gee demanded.

Alice-Miranda flew after him and snatched the toy away. 'Miss Plunkett!' the child called. 'Catch!'

'No! That's mine,' Desmond howled.

'Desmond!' Jemima shouted from the side of the stage.

'Desmond? Not that dreadful Desmond Berwick?' Aunty Gee took a closer look at him and gasped. 'What are you doing here?'

'Yes, that's him and I think I know where he's hidden all the money or at least how we can find out.' Alice-Miranda leapt onto the stage.

Desmond Berwick was still on his hands and knees.

'I'm sorry, Chessie, but we can have Rodney fixed, I promise,' Alice-Miranda said and took the dog from Marjorie's hands. She pulled hard on the centre seam of the toy pup's tummy and tore it open. Alice-Miranda reached in and pulled out a little pouch. She unzipped it to find a tiny key and a piece of paper.

'My goodness, that's it!' Marjorie's eyes were huge. 'Arrest that man!' she ordered.

Agents came from everywhere, pouncing on Desmond and cuffing his hands behind his back.

'And arrest him too,' she said, pointing at Bentley Treloar.

Daisy shuffled through the crowd and took Martha from her father. Leo clung to her leg and held on to his big sister's hand. Adrienne Treloar was still standing on the stage, shaking in shock.

'What does it say?' Jemima asked, gesturing to the paper in Alice-Miranda's hand.

'It's a receipt for a safety deposit box,' Alice-Miranda said.

'This is very good news, indeed. How many millions did that swindler steal?' Aunty Gee asked.

'Eight and a half,' Jemima replied. The number was burned into her brain.

'Well, it looks like we're kicking off the foundation with an excellent amount and another million from me,' Aunty Gee announced, rousing a huge cheer from the crowd.

Jemima hurried to her daughter with her husband in tow. She hugged Chessie tight and burst into tears. 'It's over, darling. We can be a proper family now,' she sobbed.

'We have one person to thank for that,' Chessie said, turning to Alice-Miranda.

The two children embraced.

'I can't believe you worked it all out,' Chessie said. 'Not only this but the food poisoning as well.'

Alice-Miranda smiled and shrugged. 'I guess sometimes you just have to find the key. And I'm sorry about Rodney. Shilly can sew him back together and he'll be even better than new.'

Millie rushed over to join the girls and gave them both a hug as Marjorie's people discreetly removed Bentley and Desmond from the crowd.

'Wow! That was . . . unexpected,' Millie said, grinning from ear to ear.

'Daisy, I must apologise to you and the Kennington-Joneses,' Adrienne said. 'I need to go with Bentley and see if we can sort out this mess. Would you mind taking care of the children?' she asked, her voice wavering.

'Of course,' Daisy said with a sympathetic smile. She'd need every distraction technique in the book to keep the children's minds off what they'd just witnessed but she'd give it her best shot.

'Hey, look,' Millie said, nudging Alice-Miranda. She pointed to the far edge of the crowd. 'There's Miss Grimm and Mr Grump and Plumpy and Reedy. They made it. Whoa, looks like Miss Grimm's eaten a few too many donuts.'

Alice-Miranda and Millie looked at each other.

'No way!' Millie exclaimed. 'Do you really think she could be?'

Alice-Miranda smiled. 'We know she didn't have food poisoning and she has been sick. It makes a lot of sense if you think about it.'

'I would never have thought about it,' Millie giggled.

'Well, this has to be the loveliest news to top off a rather interesting day.' Alice-Miranda took Chessie by the hand. 'Come on, Millie and I will introduce you to our headmistress.'

She looked over at Jemima and Anthony Tavistock, who nodded fiercely and gave her the thumbs up.

Alice-Miranda beamed. 'Something tells me you may be getting to know her much better very soon.'

And just in case you're wondering . . .

Bentley Treloar had been so desperate to see his wife succeed that he had completely lost all rational thought in the process. He'd believed he had worked out a way to make people just a little bit sick, but things quickly got out of hand. His research into plastics recycling had indeed hit a dead end and so he had come up with this plan instead – at least one member of the family should be successful or so he'd thought. For a smart person, his actions had been especially dim-witted. He was charged with industrial sabotage and placed on a good behaviour bond with a hefty dose of community service thrown in for good measure. Hugh Kennington-Jones hated the thought of the Treloar family suffering, so he continued the man's employment under strict supervision.

During her investigations, Dolly Oliver might just have made the breakthrough Bentley couldn't. Dolly asked if Bentley wanted to undertake some additional research with her in the laboratory and it soon seemed as if they were on to something groundbreaking.

Adrienne Treloar visited the Highton-Smith-Kennington-Joneses the following day to apologise in person for the trauma she had inflicted on Alice-Miranda and her misjudgement of Hugh and his business practices. She was appalled by her behaviour and realised she had been blinded by bitterness and ambition. She offered to resign from her new role, effective immediately, but was shocked to find that Edwin Rochester refused to accept it. She had solved the mystery of the Kennington's crisis and, although her husband had made a few suggestions here and there, she had been incredibly thorough in her research. She was just the sort of woman they needed to head up the children's hospital.

Adrienne wondered if perhaps she'd misjudged Mr Rochester somewhat as well.

Fortunately, Leo and Martha were too young to understand what had happened that day. Dottie, though, felt terribly ashamed that hundreds of people had suffered at the hands of her father. Almost immediately after the garden party, he did his best to make it up to her and so did her mother. The thing about parents is that you can't help but love them, and Dottie was determined that their family would emerge from this horrible time to be better than ever. She was worried that Alice-Miranda wouldn't want to be her friend anymore, but that was the furthest thing from the truth. Once Alice-Miranda made a friend, it was for life.

Desmond Berwick's dreams of privilege and luxury turned out not to be. He'd served his time for the theft of the money from the Paper Moon Foundation and now he needed to complete his parole and get a job. Marjorie Plunkett decided that it would be best if he moved to the other end of the country, where she secured him a position in a toy factory, manufacturing stuffed animals.

Anthony Tavistock was even more in love with Jemima than when they'd first met. He believed her courage in trying to do the right thing was extraordinary. Jemima decided that Bedford Manor was just fine as it was, although she and Anthony did raid the attics and cellars for an auction with startlingly good results. Dally was initially poised for sale but, oddly, Jemima had a last-minute change of heart and he's now back in his usual place. Jemima realised that, despite not everything being to her taste, Bedford Manor's history was important and she and Chessie were now a part of it. She even took up Prigg's offer to show her the strange cabinet in the Great Room. The man was stunned when Jemima challenged him to a round of chequers – it seemed the frost was finally beginning to thaw. In fact, now that she was no longer worried about her brother, Jemima wondered if perhaps she could help Anthony by opening the house to the public. Maybe they could run a tearoom or even some weekend house parties for paying guests. The best news of all was that she and Chessie and Anthony were now a proper family.

Alice-Miranda and Millie rode Bony and Chops over to visit Chessie the day after the garden party. Under strict instructions from Hugh and Cecelia, they took things very slowly and Bonaparte behaved like a perfect gentleman.

Francesca Compton-Halls couldn't believe her luck. She had made two wonderful friends in Millie and Alice-Miranda, and her stepfather was everything she could have wished for and more. But the best thing was that her mother and Anthony didn't want her to go all the way back to Bodlington. Although she was sad to be leaving Mrs Fairbanks, she was equally thrilled to be saying goodbye to Madagascar. Ettie Fairbanks reorganised her linen cupboard and had a long chat with Peggy Howard about her new charge.

Chessie had a lovely interview with Miss Grimm, who was happy to report that she was over her morning sickness and expecting an addition to the school community in five months' time. But there was to be another one earlier than that, when Chessie started next term.

Mrs Shillingsworth fixed Rodney just as Alice-Miranda said she would. But Chessie decided that perhaps the old dog needed a new adventure, so she bundled him up and posted him to a special little friend called Imogen.

Aunty Gee was pleased to have her larder restocked and was relishing her orange marmalade toast – even more so when she got to make it herself for a midnight snack.

Cast of characters

The Highton-Smith-Kennington-Jones household

Alice-Miranda Highton-Smith-Kennington-Jones	Only child, nine years of age
Cecelia Highton-Smith	Alice-Miranda's doting mother
Hugh Kennington-Jones	Alice-Miranda's doting father
Aunt Charlotte	Cecelia's younger sister
Marcus and Imogen Ridley	Twin toddlers of Charlotte and Lawrence
Dolly Oliver	Family cook, part-time food technology scientist
Mrs Shillingsworth	Head housekeeper
Mr Harold Greening	Gardener
Mrs Maggie Greening	Mr Greening's wife

Daisy Rumble	Current juggler of three jobs – maid, receptionist and nanny
Heinrich Bauer	Runs the farm at Highton Hall
Lily Bauer	Heinrich's wife
Jasper Bauer	The Bauers' eleven-year-old son
Poppy Bauer	The Bauers' seven-year-old daughter
Max	Stablehand
Bonaparte	Alice-Miranda's pony

Friends of the Highton-Smith-Kennington-Jones family

Aunty Gee	Queen Georgiana
Marjorie Plunkett	Head of the Secret Protection League of Defence
Pippa McLoughlin-McTavish	Millie's mother
Chops	Millie's pony

Winchesterfield-Downsfordvale Academy for Proper Young Ladies staff

Miss Ophelia Grimm	Headmistress
Miss Livinia Reedy	English teacher
Mr Josiah Plumpton	Science teacher
Miss Benitha Wall	PE teacher
Mr Cornelius Trout	Music teacher
Howie (Mrs Howard)	Housemistress
Mrs Doreen Smith	Cook
Charlie Weatherly	Stablehand
Fudge	Much-loved cavoodle puppy

Students

Millicent Jane McLoughlin-McTavish-McNoughton-McGill	Alice-Miranda's best friend and room mate

Sloane Sykes	Friend
Caprice Radford	Friend of sorts
Sofia Ridout	Head prefect
Mimi Theopolis, Anna	Students

Bodlington School for Girls

Mrs Fairbanks	Housemistress
Francesca Compton-Halls	Student
Madagascar Slewt	Student and full-time troublemaker

Chattering Children's Hospital staff

Dr Adrienne Treloar	Pediatrician
Edwin Rochester	Hospital administrator
Dr Miller	Alice-Miranda's doctor
Mrs Tigwell	Tea lady

The Bedford Manor household

Jemima Tavistock	Lady of Bedford Manor
Anthony Tavistock	Lord of Bedford Manor
Mr Prigg	Butler
Mrs Mudge	Cook

Others

Stanley Frost	Owner of Wood End
Ursula	Stan Frost's daughter
Myrtle Parker	Village busybody
Reginald Parker	Husband of Myrtle
Mrs Marian Marmalade	Queen Georgiana's lady-in-waiting
Bentley Treloar	Husband of Adrienne Treloar
Dottie Treloar, Leo Treloar and Martha Treloar	Children of Adrienne and Bentley Treloar
Desmond Berwick	Swindler
Isabella	Kind tea lady

About the Author

Jacqueline Harvey taught for many years in girls' boarding schools. She is the author of the bestselling Alice-Miranda series and the Clementine Rose series, and was awarded Honour Book in the 2006 Australian CBC Awards for her picture book *The Sound of the Sea*. She now writes full-time and is working on more Alice-Miranda and Clementine Rose adventures.

www.jacquelineharvey.com.au

Jacqueline Supports

Jacqueline Harvey is a passionate educator who enjoys sharing her love of reading and writing with children and adults alike. She is an ambassador for Dymocks Children's Charities and Room to Read. Find out more at www.dcc.gofundraise.com.au and www.roomtoread.org/australia.

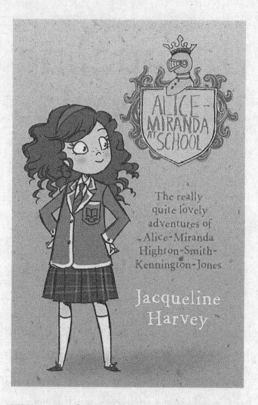

Want to know how it all began?
Read on for a sample of
Alice-Miranda at School

Chapter 1

Alice-Miranda Highton-Smith-Kennington-Jones waved goodbye to her parents at the gate.

'Goodbye, Mummy. Please try to be brave.' Her mother sobbed loudly in reply. 'Enjoy your golf, Daddy. I'll see you at the end of term.' Her father sniffled into his handkerchief.

Before they had time to wave her goodbye, Alice-Miranda skipped back down the hedge-lined path into her new home.

Winchesterfield-Downsfordvale Academy for

Proper Young Ladies had a tradition dating back two and a half centuries. Alice-Miranda's mother, aunt, grandmother, great-grandmother and so on had all gone there. But none had been so young or so willing.

It had come as quite a shock to Alice-Miranda's parents to learn that she had telephoned the school to see if she could start early – she was, after all, only seven and one-quarter years old, and not due to start for another year. But after two years at her current school, Ellery Prep, she felt ready for bigger things. Besides, Alice-Miranda had always been different from other children. She loved her parents dearly and they loved her, but boarding school appealed to her sense of adventure.

'It's much better this way,' Alice-Miranda had smiled. 'You both work so hard and you have far more important things to do than run after me. This way I can do all my activities at school. Imagine, Mummy – no more waiting around while I'm at ballet or piano or riding lessons.'

'But darling, I don't mind a bit,' her mother protested.

'I know you don't,' Alice-Miranda had agreed, 'but you should think about my being away as a holiday. And then at the end there's all the excitement of coming home, except that it's me coming home to you.' She'd hugged her mother and stroked her father's brow as she handed them a gigantic box of tissues. Although they didn't want her to go, they knew there was no point arguing. Once Alice-Miranda made up her mind there was no turning back.

Her teacher, Miss Critchley, hadn't seemed the least surprised by Alice-Miranda's plans.

'Of course, we'll all miss her terribly,' Miss Critchley had explained to her parents. 'But that daughter of yours is more than up to it. I can't imagine there's any reason to stop her.'

And so Alice-Miranda went.

Winchesterfield-Downsfordvale sat upon three thousand emerald-coloured acres. A tapestry of Georgian buildings dotted the campus, with Winchesterfield Manor the jewel in the crown. Along its labyrinth of corridors hung huge portraits of past headmistresses, with serious stares and old-fashioned clothes. The trophy cabinets glittered with treasure and the foyer was lined with priceless antiques. There was not a thing out of place. But from the moment Alice-Miranda entered the grounds she had a strange feeling that something was missing – and she was usually right about her strange feelings.

The headmistress, Miss Grimm, had not come out of her study to meet her. The school's secretary, Miss Higgins, had met Alice-Miranda and her parents at the gate, looking rather surprised to see them.

'I'm terribly sorry, Mr and Mrs Highton-Smith-Kennington-Jones,' Miss Higgins had explained. 'There must have been a mix-up with the dates – Alice-Miranda is a day early.'

Her parents had said that it was no bother and they would come back again tomorrow. But Miss Higgins was appalled to cause such inconvenience and offered to take care of Alice-Miranda until the house mistress arrived.

It was Miss Higgins who had interviewed Alice-Miranda some weeks ago, when she first contacted the school. At that meeting, Alice-Miranda had thought her quite lovely, with her kindly eyes and pretty smile. But today she couldn't help but notice that Miss Higgins seemed a little flustered and talked as though she was in a race.

Miss Higgins showed Alice-Miranda to her room and suggested she take a stroll around the school. 'I'll come and find you and take you to see Cook about some lunch in a little while.'

Alice-Miranda unpacked her case, folded her clothes and put them neatly away into one of the tall chests of drawers. The room contained two single beds on opposite walls, matching chests and bedside tables. In a tidy alcove, two timber desks, each with a black swivel chair, stood side by side. The furniture was what her mother might have called functional. Not beautiful, but all very useful. The room's only hint of elegance came from the fourteen-foot ceiling with ornate cornices and the polished timber floor.

Alice-Miranda was delighted to find an envelope addressed to 'Miss Alice-Miranda Highton-Smith-Kennington-Jones' propped against her pillow.

'How lovely – my own special letter,' Alice-Miranda said out loud. She looked at the slightly tatty brown bear in her open suitcase. 'Isn't that sweet, Brummel?'

She slid her finger under the opening and pulled out a very grand-looking note on official school paper. It read:

Winchesterfield-Downsfordvale Academy for Proper Young Ladies

📖

Dear Miss Highton-Smith-Kennington-Jones,

Welcome to Winchesterfield-Downsfordvale Academy for Proper Young Ladies. It is expected that you will work extremely hard at all times and strive to achieve your very best. You must obey without question all of the school rules, of which there is a copy attached to this letter. Furthermore you must ensure that your behaviour is such that it always brings credit to you, your family and this establishment.

Yours sincerely,
Miss Ophelia Grimm
Headmistress

Winchesterfield-Downsfordvale Academy for Proper Young Ladies
School Rules

1. Hair ribbons in regulation colours and a width of $^3/_4$ of an inch will be tied with double overhand bows.
2. Shoes will be polished twice a day with boot polish and brushes.
3. Shoelaces will be washed each week by hand.
4. Head lice are banned.
5. All times tables to 20 must be learned by heart by the age of 9.
6. Bareback horseriding in the quadrangle is not permitted.
7. All girls will learn to play golf, croquet and bridge.
8. Liquorice will not be consumed after 5 pm.
9. Unless invited by the Headmistress, parents will not enter school buildings.
10. Homesickness will not be tolerated.

Alice-Miranda put the letter down and cuddled the little bear. 'Oh, Brummel, I can't wait to meet Miss Grimm – she sounds like she's very interested in her students.'

Alice-Miranda folded the letter and placed it in the top drawer. She would memorise the school rules later. She popped her favourite photos of Mummy and Daddy on her bedside table and positioned the bear carefully on her bed.

'You be a brave boy, Brummel.' She ruffled his furry head. 'I'm off to explore and when I get back I'll tell you all about it.'